SEEDS OF BLISS

by

J. Andrew Rice

DORRANCE PUBLISHING CO
EST. 1920
PITTSBURGH, PENNSYLVANIA 15238

Dorrance Publishing Co
585 Alpha Drive
Suite 103
Pittsburgh, PA 15238
Visit our website at *www.dorrancebookstore.com*

ISBN: 979-8-88683-464-2
eISBN: 979-8-88683-552-6

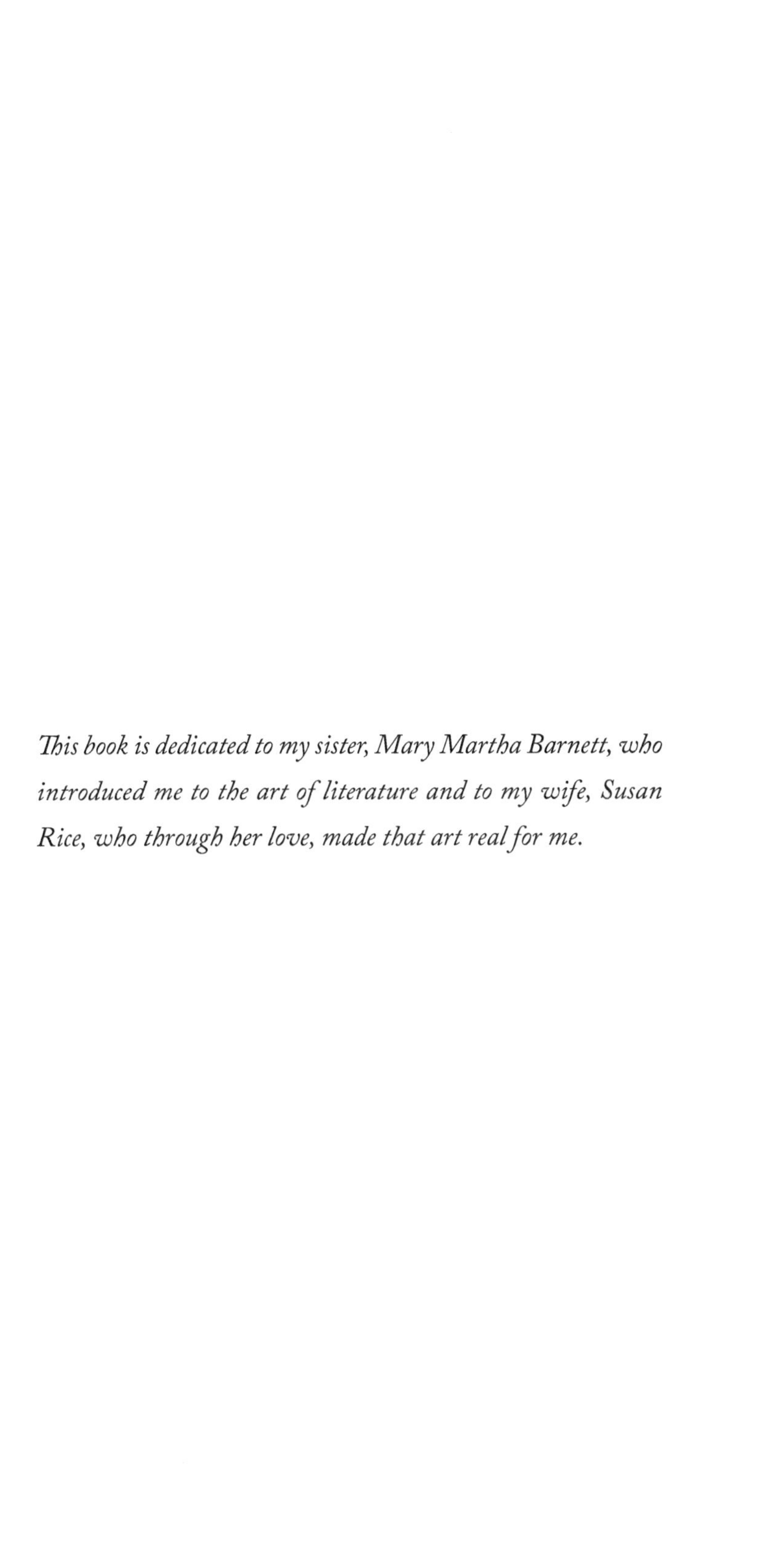

This book is dedicated to my sister, Mary Martha Barnett, who introduced me to the art of literature and to my wife, Susan Rice, who through her love, made that art real for me.

"This is a work of fiction. Names, characters, places and incidents either are products of the author's imagination or are used fictitiously. Any resemblance to actual events or locales or persons, living or dead, is entirely coincidental."

PART I

Every god, every mythology, every religion, is true in this sense: it is true as metaphorical of the human and cosmic mystery. He who thinks he knows doesn't know. He who knows that he doesn't know, knows.

Joseph Campbell

Chapter 1

It was the wind that reminded him. As he stood at the burial site and looked around, he felt it. It brushed past his cheek, moving his fine, blond hair all over his head. The old man had been his friend for many years. What was it about the wind? It was constant and dependable, and it was always there to remind him of something that was permanent. He just couldn't put his finger on it.

His reverie was soon gone. The minister was winding up his portion of the graveside service. The Masons were beginning their ceremony. Some middle-aged people were softly sobbing. He felt the welling up in his throat. It always happened when one of his old friends died. He would miss the old man. Every time a member of his parents' generation passed away, he was like a little boy again. It was the same as when his mother left him for the first time, and he had to do something that was new to him. He knew he had to grow up and do what she wanted him to do, but he always had an empty spot inside.

The old man's advice and friendship had been essential to him. He wasn't looking forward to facing his job, his family or his community without the presence of this valuable friend. The wind blew his pants leg around as he bowed his head for the final prayer.

People began moving and talking. The service was over. Scott Mitchum knew he had to go back to work. The wind was still blowing. Even though it was October, the Texas sun drove into him like a knife. The weather was pleasant enough, but the sadness of this funeral and the contemplation of his immediate responsibilities were enough to give him a headache.

Bruce Jones, the minister, walked toward him talking to one of the members of the family and stopped when he saw Scott.

"Are you coming to the church, Scott, to eat with the family? There is plenty of food" asked Bruce.

In a low voice Scott replied, "No, I've got to get back to work but thanks anyway. I'll see you Sunday, Bruce."

"Okay, hey—remember that the quartet is singing Sunday morning."

"Yeah, I'll be there."

Scott smiled to himself. He loved singing, and the quartet was a good release from the day-to-day grind of living. But to Bruce, it was part of the Sunday morning production that was called a worship service at Whispering Hope Church.

He walked down through the gravesites looking at headstones of all these people from solid East Texas families. He had known many of them or at least their descendants. He was a fourth generation Mitchum who had lived in this rural East Texas community of Lyric for 135 years.

Scott Mitchum was also the Mayor of Lyric. It was a community position that suited him, but it had become burdensome especially with the wants and needs of people like Mary Jo Breeden who was approaching him from the right.

"Hi, Scott." Mary Jo said in a soft voice looking down after she said it.

"Hi, Mary Jo," Scott replied with an anguished look.

Mary Jo's daughter, Amy, had been missing since yesterday. An Amber Alert had been sent out this morning. The police chief had given Scott all the details. Yesterday afternoon, Amy had gone to the nearby junior college to pick up a book from the library. Several college employees and her friends had seen her at the library. She never returned home. Her car was still in the parking lot.

Coincidentally, Buddy Parker, an acquaintance of Amy's had also gone missing since about the same time. Not that Amy was a good friend of Buddy's. They hardly ran in the same circles. However, they were both seniors at the local high school and knew each other.

Mary Jo and her husband, Richard, were well respected in the community and Mary Jo's family had lived in Lyric for four generations. Conversely, Buddy's family had been rather transient moving from Beaumont to Lyric only two years ago. Buddy was living with his mother and stepfather.

Scott and Mary Jo had been friends for many years and had dated in high school and college. It was particularly difficult to talk to her now. Scott's empathy had always been his strength and his weakness. People loved him because he cared about them. But they used him and took him for granted many times.

"Scott, I know that this is not a good time, but I am barely holding on to my sanity. Have you heard anything about Amy? Has Chief Henderson told you anything confidential that I should know?"

Scott looked at the drawn face, which still reflected the inherent goodness of his long-time friend. "No, Mary Jo. I haven't heard anything more than what I talked to you about last night. I wish I could tell you something, but there is nothing to tell."

Mary Jo was downcast but kept her composure. "I guess life has hit us both hard at the same time. You've lost your best friend, and I've lost my daughter."

Scott reflected on that a minute and replied, "Yes, but we don't know she is lost, yet. Give it some time, Mary Jo."

Mary Jo walked away, and Scott let his eyes follow her. She still looked exceptionally good and walked with a sure step. Scott often wondered why they had never become closer in their young adult years.

As he walked on toward the cemetery gate, the wind continued to blow. The tops of the pin oak and white oak trees were swaying gently. The wind whispered through the pines. It was a good feeling. Robert Ward, the man he had just help to bury, would have been proud of him. He would have said, "It's the little things in life that make it worth living, Scott—a cold glass of tea, the wind blowing through your hair, the smile and touch of a beautiful woman." God, he was going to miss him. This man had been his soul mate since he was a boy. Scott's father had died when he was twenty-five. Scott had only been married two years, had a one-year-old child and was just starting his career. Robert had become his mentor, his sage, the person he leaned on when he couldn't find the right answer. What was life going to be like without him?

His thoughts were broken near the gate by Bucky Taylor who accosted him before Scott knew he was near.

"Scott, how ya doin?" asked Bucky.

"As well as can be expected, Bucky," replied Scott.

"Hey, I'm real sorry about Robert. You know he taught me how to hunt armadillos. He was a real good man. Take care of yourself, Scott."

"Thanks, Bucky."

Scott had heard the armadillo story from Robert. He couldn't help but smile to himself. The town was full of characters.

As he approached his car, someone called his name. The voice was recognizable and as he turned, his intuition told him that it was John Marsh. It was. John was older, more distinguished looking than he had been when they were in high school. Although Scott saw John from time to time, he had never really looked at how he had aged. It wore well on John, but it didn't give him the substance he needed. John just never seemed to have it, ever since he became a congressman.

"Scott, I'm really sorry about Robert. I know he meant a lot to you."

"Thanks, John," Scott replied. "I'll miss him."

"It seems like that generation just drifts away more rapidly as the years go by," mused John as he straightened his hair and moved his head slowly while looking at people and potential voters.

Scott couldn't help but notice John's wife, Paula, standing next to him. She had always been a pretty, vibrant woman. John had met her in college. She looked too thin—unhealthy, now. Scott wondered if John had noticed.

"Say, Scott, I was wondering if you might have a minute this evening to talk to me about this tragic situation with Richard Breeden's daughter, Amy?" asked John.

"Look, John, I don't mind talking to you about it, but tonight is not a good time. Come by my office tomorrow and I will tell you what I know, which is not much more than most everybody in this community.

"Okay, I'll see you tomorrow about 9:00 a.m. I've got to catch a flight from Houston to Washington at noon."

"See you tomorrow," Scott replied as he watched John walk away and most of the other people attending the funeral. Just a few were standing around renewing acquaintances, talking about the past, discussing how things used to be. Scott felt the wind again.

Chapter 2

Amy Breeden knew that she was still in East Texas. As she lay in the bed of the pickup truck on a piece of plywood, she could smell the pine trees. The pickup was on a pretty rough road—further indication that she was back in the woods. Her head was pounding. The last thing she remembered was talking to Buddy Parker in the parking lot at Lee College. She was scared but not so much that she couldn't think. Her mother had told her to use her head and her instincts in this kind of situation. They had talked about it while watching NCIS. She needed to make an assessment. She was blindfolded and had her hands tied behind her back. Her feet were also tied together. Her head hurt and she thought she had been drugged. She knew that about ten minutes ago the pickup had gone over a cattleguard. Intuitively, she figured that the truck was old. As it hit the bumps and holes in the road, the shocks creaked and groaned with each jolt. Occasionally, on a large hole, the sideboards of the pickup bed and the camper would shudder and rattle ferociously.

She also knew that this must have something to do with Buddy Parker. That she could not understand. She and Buddy didn't know each other well, but they had always had a mutual respect for each other. She thought he was cute, but never considered going out with him. He was too distant, and there was something different about him.

The pickup stopped. Upon opening, the doors creaked and groaned as metal rubbed against metal. And then there was silence. Amy heard something like water being poured out on the ground. It stopped and then started again for only a moment. She realized that somebody—a male-- must have been peeing. Although she was scared, she couldn't help but laugh to herself. Whoever it was had to be from East Texas. It was a male ritual in this part of the world to pee outside. Her father and brother even did it with loud protests from her mother and grandmother. What was funny about this maleness was that most of them tried to be somewhat modest. They would open a car or truck door and stand behind it, stand behind a tree, or go to the corner of a house or barn. There was not much success in their modesty because she had seen men do it plenty of times.

Amy heard the camper door open and then heard a voice say, "You think she's awake?" The voice was mid-range and definitely had the East Texas twang.

To which Amy responded, "Yes, I'm awake. Who are you?" (Stay in control. Don't lose your head.)

"Well, I'll be," said the voice, "I believe we got a live one, Buddy."

So, thought Amy, Buddy is a part of this criminal act. It was time to make him start thinking.

"Buddy Parker, why are you doing this to me?" demanded Amy, "I thought we were friends."

"Now—now Amy, this ain't like it seems," responded Buddy, "you're goin' have to let me explain."

"Aw, shuddup Buddy," said the voice, "fore I pop you one. We've got work to do. Now git her out of that pickup."

Amy felt two hands on each of her ankles and then she was pulled toward the back of the pickup bed. (Keep them on the defensive. Don't scream. Look for an opening.) They pulled her feet off the tailgate and then they put their hands on her shoulders and pulled her to a sitting position.

"She shure is a pretty little heffer," said the voice.

"Why don't you just shut up, Jack," said Buddy.

Amy then heard what sounded like a slap and then she heard Buddy say "Shit!"

Jack said, "Don't you ever tell me to shut up again, you little turdhead, or I'll whip your ass into the next county."

"Take that blindfold off her and let her see my beautiful face," Jack told Buddy.

Amy felt Buddy's shaking hands on the back of her head as he fumbled with the knot to the blindfold. After about two minutes, he was able to loosen it and it slipped off her head.

In front of Amy stood the ugliest man she had ever seen. He was at least six feet four inches tall and weighed about 275 pounds. He had a small beer gut on him, but he looked in good condition. His arms, shoulders and chest were massive. He had coal black hair that touched his shoulders and a black beard. His forehead had lumps in it and old acne scars covered the rest of his face. Down the left side of his face was a scar from the temple all the way to where his neck met his shoulder. His nose was flat and large and had been moved from its original location to one side of his face. He was smiling and his teeth were brown stained with a couple missing on the top. If there was a redeeming feature about him, it was his eyes. They were piercingly blue. There was a mission in those eyes. I'll at least be able to identify him if I get the chance.

"Buddy, what is this about?" asked Amy.

"I'll answer that question, little lady," answered Jack, "you see, your daddy owes me some money. Now, I been trying to collect it for two years and he ain't paid it yet. So, me and Buddy decided to take you as a down payment. We figger that he'll pay the rest with some big interest pretty soon." Jack laughed with a high-pitched cackle that just did not fit his body type. Amy thought things were seriously weird.

"Who are you?" retorted Amy.

"I can answer that question, too," replied Jack. "I'm Jack Rocker or some people call me 'Crazy Jack'."

Amy looked at Buddy and said, "Buddy, what are you doing with this guy?"

Buddy hung his head and said softly, "He's my stepfather, Amy."

Jack laughed once again with a high-pitched cackle.

Chapter 3

Sunrise was spectacular on this morning in Lyric, Texas. The yellow combined with blue and red conjured a myriad spectrum that was beyond description. Scott always welcomed the new day. It was full of possibilities and challenges and this sunrise made it that much better. When his son, Matthew, was small he called the sunrise "God's artwork"—Scott agreed completely.

The traffic into Lyric was especially heavy this morning. It appeared that there was a fender bender at the school entrance. Buses were stacked up and couldn't access the school driveway to drop off the kids. Scott waited in the traffic and mused on his bus riding days when he attended Lyric schools. He could not help but remember the confrontations and fights, especially those with Orie Terrell, bus terrorist. Orie stayed in school forever and struck fear into the heart of every kid from Scott's age to ten years younger. He got his comeuppance one day though. Two brothers, Edward and Gerald Morgan, who were Scott's age, conspired to set things straight with the bully. They were among the last ones off the bus along with Orie. They buddied up to him as soon as they got on the bus that afternoon telling him they would give him a dollar if he would steal some candy at Woodrow's store. When most of the kids were off the bus, Edward told Orie that he wanted to show him something at the back of the bus. Edward sat in the back seat, and he directed Orie to sit in the seat in front of him. Gerald slipped into the seat in front of the bus terrorist. As soon as Gerald sat down, Edward punched Orie in the nose. The bully pulled his fist back to hit Edward and Gerald brought a heavy history book upside Orie's head. The bus terrorist turned to hit Gerald and Edward hit Orie in the ear. And it continued like that until the bully ran to front of the bus. Orie never fooled with Edward and Gerald Morgan or their friends again. Scott had been glad that he was in that lucky group of people.

Scott remembered that John Marsh was on his agenda today. He really did not want to spend a lengthy time with him and since he had to be back in Washington, Scott assumed it would be a short meeting. As he moved through the traffic, Scott thought about the rest of the things he would have to do today. His firm, Mitchum Engineering, was growing. More business was coming his way every day. He personally had to finish the plans and specifications for a twelve-inch water line and elevated water storage this week. It was for the nearby City of Pelican, a town of about 6,000 people. Additionally, he was still the Mayor. This was his fifth year and if his wife had anything to say about it, he would be Mayor only one more year. He liked the job, but it did take time away from her and their two kids. Especially when there was a major situation, like two missing teenagers. The Amy Breeden case weighed heavily on him. He had grown up with Richard and Mary Jo Breeden, and Amy had been to his house visiting his daughter on several occasions. He was confident that Jesse Henderson, the police chief, was handling the case in a professional and competent manner. However, he felt a tremendous sense of responsibility for bringing her home safely.

"Hey, Scott," a tall lanky man said to him as it came into the office building. It was Ben Smith, the firm's surveyor, "What's the good word."

"Beat the Wildcats," replied Scott.

It was a running joke between them. Ben was from New York. He had lived in Texas for twenty-five years and loved Texas high school football. Cheerleaders were always yelling to people in the stands "What's the good word" and of course the spectators were supposed to yell "Beat the (other team's mascot)". Ben just loved that phrase and he greeted everyone with it. Scott, knowing that he was from the North, always responded in an appropriate Texas way with the scheduled team for the week's game.

"Scott," Ben continued, "we've finished the surveying on that road project in Lum. Are you going to turn that over to Allen?"

"Yes," Scott replied. Allen Marshall was an Engineer-In-Training (EIT) and this would be his first project to design as a member of this firm. As a recent college graduate and EIT he had to train under Scott for a period of four years before he could take his test to get his Professional Engineer's license

Scott walked in his office and took a cursory look at his desk. Since he was out yesterday, the phone messages had piled up. Most of them were business related although a couple of them were personal. He decided to return those calls after his meeting with John.

He had just sat down when Allen Marshall walked in his office. "Hey, Scott," said the young man. "I just got a call from Kit Johnson over at Eminence. He was telling me that the meeting on the new surface water treatment plant did not go well last night. It seems that some guy is whipping up hysteria over there about how Jefferson County Fresh Water Supply District #1 is going to be taking them to the cleaners over the purchase of water. He doesn't want the Eminence Special Utility District getting involved with other systems. Kit said he started quoting George Washington and something about 'entangling alliances'.

Scott smiled. The joys of local government were beyond description. Where else could people say their piece, misinterpret the sayings of a former president, be completely wrong and still convince people that they are right? It was classic and believable but certainly not logical.

"Well," Scott replied, "it appears that project will be on hold for a while. Why don't you go ahead with the Lum project?

"Okay but keep me out of the politics. That Mayor and I might get into more than an entangling alliance."

Allen left the room, and Scott looked at his schedule and tasks. He was hoping he didn't have a lot to do. Ever since Robert died last week, he just did not have the energy to get motivated about his work.

John Marsh stuck his head in the door. "I'm here a little early. Do you have time to see me now?"

"Sure, come on in John."

John sat down and looked at Scott intently. "Tell me what's going on with the Amy Breeden case."

John had never been one for small talk. Get right to the point.

"I don't know much about the details, but generally we know that she and Buddy Parker are both missing."

"Who is Buddy Parker?"

"He and Amy are the same age. He has been reported missing by his mother and what links the two together is that a witness, who is the last known person to see Amy, saw Amy talking to him right before she disappeared."

"Well that pretty much tells you what happened," noted John.

"Not really," Scott said bluntly. He did not like presumptuousness and John had a lot of it.

"Buddy Parker is a member of our church and would come quite a bit without his parents. They don't go to any church. I talked with him some, and I don't' think he would try to deliberately hurt anybody."

"And I thought I was the bleeding-heart liberal," replied John, "I bet Bruce is thumping that Bible real hard now that one of his flock is implicated in a kidnapping."

Here we go again thought Scott. He knew that John would get around to talking about Bruce Jones. Although all three of them had grown up together and had been friends, their adult lives had taken different directions. John had gone to college at the University of Texas and became enamored with politics. He got his law degree, practiced as a personal injury litigator and then ran for the state legislature and was elected. He stayed in state politics for ten years and then ran for U. S. Congress. He had been a congressman for ten years. He was on important committees and made the Sunday talk show circuit frequently. He was an influential person and a leader in his party.

While they were teenagers, Bruce had been called into the ministry and had gone to East Texas Baptist University. From there, he went to Southwestern Seminary where he received his Doctor of Ministry. Bruce had become a Southern Baptist pastor. He had been the pastor of two churches before he came back home and began his pastorate at Whispering Hope Baptist Church of Lyric. If success was measured by number of people attending, Bruce Jones had broken all the records. Whispering Hope Baptist Church had grown from a small rural church to a church attended by many people throughout the surrounding area. Bruce had done well with the Southern Baptist denominational hierarchy. He served on important boards and was given high media exposure positions. Bruce Jones was well known in denominational and secular politics.

Scott had always liked his two friends, but he knew that they were different. And he was different from them. He had liked to build things when he was younger, and it was just natural that he would become an engineer. He had also been a good student and a good athlete, which was the right combination to get him a scholarship to Rice University. After he left Rice, he worked in California for a large civil engineering firm for several years where he received his professional engineering license. He also became a partner in the firm. However, after ten years of it, he was tired of the massiveness of the projects he worked on and wanted to make and see a noticeable difference with his work. He sold his share of the partnership and moved back to Lyric to set up his own small civil engineering firm. He struggled at first but after fifteen years he had made a good reputation north of the Houston area for his quality work and his honesty. Scott had also become involved in community activities. He had served on the City Council for two years when several community leaders asked him to run for Mayor. He liked the idea of serving his hometown and using what talents he had to make Lyric a good place to work, play and live. He signed up and ran unopposed his first and second elections.

"You know, Scott, Richard Breeden is a big contributor to my campaigns and avid supporter."

"Yes."

"Well that's the reason I'm here. I want to offer whatever assistance I can to help with this investigation. If it becomes a federal case, I want to do everything I can to help. I know it is in capable hands with you and your staff. You know you have always had my respect. However, I think something needs to be resolved soon, or some people are going to start pulling other strings."

Scott contemplated that a moment. "Is that an ultimatum?"

"No, just a fact. Richard Breeden is going to see that every possible resource is used to find Amy. If someone is in the way, then they will probably be pushed aside."

"Thanks for the warning, but I already knew that. I want to find her as much as anybody, but I want to do it right."

"I've got to go. Wish me luck with the Washington crowd."

"Good luck. See you whenever."

"I'll stay in touch."

Chapter 4

Bucky Taylor had fallen face down when he lost his balance using his shovel. He was spitting the dirt out of his mouth when he saw it. The biggest timber rattler he had ever seen was coiled and ready to strike him only five feet away. Bucky thought about why he always seemed to get in these hairy predicaments. He was on his knees and started slowly backing away from the snake. The snake was still coiled, but it had not moved and when Bucky got out of striking range, he stood up and rushed back to his pickup.

On the gun rack was a .22 rifle. He grabbed it and walked back to where the snake had been. He looked for a while and couldn't find it. Bucky sat down and contemplated his situation.

Ever since he had heard that old legend about Santa Anna's gold, he could not get his mind off of it. That had been two years ago. Bucky had never been the brightest person but had always worked hard. He had been visiting Robert Ward one day and as they sat on the porch, Robert told him the story of Santa Anna's gold.

It seems that Santa Anna, the Mexican dictator during the Texas Revolution, always carried a great deal of gold with him when he traveled. Supposedly his instructions to his gold bearers, who each had two donkeys laden with gold bullion, was for them to flee any fighting where it appeared that Santa Anna's army may be losing and then head back to Mexico. He did not want the gold to be captured by the Texicans under the command of Sam Houston since the gold could be used to buy arms and assistance from outside sources.

During the Battle of San Jacinto, the legend goes that the gold bearers could immediately see that the battle was going bad for the Mexicans. They quietly slipped away and headed north into the east Texas forests. They followed the San Jacinto River and then one of its tributaries until they came to Rice Creek. They had traveled about thirty miles and knew that it was a long way to Mexico and had no idea what had happened to Santa Anna. Afraid that they might be captured or killed by the Texicans, they buried the gold somewhere on Rice Creek by a marker so that they could retrieve it at a later date.

Of course, the Texicans won the Battle of San Jacinto and sent Santa Anna back to Mexico. The gold bearers fearing the Texicans and Santa Anna, since they did not return to Mexico as instructed, fled to California. Years later some Mexican gold coins were found near Rice Creek after a spring rain and the search was on. One man even found one of the gold bearers, who was an old man living in Los Angeles. He told the man that neither he nor the other gold bearer had ever returned to Texas for the gold—they were too afraid of the Texans and Santa Anna.

Nobody had ever found the gold, and Bucky was determined that he would be the one. Bucky had grown up in a home where his mother and father were poor and ignorant. Bucky remembered going to school with just the bare essentials. He had two pairs of blue jeans and two shirts. Each night his mother would wash his shirt and jeans he had worn that day and he would wear his other shirt and pair of jeans the next day. His dad was a sawmill hand, and his mother cleaned houses for people during the day.

They were dead tired when they came home each evening. His dad drank a lot but was never mean.

From the time he was little, Bucky knew that he did not have some of the advantages many other people had in Lyric. He accepted it and did the best he knew how to do with his life. But there was always something nagging at him to improve his stature. He had graduated from high school, an advantage he had over his father and mother and had gone to work for a local logging company. First he felled trees with a chain saw. Then he ran the skidder. He worked his way up to running the loader. His boss had noticed his hard work but was a little skeptical of Bucky's continuing ability to get into dangerous predicaments. He wouldn't let Bucky drive the log trucks or stay on the loader more than an hour. He had already pulled down five hundred feet of fence when he ran the skidder, dropped a twenty inch log on the cab of a truck while running the loader and almost cut his leg off with the chain saw.

Bucky also did a little cowboying. A local ranch hand would hire him from time to time to help round up cows in the East Texas woods for various ranchers. Bucky enjoyed the work. He liked riding a horse and was rather good at flushing cows out of briar and yaupon thickets. One day while he was trying to move an old mama cow and her calf is when he saw the gold piece. He was working near Rice Creek. The sun was shining bright. A flash of light caught his eye and he looked in its direction. There on the ground he saw it. Bucky would have been simply curious if had not heard the legend from Robert Ward. But it had not been two weeks since Robert had told him the story. He jumped off the horse, picked up the coin and he immediately knew it was old. He took out his machete and marked a big white oak with an X, made a note of the spot and got back on his horse. By now the cow and calf were moving in the direction he wanted them to go. He got behind them and started observing the coin. Bucky felt like he had just met his destiny.

But the search was getting old. He had become obsessed with it and now was downright discouraged. He had dug up everything in this part of the woods and had found nothing else for two long years. Contemplating his future was not an exercise that Bucky did often but he was doing it today. He was twenty-five years old and had always been a logger or a cowboy. He had no financial worth, no wife, no children. If he didn't find this gold, he had no idea what he could do to distinguish himself.

A noise came sharply through the trees. It was north of him and sounded like somebody laughing. Bucky was pretty far back in the woods, and he was curious why someone else might be back here in the middle of the day. He decided that the gold hunting could wait, and this unexpected diversion would give him a break. He started walking north.

Bucky had walked about a half mile up Rice Creek into Rice Creek Flat when he heard voices. One was a man and the other was a woman or a girl. The tenor of the conversation was strained at best because the voices were raised above a normal level. Bucky decided to be discreet, if not invisible. He slowly walked through the small pine trees using the yaupon thicket as cover. He saw the white pickup before he saw the people. They were standing behind it. He moved over to his right and they came into view.

He couldn't believe it. There was Amy Breeden talking to Crazy Jack Rocker and Buddy Parker. It looked like Amy's hands were tied behind her back. He knew that Amy had been missing but hadn't paid much attention to it because he figured that she had probably run away from home or something like that. He could clearly see that she was here against her will.

She was having some heated discussion with Crazy Jack. Buddy had a hang dog look about him. Crazy Jack was mostly laughing at her and it was making Amy mad. Her voice was getting louder. Bucky moved in closer to hear what they were saying.

"What makes you think you will get away with this? My father will use every resource at his disposal to see that you are caught and prosecuted." Amy said.

"You know little girl, you sure do use a lot of big words for someone that is in deep shit. I could take care of you right now and it wouldn't make me no never mind. I just want your daddy's money" answered Jack.

"Buddy, why did you do this?" yelled Amy. "I thought we were friends." Amy started crying.

"Aw, Amy don't do that" replied Buddy. "You're my friend. Jack forced me into…." Then Bucky saw Crazy Jack take the rifle he was holding and crack the butt of it against Buddy's head. Buddy went down in a heap.

Bucky was getting anxious. What should he do? He had worked with Crazy Jack Rocker and knew how tough and strong and how crazy he really was. The man had no fear. He and Crazy Jack were logging one day together and ran onto a couple of cottonmouth water moccasins. Bucky had never forgotten it. Crazy Jack told Bucky, "Watch this" and as quick as lightning, Jack had stepped on one of the snakes, reached down and picked it up behind the head and proceeded to squeeze the snake until blood ran out its mouth.

He looked back over at Crazy Jack. He put the gag back on Amy's mouth and had rolled Buddy over on his stomach. He was tying Buddy's hands behind his back. Bucky knew things were getting too serious, and he knew he wouldn't be able to take on Crazy Jack Rocker himself without him or one of those kids getting hurt. He decided to go for help.

He turned to go, and a limb of a yaupon tree hit him right in the ear and temple. He grunted. He whirled around to see Crazy Jack looking up and starting in his direction. Bucky hunkered down and stayed completely still. He was barely breathing and felt his heartbeat pounding in his ears. Crazy Jack took a hunter's stealthy steps, extremely quiet for a big man, as he walked and got closer. Bucky started running. He lit out south and then heard the crack of the rifle. Instantly, a sharp and then numbing pain hit his arm. Bucky fell over. He had been shot. As soon as he tried to get up, Crazy Jack was standing over him cackling, "Well looky here, Bucky Taylor done decided to join our little party."

Chapter 5

Mary Jo Breeden looked out the window sipping her coffee. It was her morning ritual, but it didn't feel right. Amy was constantly on her mind—her little girl—what was happening to her. She is probably scared Mary Jo thought, even though Amy had always been pretty tough. Mary Jo knew she was alive.

Mary Jo had never worn her faith on her sleeve. She had been careful to let people know that her relationship with God was important, but it was a private matter. These special morning times had always been set aside for prayer. She was in the deep well of her soul this morning. She knew that God was there, but no answers were forthcoming.

Sleep had been fitful. She looked at the bottle of pills on the table in front of her. The family doctor had prescribed them after the first night of Amy's disappearance. Mary Jo disliked drugs—especially those that were supposed to help you with mental and emotional problems. She hadn't taken them, but she knew she had to sleep sometime, or things would just get worse. It had been two days since Amy had been abducted—she knew she couldn't stay awake much longer.

She was helpless, and she hated that feeling. All she did was sit and wait for news and listen to other people with their trite phrases such as "If there is anything we can do to help, just call me." Many people were sincere, and many had helped, but this circus was getting old. She needed to do something to find Amy.

But what? The police had made it clear that everyone who could possibly work on the case was working on it and that other people would just get in the way. People in her church were praying for them constantly. There was an Amber Alert and the Laura Recovery Center had become involved, and she knew that the effort by the community to find Amy was not lacking. There was just something nagging at her that made her feel that she should be doing something.

The doorbell rang and Mary Jo got up and went to the front door. "Who could that be at this time of the morning?" she asked herself. She opened it and a blonde headed girl stuck her head out from behind it.

"Hi, Mrs. Breeden." It was Ashley Wilson—an acquaintance of Amy's. Mary Jo had heard her speak of Ashley on occasion. Amy had been concerned about Ashley and her home life. It seemed that Ashley was in the middle of a war at home between her mother and father and had confided in Amy. Ashley, Amy told her mother, had few friends and although Amy was not close to her, she confided in Amy because she felt like she could trust her. She was a pretty girl—big sad eyes. Her long hair was parted in the middle. She was wearing hip hugger jeans and a tight shirt that was short enough to let her navel show.

"Hello, Ashley. I'm surprised to see you this early in the morning. Come in and have a seat."

"Wul, I knew that you were probably up. Amy says that you get up early in the morning. And I didn't have time this afternoon to come see you so I thought I would come before school."

Ashley sat on the edge of the couch as Mary Jo sat in the easy chair across from her. Ashley was taking her long hair and curling it around her left index finger and was bouncing her right heel up and down. It was easy to tell she was nervous.

"Okay, is there something I can do for you?" asked Mary Jo.

"Wul, I hope I can do something for you."

"What do you mean, Ashley?"

"Wul, I know that Amy and Buddy Parker have both disappeared, and I wanted to tell you something about Buddy."

"What about Buddy?"

"Wul, Buddy told me something the other day that I thought was kinda strange, and I thought you should know it. We were sitting together at lunch, and he was pretty nervous. He kept telling me that he hated his stepfather. I asked him why, and all he would say was that he was forcing him to do something he didn't want to do."

"What else did he say?" queried Mary Jo.

"Nothing."

Mary Jo was thinking. What did this mean? She needed to know more.

"When did Buddy tell this to you?" Mary Jo asked Ashley.

"I think it was last Tuesday."

"Why are you telling me this, Ashley?

"Wul," Ashley stuck her hands in her pockets and bowed her head, "Amy, before she went to college, and now Buddy are the only people at that school that seem to care about me, and I wanted to help." Tears were dropping on the floor. Ashley was shaking and said, "Oh Mrs. Breeden, I don't want to get Buddy in any trouble, I just think everybody has got this whole thing messed up. Buddy wouldn't hurt Amy. I know he wouldn't, but I want Amy to be found."

Mary Jo was stunned. This young girl had bravely relayed some information to her that might help find Amy but could implicate another friend of hers in a crime. Mary Jo took her in her arms and hugged her.

Chapter 6

The sunrise could not have been more beautiful. The green tops of pine trees were the foreground to a light gray color of the sky as it shifted into shades of red. Streaks of pink shot over the tops of the pine trees as blue became apparent in the background. The air was crisp—a norther had blown in the night before.

Bruce Jones was watching it from a hospital room. One of the elderly members of his church had fallen ill during the night, and he had come when summoned by her husband. This was a regular duty. He didn't really enjoy it, especially when the person was dying like this dear old soul. However, the comfort that his presence gave to the family was always rewarding to him. He loved being a pastor. There was something about leading people that gave him fulfillment and contentment. He also had a passion for truth, and he knew that the truth was in the Bible. It was this passion and his natural leadership abilities that had made Whispering Hope Baptist Church one of the fastest growing Southern Baptist churches in East Texas.

Bruce had known this call to preach and pastor since he was eighteen years old. It had consumed him. He sincerely believed that giving direction to the directionless i.e. bringing people to a saving knowledge of Jesus

Christ was the most important thing a person could do during his lifetime. Of course, this was confirmed in the Bible and gave Bruce the confidence he needed to pursue his dreams. As he looked out of the hospital room at the sunrise over Lyric, he thought more about the possibilities for his church's future.

Lyric was not a large town by any means, but there were many other surrounding communities that made up an area population of about 90,000 people. These people all came to Lyric, which served as a hub for these communities, to conduct business. Many of them were unchurched. Bruce knew that there was no dominant church in the area, and he intended to make Whispering Hope that church. He had talented lay ministers working at Whispering Hope. He was an up and coming star in the Southern Baptist Convention. His Baptist connections grew every day. Things could not be better.

"Bruce, could you come here a minute?" asked the husband of the patient. He was standing next to the doctor talking in a low voice. Upon Edd's direction, all three of them left the room and went down the hall to a small alcove.

"The doctor tells me that the results of the tests Lily took last week have shown that her cancer is anaplastic—it can't be cured. In other words, it has spread all over her body and she doesn't have much longer to live." He hesitated as he said the last few words. Bruce saw the single tear come out of the corner of his eye.

"I'm sorry to hear it, Edd," Bruce replied and put his arm around him.

Bruce didn't say anything. He just quietly held the man as the low sobs came from deep within him and made his body shake.

"I just thought …I just thought we would have a little more time together," replied Edd.

The doctor walked down the hall. Bruce was quiet. He knew that Edd needed consoling, not preaching.

"She and I would have been married 50 years next June. I have always been in love with her."

"I know you have, Edd. I've always admired you and Lily and your relationship. It has been an inspiration to me, even when I was a boy."

Edd was gaining his composure. "You know, she almost married another man," he said.

"Why would she do that?" queried Bruce.

"Well, I kinda got a late start out of the blocks. She was engaged to some other guy before I met her. For some reason, she decided it wasn't going to work and gave his ring back to him. I came along after that and I guess you might say I swept her off her feet," Edd replied with a grin.

Bruce laughed. "Now don't get too cocky, Edd."

Edd grinned again and then his face went solemn. "I don't know how to tell her. Will you come with me?"

"Sure." They walked toward the hospital room. Bruce saw a look of steely resolve come over Edd's face.

Edd walked up to the side of the bed and took Lily's hand. Her eyes lit up when she saw him. She smiled weakly at him. Bruce stood at the foot of the bed.

"Honey," Edd hesitated, "the news is not too good. You have cancer and it has spread all over you." His voice broke.

"I know," Lily replied. "I'm going to die, aren't I"?

Tears were streaming down Edd's cheeks. He couldn't speak. He looked at Bruce. Lily looked at Bruce.

Bruce had known these people all of his life. Lily had taught him as a Primary in Sunday School. Edd had been his Royal Ambassador leader. *God, give me strength*, he prayed.

"Yes," he replied as he looked at Lily. He walked to Edd's side, put his arm around Edd's shoulder and grabbed Lily's hand. "Let's pray."

Bruce poured out his soul during the prayer. It was cathartic and when it was finished, he squeezed Lily's hand and hugged Edd again.

"God will see us through this. I love both of you and the church loves you."

"Thank you Bruce," replied Edd.

Lily squeezed his hand and said weakly. "You go home and hug that lovely wife and two kids of yours for me."

Bruce smiled. "I will." He looked at Edd. "You call me if you need me."

Bruce walked out of the room. As he went down the hall, he thought about Lily and Edd and Robert Ward. These stalwarts of the church and the community were beginning to leave, passing the torch on to him and his generation. He was up to the task, but he was going to miss them—their wisdom, their guidance, their love—it could not be replaced.

As he came to the front door, he saw Scott Mitchum outside talking to Jesse Henderson, the police chief. The conversation looked pretty animated from Jesse's point of view. Bruce could not hear them.

Bruce ventured out and slowly walked up to them. "I'll see you later, Mayor," Jesse said as he shook Scott's hand and then noticed Bruce. "How are ya Brother Jones?" asked Jesse as he stuck out his hand.

"Just fine, Jesse, good to see you," replied Bruce.

"How's the music program over at the church, you find any singers over there with any soul, yet?" he winked at Scott.

"I'll have you know that we got a 'hallelujah' during one of our songs last week and some people were even swaying a little bit. I was stunned."

Jesse's eyes got mockingly wide. "Well, I do declare. Us black folks are going to have to come see that for ourselves—we may be close to the Second Coming."

Scott and Bruce laughed. It was a running joke between the three of them, but Bruce began to look serious and said, "There's more truth in that statement than you think there is."

"Well, I've got to go," Jesse conveniently interjected. "Law enforcement calls."

As Jesse walked off, Bruce looked at Scott. "Have you come to see Lily?"

"Yes," Scott replied.

"It's not good, Scott. She's dying."

Scott stared off in space for a moment and then asked. "Cancer?"

"Yes. It's everywhere."

Scott shook his head. "What an insidious disease. How long?"

"Don't know. The doctor didn't say."

"Is Edd up there with her now?"

"Yeah, I just left them. He's pretty shook up, but he has a look of determination on him."

"Well, I guess I better go up and see them."

"Say, how's it going with Amy?" queried Bruce.

"That's why I was talking to Jesse. It looks like there are some developments, but I can't say anything about them now. One thing I can say is that John is putting some pressure to get the feds more involved in the case. Jesse is not happy."

"I don't blame him. John needs to stay out of it and mind his own business—whatever that may be."

Here we go again, thought Scott. These two guys were getting further and further apart. How could that happen to friends who had grown up together and who had had a great love for one another?

"Listen, I'll see you later, Bruce. I need to get going."

"See you Sunday, Scott. Looking forward to hearing you sing."

Chapter 7

Reminiscing to himself had taken up a lot of Scott's time since Robert had died. He was doing it now as he waited for the doctor to finish his visit with Edd and Lily. He was thinking about the time he had his first serious talk with Robert.

"Those two friends of yours are ambitious fellows," Robert said to Scott as they watched Bruce Jones and John Marsh leave in John's Chevrolet pickup. Robert was sitting on the porch of his farmhouse in a cowhide chair. Scott was sitting in the porch swing.

"Yeah, they have big dreams. I wonder how it will turn out for them," replied Scott. Early that Saturday morning, all of them, Robert, Bruce, John, and Scott went squirrel hunting in the woods behind Robert's house. Robert invited them to go the previous Sunday at church. Robert told them he had a new squirrel dog, and he wanted to break her in. Being seventeen years old and always looking for something to do, all three of the boys had jumped at the chance. Football season was over, and Scott and John wouldn't be worn out and beat up after Friday night. Robert had also asked Scott specifically if he could stay a little while after hunting to help him with some chores on the farm. Scott had readily agreed. He liked Robert, and Robert had always paid him well anytime he worked for him.

"What about you?" Robert responded.

Scott looked at him and didn't speak for a while.

"Well, I'm not sure. I have always wanted to do something special with my life. It looks like I'm going to go to Rice University, and I'll probably study engineering. However, I never have been able to have the bravado those guys have in being so cocksure about what they are going to do as far as a career." When they were in high school, these two guys were always competing with each other on hunting, dating, fishing, vehicles, etc. Scott thought about the previous conversation while squirrel hunting that they had with Bruce and John. It was a dick measuring contest. Bruce was expounding about how he was going to East Texas Baptist University, get his degree in business administration and then go to Southwestern Seminary in Fort Worth to get his Doctorate in Ministry. He was getting his degree in business administration so that he could be a good manager for the churches he would eventually serve as pastor. John tried to "one up" Bruce by stating that he was planning to go to the University of Texas, get his bachelor's degree in political science and then go to law school. After law school, he planned to go into politics and someday be Governor of Texas. Bruce then talked about how the salvation of the world would come when people turned to God and not to institutions created by men. John countered with institutions like the United States government created by its Constitution had allowed people the freedom to worship God in their own way. A friendly debate had ensued until Bruce said that he had to get home.

"Religion and politics. Now there are two subjects and careers where you can spend a lifetime and not accomplish much," Robert said as he bent forward in his chair to spit a stream of tobacco juice out his mouth into the side yard. Scott had always wondered how long it took to get so skilled at spitting that you could hit a dime ten feet away with a stream of tobacco juice. Robert had let him try a chaw one time. As he put it in his mouth, he knew that he would never do it again. It had a biting taste. Chewing it seemed to catch his mouth on fire. He hardly worked any juice out of it before he spit it out. Some of the juice went into his stomach—later on he felt a little green around the gills.

"Why do you say that?" Scott asked.

"Well, I've known a lot of preachers and politicians. I believe that most of them have started off with good intentions. They sincerely want to change what is wrong with our society and make it better. The problem is they forget they are human. By that I mean they don't recognize their own limitations. Prestige and power go to their heads, and they lose the substance of their humanity."

"What do you mean by the substance of their humanity?"

Robert looked off at the brilliant eastern sky with its mid-morning sun. "We are complex spiritual beings but don't get me wrong--I think that evolution, even though it is a theory, has credibility. Nevertheless, there is more to the creation of this universe than mere chance and random selection. There is a Creator. However, our spiritual being is wrapped up in this body that sheds the light of reality upon us. It's a paradox, but it explains the harmony of Creation. It is the crucifixion and the resurrection. It is the Chinese yin and yang; the positive and negative forces of physics and chemistry."

"What's that got to do with the substance of their humanity?" Scott was confused.

"Everything. You have to keep them in balance. Going too far one way or the other dilutes a person's humanity. For instance, Bruce may sincerely think that he can save the world through his preaching and teaching the Bible. He will want everyone to become what he thinks is a totally spiritual person by following every precept of the Bible in the manner that he interprets it. If he is like a lot of other preachers I know, he will put limits on God. He may never consider that God may choose to reveal himself to people in manners that Bruce and those of his ilk can never accept. Bruce will get out of balance by being so confident in his human reasoning and masking it with what he perceives to be God's logic."

Scott remembered sitting on the porch and marveling at Robert's wisdom. He was only seventeen, but instinctively he knew that there was a lot of truth in Robert's words. Robert's life had always been a bit of mystery to Scott. He had grown up in Lyric but left home when he was sixteen. He fought in World War II and Scott's father had told Scott that Robert had been decorated during the war. After World War II, he attended Baylor University where he received his law degree, married, and started a career. He and his wife never had any children and his wife died when they both were in their thirties. He then bought a 250-acre farm in Lyric and moved back. He hung out his shingle in Lyric and raised cattle on his farm. He never married again. He never talked to Scott about the war, his wife, or his law career. It was as if it was another life he had lived in a different time. This other existence must have had a profound effect on Robert's attitude about life and his attainment of wisdom. As he continued reminiscing, Scott remembered what Robert had said about John.

"Now you take your other friend, John. He is a natural leader and a visionary. He sees and comprehends things that you and I may never grasp. It is a gift. How he uses the gift may determine history and the lives of many people. John may or may not know he has this gift and how powerful it can be. If he doesn't know that he has the gift, he may squander it by misusing it and destroying trust in his ability or he may blissfully ignore it and use it very little or not at all. If he knows that he has it, he may use it for good, or he may use it for evil. Ultimately, it will be left up to him."

Robert stopped looking at Scott and gazed into the sky for a few moments and said, "Most people do not think deeply. They blindly follow people who seem to know the way to go in life. John and Bruce both will probably be two of those leaders that people blindly follow. It's a tremendous responsibility."

Robert had been right about both of them.

Scott was taken out of his reverie by a presence next to him. It was Edd. He gave him a hug and walked into Lily's room. He took her hand and they all cried. Times were changing.

Chapter 8

Amy was looking at Crazy Jack. He was sitting on the ground with the gun across his lap and his back against a pine tree. Buddy was gone. Bucky lay in the back of the pickup with his arm bandaged. Buddy had managed to stop the bleeding, but Bucky felt pretty bad. Amy had been trying to comfort him as much as possible, but Jack would not untie her hands. Amy knew that Bucky would need some medical attention pretty soon. He had been shot two days ago, and he didn't seem to be getting any better.

With regard to the weather, it was a beautiful morning, but for Amy, whose fears had turned to anger, it was time to do something. Buddy was away from the camp. She had seen him and Jack talking in low voices earlier. Buddy had been protesting something Jack was telling him and then Jack had slapped him once again. In a louder voice, Jack had said "and there is more of that for your mother". Buddy had ridden away on a motorcycle, and Jack was laughing at him.

"Getting your eyes full, little lady," Crazy Jack said as he turned and faced Amy. She continued to look at him.

"Ain't I purty? I'll bet you've never had a boyfriend as purty as me," Jack said laughing as he got up off the ground. "I'd like to give you a piece of my action but the time's not right. We've got to keep you in prime condition for a little while longer."

Amy was disgusted. This evil creep not only had kidnapped her but also was threatening to rape her before it was all over. Instead of scaring her, it had the opposite effect. She had to make a plan to fight back and get out of here.

Crazy Jack sensed her determination. "Now don't be gittin' any ideas about trying to get out of here. That shore would make me mad. An' you don't wanna see me mad. I may have to fuck your tight little pussy sooner than I want to."

Amy looked down and didn't respond to him. She felt a twinge of fear from his remark, but it wasn't overwhelming. He was smart. He was trying to keep her scared so she couldn't think straight. She was going to have a tough time with this lunatic. Bucky had been asleep during the exchange between Jack and Amy. He groaned and woke up. He sat up and looked around. His face was beet red. Amy thought he looked feverish. Bucky looked at Jack and then looked at Amy. He started talking.

"Jack, we gotta get those logs out of here before it rains, or we'll never make it."

"What are you talking about, Taylor?" answered Jack.

"You know, those logs" Bucky replied, waving his good arm in a circle, and pointing toward Amy. Then he just stared at her.

"You're a silly ass, we ain't got no logs."

"Yeah we do. What's she doing here."

"What's the matter with you, Taylor?"

"He's got a high fever and is out his head," responded Amy. "He needs some medical attention."

Bucky just stared at Amy.

Jack said, "I'll give him some medical attention," and walked over and slapped Bucky in the face. Bucky yelled, tried to get up and fell down weak from exhaustion. Jack laughed that high shrill unnerving laugh and looked at Amy.

Amy didn't say anything. She knew it would provoke this insane piece of garbage. Things were getting dangerous. She would have to make a break for it soon or he would do something to her. She wished Buddy would come back.

As he drove down the highway, Buddy was facing a dilemma. He was violating everything he had learned about Christianity. His heart was sick. He knew what Jack Rocker was capable of doing. When his mother first met Jack, he had deceived her and Buddy and Kristen, Buddy's little sister. He was very attentive to Buddy's mother, Karen. He took Buddy and Kristen to the local amusement park on several occasions, played ball with Buddy and took Kristen swimming with her friends. All of them loved the attention. Buddy's father had been recently killed in a car accident, and Jack had filled the void with his kind and considerate actions. Buddy had missed his father, and Jack seemed to fit right in with their family.

Jim Parker, Buddy's father, had been successful logging contractor and Jack had known him through that business. As soon as he died, Jack came to their house to offer his condolences and started seeing Buddy's mother. Jack helped Karen Parker with the business and together they kept it successful. Within a year, Jack and Karen had married.

As soon as the honeymoon was over, Jack became a different person. He started drinking heavily and his attitude toward Karen, Buddy and Kristen turned evil. He and Karen began to fight about the business because Jack refused to work over twenty hours a week. He was also taking money from company accounts and using it to party and gamble. Karen tried to stop him and that is when he began to hit her.

Jack not only threatened to kill her if she went to the police. He also threatened to kill the kids. Karen had always been a quiet unassuming kind of person. She had no family or close friends to help her. She felt trapped and did not know what to do. Buddy, after bearing the brunt of a few of Jack's blows, tried to make himself as scarce as possible. Kristen stayed in her room all the time. Within two years, the business was bankrupt, and they had no source of income. For some odd reason, Jack stayed even though the money was gone. From time to time, he was even decent to them. They moved a lot as Jack tried several jobs and businesses. His drinking and gambling always lost any employment that he might gain. Their last stop had been Lyric.

Jack had gone to work for Richard Breeden as a truck driver hauling logs. Of all the drinking he did, Jack had never been arrested for driving while intoxicated. He had stopped drinking for a while and was halfway civil with Karen, Buddy and Kristen. One night, while hauling his last load of the day, he had an accident with a car. The driver of the car, a teenage girl, was killed. Jack's truck turned over and his face broke the windshield. The windshield also broke his face. There were no witnesses to the accident. Because the road was wet and there were very few skid marks, it was hard to tell what happened. There was an investigation, and the conclusion was that the girl had lost control of the car. Jack had tried to avoid her, and an unfortunate accident had occurred. But Buddy knew better.

Jack had to stay in the hospital a long time to get his face reconstructed. Richard Breeden's company continued to pay Jack's salary and all of his hospital bills. Buddy knew some of Jack's so-called friends from seeing Jack hang around with them at the local pool hall. One day Buddy was at the hardware store getting some items for his mother when he overheard a couple of Jack's friends talking around the corner.

"Ol' Jack Rocker got out of that pickle, didn't he?" said a tall, lanky redneck with a beak nose.

"Yeh, it sure was a shame about that girl. He shouldn't a been drinkin' and driving that truck," said a younger rotund man with overalls and a Astros baseball cap.

"He put too many away that night at Triggers. I tried to tell him myself.

"Well, I don't guess nobody will ever know now cause I'm sure not gonna tell and I understand they didn't do a breathalyzer test."

Buddy had walked away. He was ready to cry. He would have left if it were not for his mother. He wanted to know how they could continue to live with such an evil man.

He went to talk to Grace Rhoden. Grace befriended him when he entered Lyric High School. Grace always seemed to have a sweet disposition but a determined look about her. She and Buddy had talked a lot. They were not boyfriend and girlfriend. Neither one of them seemed to be interested in that. Grace always seemed to have something positive to say to Buddy.

When Buddy arrived at Grace's house, they sat down in her living room. Buddy told her what was on his mind.

Grace listened. She kept her eyes on Buddy. She was calm and was genuinely interested in his predicament. Buddy finished with his story. Grace continued looking at him. Her hands were in her lap and in a soft but assured voice, she said a remarkable thing, "I think you need Jesus."

Buddy had never heard her talk like that before and the only time he ever heard any of that kind of talk was from superficial TV evangelists and preachers.

"What do you mean?" replied Buddy.

"All I know Buddy is that Jesus is the Son of God. I know he lives, and I know he lives in me. He comforts me when I have trouble, and he gives me courage to live each day. He has saved me from a life without God. You need him in your life—he will see you through difficult times in your life."

"You don't sound like those TV evangelists or some preachers I've heard."

"Well, I think they have good intentions, but they go overboard. This is remarkably simple. You just pray and ask God to forgive you of your sins. By the way, sins are those actions you take that separate you from God. You then ask Jesus to come into your heart and life. You can do it right here. He'll be with you everywhere—lonely nights, family trouble, fights with your stepdad. He'll give you a quiet direction to go."

Buddy was ready to cry. No one was with him during those times. Not even his mother. He had been lonely and lost. He did need Jesus.

"Tell me how to do this, Grace."

Grace led him through a prayer. He asked God to forgive him of his sins. He asked Jesus in his heart and life. He knew his life had changed when he had finished.

That is why as he drove away from Crazy Jack, Amy, and Bucky, he was praying and looking for that quiet direction. Things were horribly wrong, and he didn't know what to do.

Chapter 9

Fran Mitchum was frazzled. Her teenage daughter, Elaine, had forgotten her cheerleading outfit for the pep rally that day. She had taken it to her and then got into a discussion with the principal about Project Graduation. Being in charge of that production, with the Amy Breeden case hanging over everyone's head, and being the Mayor's wife was beginning to weigh on her. She drove by the police station on the way to Scott's office and noticed Mary Jo Breeden and Ashley Wilson coming out the front door. She didn't think anything was unusual about Mary Jo being there, but Ashley was a different story. Fran knew Ashley. She was an acquaintance of Elaine's. She decided to tell Scott.

Scott was looking over the plans of the Lum project with Allen. He felt good about this project. It was the thing this community needed to do. It would give them plenty of water storage and pressure for years to come. That was the satisfying thing about his work. He knew he was doing something practical and helpful and long lasting. He wished that every person could feel that way about his or her job. His father had always told him that there was a lot of dignity in work. "God didn't put us here to wile away time by doing nothing. A person needs to have purpose, and purpose can be found in the work they do, whatever it may be."

He was also pleased with his young EIT Allen had showed that he cared about his assigned projects and the people associated with them. Maybe he would continue Scott's legacy when Scott decided to retire.

Fran interrupted his thoughts as she walked through the office door. Scott mused, as he watched her come through the door, that she was still a magnificent woman even after twenty years of marriage. It seemed like one. She had a lot of class and a lot of quiet energy. She was good for him. She knew it and he knew it. They were still deeply in love with each other.

"I need to talk with you privately for a moment," she said as she moved toward his office.

"Okay. I'll be right there," Scott replied. "Allen, make these corrections and then print ten sets. Advertise for bids as required and be sure you put it in Dodge Reports. Notify all pertinent contractors on our list. Let's have the bid opening on November 1st."

Fran was sitting with her legs crossed in one of the side chairs of Scott's office. She had on that blue dress that came to right above her knee. She was wearing her pearl necklace. Scott couldn't help but notice that her legs still looked outstanding. Her brownish gray hair was parted in the middle and fell softly on her shoulders. Her green eyes looked serious.

"Scott, I just saw Mary Jo Breeden come from the police station with Ashley Wilson," Fran stated. "I thought that was unusual and you needed to know about it."

"Well, that is interesting," he replied. "I'll call Jesse in a little bit and ask him what is up. What brings you this way?"

"Elaine forgot her cheerleading outfit for the pep rally. I swear, I don't think the child is going to make it at college next year. She'll probably be calling me from her dorm room telling me she can't find her shoes."

Scott laughed. Their daughter was notorious for her forgetfulness. But to Scott, she was perfect in every way. She was their first born. An intense child but she had a good sense of humor. She was also a good student and an outstanding athlete. She just had a few idiosyncrasies that kept her distracted from time to time.

"I also needed to talk to you about another matter."

Here is the real reason she is here and dressed in that knockout outfit, Scott thought.

"As you know, the Historical Society has been looking at the Koen house as a possible site for a community museum. It has an interesting history itself and if restored properly, has enough room for us to do a number of historical displays in it. We would also have enough room for preservation projects. I know that the City has a relatively large reserve built up with its hotel/motel tax. I was wondering if that money could be used to buy the Koen house and help with the restoration. Do you think that the City Council would consider using the large reserve for such a project?"

Fran looked intently at him. Scott knew that this meant a lot to her. She had a way of including him in things that he may otherwise have truly little interest at all. Before long, he was leading the charge and was wondering what got him interested in the first place. She had a knack for pushing the right buttons.

"All we can do is ask," Scott replied. "I'll talk to George about it and ask him to put it on the agenda." George Hanel was the City Manager. He was a quiet, determined man who had been good for Lyric. Scott had often admired George's ability to get things done in a way that did not cause a lot of attention but was highly effective.

Fran relaxed. She knew that Scott would handle this. It was what had and still attracted her to him. He had this ability to find common ground with people and accomplish wonderful things for their community. Not only was her husband good looking, but also he was emotionally and spiritually a complete person. Although she would never say it to him, he was the sexiest man she knew. She wanted him to pull her close right now and make love to her on this very office floor.

"Hey, Pretty Girl," Scott said. It was his pet name for Fran. Fran broke away from her fantasy and looked at him.

"Why don't we go out to eat at Smith Ranch Friday night." Smith Ranch was their favorite place to eat. Fran knew he must have been reading her mind.

"Sounds good," Fran replied. "I need to go; Matthew has his doctor's appointment at 1:00 p.m. and I need to pick him up. I'll see you at home."

She walked toward the door and Scott undressed her in his mind. He knew the electricity was flowing between them this morning. He liked it. One day he would close the door and make love to her on this very office floor. She turned and smiled at him as if to say she knew it too and walked out.

Chapter 10

Buddy Parker pulled into Pelican. Although it was forty miles from Lyric, Buddy was being careful. Pelican was in the same county with Lyric and there were people from Lyric who came there from time to time.

Pelican was a small farming community that only had a school going through the eighth grade. After eighth grade, students would go to nearby Devers Prairie High School. There was a small convenience store in the town and Buddy parked at the very edge of the parking lot.

He sat on the bike for a few minutes fiddling with the handlebars like he was doing something while a group of people dispersed off the front porch.

Buddy knew that Jack was using his intimidation and fear tactics to keep him from telling somebody about the kidnapping. It was a heavy burden. He was scared that Jack would somehow find out and he would then hurt his mother. He was concerned that the police may botch something and make it worse. Although, Buddy rationalized that the odds of these things happening were remote, it virtually paralyzed him.

But the terror was fading. Buddy kept thinking about Jesus. What would he do? It came to him from the deep well of his soul. It came bursting through the fear and the trepidation. Buddy walked in the store.

He bought several food items, some medicine for Bucky, a small writing pad and a small box of envelopes. He walked up to the counter and was waited on by a young man who was about his age. They were the only people in the store.

The clerk looked at him and said, "How ya doin today?"

"Just fine," Buddy answered. Then he wondered why he said it.

The clerk ran the items through the scanner and told Buddy that it would be $66.82. Buddy handed him $70.00. He took the change and receipt that the clerk gave to him and walked away.

"Have a nice day," the clerk said as he left. Buddy wondered why people were always saying that. He figured they just didn't know what else to say.

Buddy stowed the food and medicine, sat on the motorcycle, took the paper, and began to write. He finished the note, took an envelope, and sealed the note in it. He looked around. One man was coming into the store to pay for gas. Buddy looked at the note in his hand. It was shaking. His hand was shaking. He felt light-headed. It seemed as if he could hear his heart beating. He knew it was now or never. He had to overcome this tyranny of fear that was ruling him. The man in the store went back to his car and drove off.

Buddy made deliberate moves getting off the bike and walking into the store. Every inch of him wanted to bolt and run, but with willpower he could not shake, he opened the door and walked up to the clerk.

Buddy stammered, "I—I need your help."

The clerk looked at him and said, "Got vehicle problems?"

"No—No." Buddy replied.

Then hesitating for a moment, he thrust the note in the general direction of the clerk and said, "I need for you to take this note to the police chief, Jesse Henderson, in Lyric. It is extremely important. If you don't believe how serious it is, you can open it, but please don't open it until I have been gone for five minutes and please don't give it to the chief until tomorrow. It is a matter of life and death."

Buddy turned and walked out. The clerk called out to him, but Buddy ignored it and walked to his motorcycle. He started it and drove away.

Another person came into the store to pay for gas, then two people bought some grocery items. When they left, the clerk figured it had been five minutes since the strange encounter with the note bearer. He opened it and read:

> My name is Buddy Parker. My stepfather, Jack Rocker has kidnapped Amy Breeden. He has also shot and wounded Bucky Taylor. He is holding both of them in the Tanner Woods near the old Tram Road. He has enlisted me to help him by threatening my mother's life. I do not know what to do. Please help.

Chapter 11

As Scott looked at the lights above the horizon, he thought there is nothing like Friday night football in Texas. His entire family was with him. Elaine was in her cheerleading outfit, Matthew was ready for the other football game behind the stands, and Fran was enjoying the cool fall weather. It was homecoming, and there was excitement in the air. Scott knew he would see a lot of his old friends including, John and Bruce.

The ambience of the evening reminded him of Robert. There were times when he would go to Robert's house on Saturday afternoon without anyone else around. They would sit and talk and watch the fall evening wile away. Robert had one of those old Texas farmhouses with a forty-foot porch across the entire front. There were four rocking chairs and a porch swing. Scott would sit in one of the rocking chairs.

Robert had kept many of the native East Texas trees in his front yard. Some of the leaves would be green but others had begun to turn orange and red—a kaleidoscope of fall colors. Some would be falling, especially if a strong breeze came through. They made a deep carpet underneath the trees. The pungent odor of wet leaves and dirt was a part of the Lyric landscape.

Scott noticed that Robert would get more philosophical in the fall. It was like he knew his life was in that stage and he needed to pass on some of his wisdom. Scott was now grateful for the impartation of that knowledge. At the time, he just felt that Robert wanted to talk.

There was one day in particular that ran through Scott's mind. He and Robert were talking about the Friday night football game and Robert told him about a friend he had in high school named James Roberts who was a brilliant football player. Robert went into detail about how much athletic prowess this young man had possessed and some of the outstanding plays he had made on the field. Scott asked him where the man was today. Robert became silent for several moments and then he answered.

"He was killed in a car accident after the last football game in our senior year. We had just won the state championship. He was driving home, and a drunk driver hit him. He was killed instantly, and the drunk walked away. James is in heaven."

"I was shook up after his death. I found it hard to understand, especially how such a good guy like James could be taken from this world and some other people left behind—like that drunk."

"I was mad at God. Over the years, though, I began to understand tragedy much better. I know that I will never understand it all, but I do think we learn lessons from it. Take for instance, James' death. There had been several people killed in our area by drunk drivers. In fact, it had almost become an epidemic nationwide. James' death not only raised awareness in our community but everywhere in this country to the problem. Here you have a stellar young man killed in a senseless act. Something needed to be done. Stricter laws have since been passed. Organizations like Mothers Against Drunk Driving are continually active. I know that there is still a problem but nothing like when I was growing up. You used to see people weaving all over the road on many occasions. That is a rarity now. James' life stood for something. He made us all more aware—much like Jesus did. He sacrificed his life."

Scott thought for a moment and asked Robert, "You said that James is in heaven now. I keep hearing these sermons at church about how people go to heaven when they die, but then I will hear another sermon about the Second Coming where the dead in Christ will rise when He comes again. That seems contradictory."

Robert grinned. "It is," he replied.

"Over the years, theology has taken some complicated routes on the Second Coming and the end times i.e. eschatology. There are basically three philosophies—premillennialism, amillennialism, and postmillennialism. Amillennialism generally states that Jesus will come again and that will be the end of the world and all believers will go to live with him in heaven. Postmillennialism generally states that Jesus' Second Coming was His resurrection and that we are living in the millennium described in Revelation. Premillennialism is what you usually hear. It is somewhat complicated and there are differing beliefs even within that following. Primarily, it states that Jesus will come again, and believers will be raptured or taken into heaven. This includes those who are dead—in other words, they will rise first. Then after this rapture, there will be a time of tribulation when the Anti-Christ or Satan will rule the world. Supposedly some people will be saved during this time and present a resistance to this Anti-Christ. This tribulation will go on for a period of time and then Jesus will come again and reign on earth for the millennium."

"I personally don't put much stock in any of them. I'm a panmillenialist."

"What's that?" Scott asked.

"I think it is going to all pan out in the end," Robert replied.

Scott laughed. Leave it to Robert to make something like the Second Coming into a simple matter. "You are really not serious about that, are you?" Scott asked.

"Well, let me say this. Jesus made a pretty simple entrance into this world. I expect that if we go by what is in the Bible, we will know when he is coming again. I believe it is counterproductive to speculate on it. You will know it just like you know the wind is going to blow in Lyric.

"I do think that there is some precedent here that theologians and preachers never consider or dismiss. I have watched many older people who have been ill for some time die. They know they are going to die. Most are at peace with it. I think they know that Jesus is coming for them.

"I believe that Jesus comes again many times every day to take believers home to heaven with Him. To me that is the Second Coming.

"Just like he saves us individually in this world, he comes and takes us individually out of this world. I think there is a lot of confusion in this big corporate hauling off to heaven like the rapture. It makes for good stories and exciting preaching, but I don't believe it rings true with the way God operates in his creation."

Scott parked the car. They were early, of course. Cheerleader parents always had the duty to see that their cheerleading children were at the game early. Scott remembered all the excitement surrounding football games when he was in high school. Now that he was grown, he wondered why there was such a large amount of energy and time invested into a football game. It was worth some thought but he wasn't going to analyze it tonight.

They passed the concession stand along with all of the other food vendors raising money for various organizations. Kids were walking back and forth. Many people said hello or nodded their heads. Scott knew many of these folks but certainly could not remember all of their names. He and Fran headed for the stands. Matthew had found a friend. He wanted to roam with him during the game, and Scott had given him the standard lecture about staying within the stadium fence and going nowhere else.

It was a beautiful evening. The sun was going down over the home stands. It had turned the sky into a cream color with some blue and splashes of orange. There was a cool breeze blowing—a perfect night for football.

Scott could not help but think about Amy Breeden. She would be here tonight if it weren't for the kidnapping. In the stands, she would be cheering with Elaine because her older brother, Eric, was the star quarterback for the football team. Scott had heard that he was still going to play tonight. When he walked into the stands, he noticed Richard and Mary Jo Breeden sitting in their usual place. Scott knew he would have to talk to them.

A voice came over the public address system reminding people of the Rotary Club raffle for a four-wheeler, the Alumni Reunion the next day and that the concessions tonight were sponsored by the Band Booster Club. Scott decided he would have his discussion with Richard and Mary Jo now and not let it fester.

"Hi Richard," Scott extended his hand.

Richard took it and gave him a firm grip. "Hi Scott,"

"Mary Jo" Scott said.

Mary Jo stood up and gave him a hug.

After she finished her embrace, she said, "Scott, did the information from Ashley Wilson help any in the investigation?"

Scott mulled this over momentarily. "Yes. I think we suspected that Buddy may be involved but gave little consideration to Jack Rocker. Didn't he work for you?"

Richard's eyes narrowed and he replied. "Yes, he did, and I fired that crazy sonofabitch. I'm expecting a ransom note anytime. He's been after me for a year now about some money he thinks I owe him."

Scott knew Richard was mad and chose his words and his expression carefully. "Can you tell me what money?"

"We cut some timber up on Rice Ridge. Jack was in charge. I always thought he was a little nutty, but he knew how to handle men and equipment. As you know, he was subcontracting to me and I have to give him a certain amount of free hand. He decided to make a little extra money by easing over on the adjacent property belonging to International Paper. He cut some fifty acres of prime timber belonging to IP, and they found out about it a month later. They had no idea who had done it, but they knew we had been on the neighboring six hundred acre tract recently. They immediately called me. I told them I would investigate. I called Jack and he said he knew nothing about it.

"I never trusted the guy, completely. So, I decided to investigate it further. Bucky Taylor had been out there, and I've known Bucky all his life. I asked him into the office. He acknowledged that they had crossed the property line, and that Jack said he had approval from me. I thanked him and promptly fired Jack Rocker. I told him that his next payment would have the IP timber deducted from it. He went ballistic and told me he would get even. It was the last time I ever saw him."

Scott was silent. Things were getting loud. The football game was about to begin. He looked at Mary Jo. She was quiet but had a pleading look in her eyes. Richard still looked mad.

"Thanks for letting me know that, Richard. I suppose you have told Jesse?"

"Yes," Richard replied. "I gave him a complete statement, today."

"Well, we're all still praying for you. I hope we have a good game tonight and Eric can overcome this psychological burden."

"I don't know, Scott." Mary Jo replied. "He and Amy are awfully close. It's weighing on him."

"I can imagine," Scott said not knowing what to say. The announcer was asking everyone to stand for the invocation. "I'll talk to you later."

Scott walked off contemplating what he just heard. The invocation was being given but he couldn't help thinking about how 50 acres was a lot of timber to steal without somebody besides the thief finding out about it.

Eric wasn't having a good game. The Lyric Buffaloes, a perennial state playoff team, was having a tough time with the lowly Nineveh Wildkats. At half time, the score was Lyric 10, Nineveh 7.

Scott liked Texas high school football games. It was a community event. Sometimes he thought that people came more for the socialization than to watch football. People in the stands were constantly talking about everything from some couple's pregnancy to the latest political events in Washington D.C. Scott had even had a discussion about gay rights during one Friday night football game.

He wasn't sure the players or the coaches ever understood this concept. He believed, like he did when he played the game, that coaches and players thought the people in the stands were there to see them carry their school to glory. That was some part of it, but Scott was fairly sure that even if the team had a bad record, there would be a good crowd.

Game attendees would walk up and down the stands looking for friends and family. The self-appointed male football analysts would never come into the stands but would stand at the fence around the thirty or forty yard line. This gave them some serious time to study the home team and its opponent without being disturbed by the social pressures in the stands. In addition, other topics were discussed such as the football seasons of favorite college teams and pro teams. Occasionally, some banter about work would enter the conversations. Pregnancy and gay rights were taboo subjects in this area of the stadium. Any reference to these subjects was greeted with blank stares and some spitting.

Behind the stands, at least one other football game was going on. This game was usually dominated by boys fourteen years old and younger. Someone would bring a football and something resembling a football game would begin. Sides were chosen by friendship—no equal opportunity existed. If all of your friends were big and the other guys were little, so be it. Everybody just had to make do. The game was more like "keep away" than football because no one was quite sure about all the rules. If one of the big guys was confident about the rules and wanted to enforce them, then everyone played by his rules. Generally, though, there was lots of random running and lots of tackling and lots of seeing who was the toughest.

Down near the concession stand, all kinds of organizations were having fundraisers. The band boosters usually had the concession stand, but nowadays there were other organizations that sold raffle tickets, barbecue, and a variety of trinkets. The organization with the barbecue always had the full blown barbecue rig, i.e. a trailer with a large barbecue pit made from thick stainless steel metal along with preparation and serving areas. When it came to barbecue, East Texans were serious connoisseurs. You didn't just cook the meat. You nurtured it through a long process of smoking, swapping stories, drinking beer, and serving with a Mother Teresa satisfaction of a work well done.

It was truly an American event. Scott relished it. Although he had not liked what the game of football had become, he still enjoyed the atmosphere of the Friday night Texas high school football event.

He went to look for Matthew at the other football game. He found him arguing with another kid about who tackled whom and who had the ball. Scott stopped and observed his son in action. It appeared that Matthew had the upper hand in this argument, since he had the ball. Each boy had his respective "team" gathered around him. The other boy was bigger and was trying to take the ball from Matthew. Matthew kept backing off and then started running. His team began blocking the other boy's team and it looked like Matthew was going to remain untouched. He got to a certain point on the field and raised his hands with the football in one of them. Scott laughed. Matthew had pulled the old "I don't care what you say—we still scored a touchdown" trick. The other boy caught up with him. Matthew let the ball go. The other boy then pushed Matthew and Matthew plowed into him. Scott ran over and separated them. He held Matthew.

"That's enough," Scott said.

"He started it," Matthew replied.

"No, I didn't, cheater," the other boy stated.

"That's enough—both of you. Either you cut it out or quit playing," Scott demanded.

"It's okay by me," said the other boy. "I don't want to play with this pip squeak, anyway."

He turned around and walked off.

"I hate that jerk," Matthew said.

"Who is that boy, Matthew?" Scott replied.

"Oh, he's a new kid who thinks he knows everything. His name is Evan Thomas."

"Where did he come from?" Scott queried.

"Deer Park. He's always putting down Lyric and telling us we're nothing but a bunch of hicks and hayseeds. He can't stand it when we do something better than him."

"How does he make friends with that kind of attitude?"

"Well, there are other new kids that are like him. All of us try to make friends with them but some of them get mad, like him. I guess he doesn't want to be here."

"Give him some space and mind your own business. He'll eventually come around," Scott advised.

Chapter 12

John Marsh sat in his Lyric office looking out the window at the two white oak trees in the back yard. He had always liked Saturday mornings in his hometown. It seemed that the pace of life slowed somewhat. This morning was particularly beautiful. A slight hint of chill was in the air. There was fog across the pasture east of the office and as the sun rose from behind the veil of earth and trees, he could make out the cattle walking through the fog. The scene was inspirational and humbling. He did not spend as much time here as he did when he was first elected. He had told himself at that time he would be an at-home representative and had meant it. He had held town hall meetings, listened to his constituents, and went to D. C. with their dreams and hopes for the nation. He had been a successful legislator. He knew how to build political coalitions, even with members of the other political party. He had been able to find ways to bring funds back to his district that were needed for police work, firefighting, parks, community, and economic development.

Now he was fighting for his political life. He had handily won his last election, but there was a movement in the country and in Texas to destroy anyone who associated himself with his party. The other party had found the right issues to outflank his party and the only reason John was still in office was his beginning years as representative when he spent so much time at home. People in his district still loved him and respected him.

However, he knew he was changing. He knew that he needed to shore up his voting base at home, but he had responsibilities in D.C. that ultimately helped his constituents. It was the age-old political dilemma— how do I keep the power that I have obtained without losing the way that I obtained it?

The situation with Amy Breeden did not help matters. One of his major financial supporters, Richard Breeden, wanted his help and he wanted to give it to him. However, he knew that encouraging the FBI to work on this case would alienate his old friends, Scott Mitchum and Jesse Henderson. To top that off, the Agent-In-Charge of this FBI district was Philip Fitzpatrick. John suspected that Fitzpatrick was the child of G. Gordon Liddy. He had the same arrogant no-holds-barred mentality. There was no caution in the man and no tact. He had risen in the ranks because of his flag-waving nationalism and his political connections.

John thought about his old and probably former friend, Bruce Jones. He wondered where he stood on this case. Was he ministering to the Breeden family like he should be doing? Or was he undercutting John for his stand on prayer in schools? John was sure that Bruce was making political hay over this situation and the inability of Amy's school friends not being able to pray for her and Buddy at school.

Ten years ago, Bruce had come to John and told him he could no longer vote for him. John was aghast. They had been friends since they were toddlers. Bruce had told him that it was because of his political party affiliation. He also said he could not support anyone who allowed the killing of innocent babies through abortion, who believed that there should be no prayer in schools, who wanted to take away his guns and who believed that homosexuality was an acceptable lifestyle.

John had tried to reason with him. He told Bruce that he was a pragmatist and that such issues were idealistic in their essence. He understood Bruce's position but as a representative he had to try to consider all of his constituents' needs and the needs of the nation. Bruce responded by dismissing his pragmatic approach as a cop out. He was interested only in changing minds to follow biblical principles.

John asked him why the government had to be involved with that mind change. Bruce's answer was that the Lord uses all kinds of ways to see that his work is done on this earth. John told him that he couldn't argue with that, but he wanted to know why Bruce was so sure about his stance on these issues.

"Because the Bible is very clear about them," Bruce said.

"According to your interpretation," John countered.

"No, it is very clear. There is no room for interpretation."

"What do you mean, Bruce? I can take any scripture and get at least three interpretations from leading theologians."

"That's the problem. There is a simple clear message with each scripture, and anyone can see it. Satan is at work in this world and he works even through theologians."

"What about people who don't read very well or can't read at all, sort of like the disciples? What if they don't agree with you about their own spiritual discernment of these issues and how they relate to the Bible?"

"Then they have to study and become knowledgeable so that they won't be lost through their own ignorance."

"I can't believe that I am hearing this—your own father couldn't read very well but was one of the finest spiritually mature people I have ever known. I happen to know he didn't have your same view on prayer in schools."

"You know, John, you would argue with a fence post. I guess that is why you are a politician. This is not personal—it's about the Word of God."

"What do you consider the Word of God, Bruce?"

"The Bible."

"I thought it was Jesus."

"You've been spending too much time looking for votes, John. You need to be reading your Bible more often. Listen, I have to go. Give my best to Paula. I'll be praying for you and your family."

"Yeah. Thanks, old buddy."

Bruce left without shaking his hand. John was angry and confused that his old friend had changed so much that he had virtually no connection with him anymore. What had happened to friendship and civility?

In thirty minutes, Fitzpatrick would be in John's office. John was not sure what to tell him.

Chapter 13

Skinny Merritt and Joe Bob Presswood were depressed—mostly from the alcohol that they had consumed the previous evening but also because they had not seen Bucky Taylor in three days. Skinny, Bucky and Joe Bob were kindred spirits. They knew that their long term health and wealth was just one lottery ticket away or just one financial scheme from becoming the next Bill Gates. They also knew that they would betray each other in a New York minute if it meant that financial freedom was to smile individually on them.

They were riding along in Skinny's 1978 Ford 150 pickup. Skinny loved his truck. It had dual exhausts and a headache rack that a welder had built for him. The headache rack had his name "Skinny" on each side of the rack. The truck was cherry red and Skinny was always entertained with personal visions of his own NASCAR fame because of his fine piece of vehicular machinery that could outrun anything in Lyric.

But Skinny was not happy this morning. They suspected that Bucky found Santa Anna's treasure and left town to find someone to help him claim it. Although they had never been out in the woods with Bucky to look for the treasure, they claimed part ownership because they had encouraged him and had given him some sage advice.

"Where do you think he is?" Skinny asked as he looked at his rotund companion.

Joe Bob was not obese but was quickly approaching it. He was having trouble with his jeans this morning. They were getting a little tight and he couldn't quite get them over his growing butt. His tee shirt also did not cover his gut. That didn't keep him from eating the crème filled donuts from Cednak's Donut Shop. He looked at Skinny with a powdered sugar mustache.

"I think he's still in the woods." Joe Bob retorted as he smacked down the last of the donut.

"You know he don't have the balls to stay out in the woods two nights in a row" Skinny sneered. "He shot his dog one night because he thought it was a wolf looking through his window."

"Yeah, but Bucky has a real passion for that treasure. If he's onto something, he'll stay there till he gets enough of it to take to some expert for verification. He's tenacious." Joe Bob was proud of his vocabulary. He had just used three big words.

"Shut your smart-ass mouth," growled Skinny. He hated people who talked smart and especially a big oaf like Joe Bob.

Joe Bob got quiet. He knew Skinny was about to explode and he didn't want to be on the receiving end of it.

"If he's out there, we're going to go get him." Skinny said.

Joe Bob smiled inwardly. He had convinced Skinny. He knew he was really the smartest of all three of them.

"And I've got the answer. We're going to find all that treasure once and for all." Skinny said as he drilled his piercing blue eyes into Joe Bob.

"What do you mean?" Joe Bob was querulous and a bit anxious.

"I mean the final solution"

"You can't do that. We'll wind up in prison"

"Nobody will know it. We'll be so far back in the woods, not even your Mama can hear it"

Mrs. Presswood had legendary hearing. When Skinny and Joe Bob were fourteen, Skinny had spent the night with him. They were in the living room watching television about midnight when they started belching and farting. Mrs. Presswood had gone upstairs to bed two hours before. Skinny thought it would be funny if they tried to light a fart. Joe Bob wanted to see it, too. Skinny convinced Joe Bob to pull down his pants and to bend over and turn his head so that he could observe. Joe Bob had some especially raunchy gas that night and when he told Skinny he was about to release a major quantity, Skinny stuck the lighter close to his butt. Sure enough, it flamed and as Joe Bob looked, he saw his mother looking at his rear end from the door. Not only that, but the flame went up his anus. Joe Bob screamed, jumped, and ran around the room holding his cheeks with his mother watching his naked bottom half. Joe Bob learned later on that his mother had heard them belching and farting and had come downstairs to tell them to quit.

Joe Bob was nervous. While drinking, all of them had talked about building a bomb out of nitrogen fertilizer and how easy it would be. They called it the final solution. The final solution for what was never decided. It just sounded good. But he was really nervous about his mother. She could hear anything.

Skinny pulled into the Lone Star feed store and backed his truck up to the loading dock and got out. He walked up the stairs and met Johnny Bush.

"Hey, Skinny, what are you doin here?" queried Johnny.

"Whaddya you think I'm doin here, dog breath? I'm buying some fertilizer."

Johnny was curious. He had seen Skinny and Joe Bob in the store on occasions but only with old man Beathard for whom they worked from time to time.

Skinny walked up to the counter and looked at Bones Johnson, the owner of the feed store, right in the eye.

"I need some nitrogen fertilizer" said Skinny.

Bones was a tall man, about six feet five inches tall and didn't weigh more than one hundred and seventy-five pounds. He was skinnier than Skinny. He had owned the store for ten years and had worked in it for twenty. He was a quiet, direct man with good business practices and didn't put up with a lot of nonsense. To him, Skinny represented a good deal of nonsense.

"What do you need it for?" he replied. That was not something that he usually asked his customers.

"I'm picking it up for old man Beathard so we can fertilize his hay pasture on Doc Winston Road."

"Mr. Beathard just came in late yesterday afternoon and picked up a load of fertilizer and said he wouldn't need any more fertilizer for six months."

Skinny was flummoxed. Joe Bob stood behind him talking to Johnny. Skinny needed some corroboration.

"Joe Bob, didn't Mr. Beathard tell us to pick up some fertilizer for him?"

Joe Bob stopped talking to Johnny. He didn't know anything about fertilizer for Mr. Beathard. But the way Skinny asked the question seemed a bit leading. He knew if he answered the wrong way, Skinny would knock the crap out of him when they were alone.

"Yeah" he replied.

"See there. Bones, you know I wouldn't shit you."

Bones didn't like it, but he couldn't turn down a sale for no reason. He looked at Skinny and asked him how much he needed.

"Fill up the back of my pickup," Skinny retorted.

"And who is going to pay for it?" asked Bones with a sternly reserved look on his face.

Skinny had to think fast. He didn't have the money and Bones wouldn't let him charge it to old man Beathard's account now unless he had a confirmation from him.

"Joe Bob is going to use his credit card" replied Skinny.

"No, I'm not," replied Joe Bob.

Skinny looked at him menacingly. Joe Bob was having second thoughts.

"Just a minute, Bones, I need to talk to Joe Bob." Skinny said.

Skinny motioned for Joe Bob to follow him outside. Joe Bob walked out with a deer in the headlights look.

"You fat butthead. How in the hell are we goin' to buy that fertilizer unless you use your credit card?"

"I don't know, but my Mama isn't going to like it."

"You're twenty-two years old. When will you quit being a titty baby? Now go back in there and buy that fertilizer."

Joe Bob was getting a bad feeling about all of this fertilizer business. Skinny was his friend, but his Mama was getting involved more deeply as each new decision was made about the final solution. However, he did not want an ass stomping from Skinny.

He walked inside and went to the counter and gave Bones his credit card. Bones looked down his nose through his cheater glasses he bought at Walmart.

"That'll be $247.52."

Joe Bob flinched. He looked at the credit card slip and hesitated before he signed it. His mother was going to kill him. But that would be later. Skinny will kill him now.

Bones looked at Johnny Bush and said, "Load 'em up, Johnny."

As Johnny was loading the fertilizer, Skinny and Joe Bob watched him from the loading dock. Joe Bob was silent and Skinny was smiling inwardly. Joe Bob looked at Skinny.

"Who's going to pay for this fertilizer?"

Skinny sneered and quietly said under his breath, "If this works, we won't have to worry about paying for anything anymore."

Skinny started walking down the wooden steps and motioned for Joe Bob to follow him. He got in the driver's side of the pickup and started the engine. Joe Bob got in the passenger side. Skinny put it in first gear and the truck was barely moving. He gave it more gas, and it barely responded. He stopped and looked at Joe Bob. They got out and looked at the rear of the truck. Both tires were flat.

Chapter 14

Jesse Henderson was working on Sunday morning. The Breedens were the reason he was here. Just before 8:00 a.m., the dispatcher had called him on his cell phone and told him that there was a man there to see him. Jesse asked her if it could wait, and she had told him that the man had something important to tell him about the Amy Breeden case. The man was insisting that he tell the Chief only. Jesse had come to the police station immediately.

It was the break he needed. The man had handed him a note and told him a guy had given it to him while he was at work in a store in Pelican. The note was from Buddy Parker. Jesse had asked the clerk if he could describe the person who gave him the note. The description was a dead ringer for Buddy. Jesse took him to one of the detectives so that they could get an official statement from him.

The note was enough information to help them find Amy. Now Jesse needed to figure out what to do. Being the first black police chief in Lyric and one of the few high ranking black police officials in the area, he always had to be extra good to get the attention of white people. He had been in the job for ten years and had gained the respect of people from all races and all walks of life. However, it had not been easy. He had been openly ridiculed from the beginning and even as he proved himself, there had still been those who silently doubted his ability.

The Breeden affair was his biggest case. He knew it was selfish, but he would like some credit. He had worked hard to change this police department. When he came here, it was a bunch of good ol' white boys who never understood the term racism. The reason they couldn't understand it was that they always perceived a difference in the level of humanity between a white person and a black person. Jesse knew that some black people were different from some white people. The good ol' white boys wanted to treat blacks with the respect that you give one human being to another. They just knew they were superior. However, they would fall all over themselves if they were around a white person, especially female, who had a lot of money. Jesse had marveled at how these guys could carry on a decent conversation with him about the many things they had in common—family, school, football, etc. But when it came to the issue of race, they took on a whole different persona. They wanted the separation— it was almost Darwinian in that they had evolved to this point and did not know how to change. Jesse had more in common with these guys than they had with their upper income idols. However, he could never command the same kind of respect.

The good ol' white boys also could not comprehend competent law enforcement. It was generally an attitude of "guilty until proven innocent" whenever an arrest was made. Civil rights did not enter the picture. Most of these guys had received the minimum required basic law enforcement training with little or no advance training or continuing education. Jesse had received a criminal justice degree from Sam Houston State University. His perception of the law was that it was to protect people first and then to punish those who were proven to violate it. He could never seem to convince the good ol' white boys that everyone had rights, including the criminal.

He had had to make some changes. It had not been popular. He was even accused of being a reverse racist. But he had persevered, and the Lyric police department had become a model for its effectiveness and efficiency. He still had some vestiges of the good ol' white boys' days, but they were slowly going away. Some white officers had actually proven to be quite capable and had given him his due respect. Harry Jenkins had become the department's chief detective and Jerry White had become a patrol officer captain. There were a good mixture of whites, blacks, and Hispanics among the officers, and all had received not only basic law enforcement training but had advanced training as well. It was also a young group of officers. Most of them were in their late twenties or early thirties.

The Amy Breeden case had not been officially a kidnapping. It was a missing persons case, but the note shed new light on the case and Jesse knew that it probably should be considered a kidnapping. That meant he should call the FBI, even if the suspects and victim had not crossed state lines. He was reluctant to call them or the Texas Rangers. He had worked with both agencies previously, and they sure liked to step in and take over. He wanted to get Amy back, but he knew the either of these agencies might muck it up. His hold card in this decision was he didn't know if the note was authentic. It could be a diversion. He needed to investigate it.

He went down the hall to talk to Harry. Harry had been raised in Lyric. He knew lots of people and had lots of knowledge about the geography. He also wanted to get Harry's opinion about calling the Texas Rangers and the FBI.

Chapter 15

Scott Mitchum was early for church. He liked being in the sanctuary early in the morning. Robert had always told him that God gave people wisdom in the morning and grace in the evening. He needed a lot of wisdom this morning. He was concerned about Amy and about how the City of Lyric was responding to her predicament. Now the FBI and Texas Rangers possibly could get involved, and the tension was growing throughout the community.

He sat down in one of the pews and looked out the stained glass window. He found it peaceful in here. There was a sense of completeness and overwhelming power. His faith was always strengthened when he gathered with other people of faith. He knew that there was pressure on preachers and churches to have good programs and minister to people. This in turn attracted more people to church, but he wondered if the real purpose of church got lost in this busy shuffle.

Robert told him that people came to church because they had a deep need for connection with God and his creation. He said that when a church forgot that fundamental principle, it may live for a few years due to a charismatic leader but that it eventually would disappear. Robert said that the church was built on faith—a mystery to all but nonetheless very apparent in every human being. Some subvert it, others pay little attention to it and some make it an important part of their lives, but all have it. Scott had asked Robert for a definition. He had replied with scripture—"the substance of things hoped for, the evidence of things not seen".

Scott knew he was relying on his faith to find the "hoped for" conclusion to this matter with Amy Breeden. What, he prayed, was he supposed to do? He had people demanding action and he wanted to make sure that anything the City did was legal and kept people from getting hurt. He was afraid of the FBI. Not that he feared for his own life or career but of the weightiness that they brought to the case and how it may affect his community. In the silence, he felt peace, and his mind was directed to wait. His faith told him it was the right thing to do.

His contemplation was broken when Bill Westcott walked up next to him. Scott saw Bill and stood up.

"Scottarino, how are you?" asked Bill. Bill had known Scott and his family since before he was born. Although he had never been called Scottarino by anyone, Bill called him that.

Scott smiled. Bill was a priceless character. He loved the old coot, but he could be a pain in the butt sometimes. He shook Bill's hand. Bill moved in close. It was a characteristic that was annoying and unusual. Bill was a close talker.

"Scottarino, how's the voice? Are you ready to sing that git down gospeling music this morning"? Bill asked as Scott drank in a combination of bad breath and breath mints.

"Yeah, Bill. I think we've got something good in store for the folks this morning."

"The Lord is good, ain't he?" Bill said in a lower voice about three inches from Scott's mouth looking Scott straight in the eye.

"Yes, he is." Scott replied as he took a step back and Bill stepped up to meet it.

"Scott, you know that ol' cancer is going away on me and I'm just praising the Lord."

"I know you are, Bill, and I'm thankful you are better."

"The Lord has wisdomized me, Scott, to know that all things work together for them that love the Lord," replied Bill.

Scott could barely hide his inward laughter. Bill was generally good for a new word in the English language, especially if it sounded important.

Bill walked away and Scott sat down again to see if he could regain his meditation and get some answers.

Scott had remembered something that Robert had told him about faith. He said that we all obtain it in different ways and that was the beauty of it. No person could tell you how to relate to God, but we could all agree that we had faith in common. Some recognized it fully and built beautiful lives because of it. Some made use of it sporadically and others knew it was there but either did not understand it or refused to see it.

He watched Bill walk through the otherwise empty church and understood this concept better. Bill, in his own way, had nourished his faith and had the fruits of the Spirit in his life. He was much different than Scott, had little education and had made many mistakes because of his ignorance, but he had persevered and had been a good person throughout his life. Scott knew that faith and grace saved people from lives of misery, and Bill, who would readily admit it, was a good example

Scott came to a conclusion. If he could lead this community with his faith and accept God's grace through whatever may happen, everyone would be much better for it. He certainly didn't want to wear religion on his sleeve. He just wanted people to know that living life gloriously meant engaging one's self both in the desert treks and the mountaintop experiences. It reminded him of the old Irish saying, 'Is this a private fight or can anyone join in?'

It was time to practice. The rest of the quartet had arrived. They ran through the song a couple of times and then they were off to Sunday School. Scott was not listening intently to the lesson as the teacher and the class discussed King David and his morals. He was still thinking about Amy and Buddy. As young people, how were they coping with their morals? Scott thought how ironic it was that even King David had ordered the murder of one of his finest soldiers over two thousand years ago, but he was known as a man 'after God's own heart'. He just hoped neither one of these young people would do something they would regret.

Chapter 16

It was muggy. A Lyric morning in the fall was not always cool. The summer heat would hang around. A person could wake up and go outside with the intention of accomplishing something in the cool morning air. Within thirty minutes, they would be sweating from head to toe. Jack Rocker was sweating and getting perturbed. People were moving too slow for his taste. His patience was wearing thin. For a reason he couldn't understand, people didn't see the beauty of his plan. Richard Breeden owed him money and wouldn't pay it. He took something of Breeden's that was very precious to him, his daughter, and would give her back when he got his money. He knew that was the only way he would get paid.

Forget lawyers and the courts. The law was stacked in Breeden's favor. Breeden had told him to steal timber and he had agreed to do it—for a fee. He could never prove that Breeden had told him to steal the timber and because of his standing in the community no one would believe Jack Rocker over Richard Breeden.

To make matters worse, his stepson was not cooperating. He had three people with him in the deep East Texas woods who would try to sabotage anything he attempted to do. On top of that, he was running out of meth. He had cooked up a batch about a month ago, sold some of it and kept some for himself. He had to have it to keep his energy up and keep going.

Rocker looked up into the tall pines. They whispered as the fall breeze began to blow through them. Their smell was uplifting. As wintertime approached, the wet weather would bring up the smell of the damp earth and leaves but for now the pine smell had the upper hand. He loved the woods. He knew them better than anyone in the Lyric area. They had been his solace, his livelihood, his friend. He had only turned to meth when things started getting complicated. His wife was a nice enough woman, but she had more problems that he could deal with and her kids were a pain in the ass. Buddy was a wimp. The only reason Jack had involved him in this little escapade is because he was Amy Breeden's friend.

He heard an engine and realized that it was Buddy coming back. He knew he could trust him. The boy was eaten up with morals—that's what made him a wimp. Buddy was never going to amount to anything because he considered how things affected other people. Jack knew a person couldn't do that and survive in this world. His philosophy was that he really didn't care what happened to other people, just as long as he was able to take care of himself.

As Buddy entered the camp area, he could see that things were about the same. He was afraid Jack may have tried to hurt Amy. Buddy drove up to Jack and gave him the food items and kept the medicine. He knew Jack wouldn't doctor Bucky.

"Where's my change?" Jack scowled.

"Here." Buddy thrust his hand out and walked away.

"I knew you'd come back, you wimpy piece of shit." Jack cackled.

Buddy walked away and went to Bucky. As he approached Bucky, Amy smiled at him.

"I'm actually glad to see you, Buddy" she said. "I knew you wouldn't abandon us."

Buddy thought about Jack's remark and her statement. Maybe he did have some character and it did show. He felt more confident. He looked at Bucky. He had bought alcohol, hydrogen peroxide and antibiotic ointment along with some bandages. Bucky was dozing and he woke him up.

Amy stood next to him and said, "I've had some first aid and CPR training. If you'll hold Bucky, I'll dress the wound."

Chapter 17

Robert leaned back in the porch chair. Scott had come to visit him right after he got his professional engineering license.

"Well, you're official," Robert smiled.

Scott nodded with a big smile. He was glad to be starting on his career.

"Now, don't be a damn fool," Robert said.

Scott was somewhat puzzled. Robert had always encouraged him and had never taken exception to his education or his career choice.

"Scott, very few people understand the real value of education. It's not about advancing your standing in society, either through wealth, position, or power. It's about pursuing the mystery."

Scott furrowed his brow. "What are you talking about, Robert?"

"The mystery of God's creation," Robert replied. "Have you ever met an uneducated atheist?"

Scott thought. Most of the atheists he knew had a lot of education. "Not to my knowledge."

"They are rare and there's a reason for that." Robert replied.

"Why?" Scott asked.

"Once you have knowledge, you begin to rationalize everything, and you forget about the mystery of creation—especially after you have some worldly success and you get older. It becomes easy to believe that you have the answer to most everything and if you don't have it, you, or someone else will be able to find it someday through reason. You don't need God. Atheists are like that."

"The other side of that coin is the educated and arrogant religious elite. They, too, have forgotten about the mystery. I'm not talking just about the Catholics and the older Protestant denominations in Christianity. I'm talking about all religions where there are self-appointed Pharisaical leaders purveying theology that "has the answers". This involves all religions. In many ways, atheists and religious leaders have the same view about life. They both believe in reason, but they get dogmatic about material world methodologies and never really understand the mystery of faith and grace."

"This religious elite and atheists have much in common. They have a tendency to believe that life can be explained through a system--the system of religion or the system of reason. Religious people want to pummel you with moral relativism every time you get off the beaten explanatory path of the Bible or the Koran or the Book of Mormon or some other book written by people. Atheists pummel you with not using logic or the scientific method to explain our existence. Neither group gets a lot of joy out of living and the glory of the struggle. They whine a lot."

"Life cannot be explained and that is why is important to believe in God but don't leave out the mystery. I believe you have to live every day and that you are fortunate to have the experience. This life is short when you take eternity into account, but it can be long if you devote it to conformity—the conformity of religion or the conformity of reason. There is a reason—see I'm not leaving reason out--that Jesus gave us two commandments—love the Lord your God with all your heart and all your soul and all your mind and love your neighbor as yourself. These two commandments are mysterious and simple to understand at the same time. We are to bask in the creator and his creation. There is no specific instruction other than to bask in it. It's like dancing. Do it because you are living. Religionists and atheists are not fun people—they've got corncobs up their butts."

Scott laughed long and hard. Robert had a way of bringing a deep discussion to pithy conclusion. However, he was curious. "How about the Bible, Robert? I've learned a lot from it and still live by the principles taught in it."

"I love the Bible and I read it all the time. I've read it through three times and marvel at its relevance even today. It gives us historical guidance and the ability to understand God. However, we are motivated by living spiritual forces, and they are virtually the reason people live the life they live. We are more spiritual than we are physical. We can recognize these forces, ignore them, or play a game with ourselves about them being non-existent. Purveyors of written book theology—whether it be the Bible, the Torah, the Koran or whatever—miss the point about spiritual forces. We are living now, not in the past."

"What we do now makes a difference in the unfolding of God's creation. We stand on the written book theology, but we are writing new chapters in it every day. God revealed himself to me through Jesus Christ but each day he reveals more about me and him through the Holy Spirit. I also understand spiritual warfare. There are evil spiritual forces that promote the opposite of Jesus' two commandments. These forces hate the creator and loathe the creative process. That is why we have crime. Whether a person does crime because he is motivated by evil or is driven to it by persons who perpetuate evil, the criminal act takes place because of evil spiritual forces. God eventually will prevail in this war, but Scott be wary. Those who say that God has led them to do something that reveals itself as unjust and unfair to you, stay away from it. It is evil wrapping itself in God's name to carry out its own self-centered desires. It is not part of the creation."

"Part of the mystery is what I have told you here works for me in my search for meaning. I think many parts of it work for all people, but everyone has a different life to live. That is why when my Christian friends ask me about the salvation of believers in other religions such as Islam or Buddhism, I tell them I don't know how God deals with those folks. I am a pretty finite being, and I know that I have been saved from being separated from the Creator by knowing Jesus. It is as simple as that and I'm grateful for it. I believe that God is very capable of handling all of his creation, and he just wants me to do my part."

After that lesson, Scott sat on Robert's front porch for a long time, staring into space.

Chapter 18

Joe Bob was worn out. After he and Skinny had unloaded all of the fertilizer, jacked up the truck and had taken the rear wheels off, he couldn't move. He had removed his shirt and sweat glistened on his pink skin. With his short blond hair and round face, he looked like Porky Pig. Skinny was sitting beside him on the bench right outside the feed store with his shirt off smoking a cigarette.

"That was one sumbitch," Skinny stated. "I hadn't worked that hard in a long time. Let's ask Bones if we can borrow his truck and take these wheels over to Bodittles and see if he can get some new tires on them pretty quick."

"How are we going to pay for them?" Joe Bob asked.

Skinny held the cigarette and turned slowly and glared at him. "How do you think we're going to pay for them, dumshit?"

"We ain't using that credit card again," Joe Bob said with authority.

"Oh yeah and how do you propose we pay for them?" Skinny responded. He was seething.

"Use your own money, asshole," Joe Bob looked Skinny straight in the eye.

Skinny pounced. Joe Bob couldn't react fast enough. They rolled off the bench and Skinny was pounding Joe Bob in the face. Joe Bob finally took some action and rapped his big arms around Skinny and wouldn't let go. Skinny began gasping for air as he continued to inflict some damage to Joe Bob's nose and eyes. Joe Bob turned his head from side to side and held on with a death grip. Skinny's blows became less effective until finally, he was gasping out pleas to Joe Bob to let go. Joe Bob finally released his grip and Skinny rolled off him and lay out on the asphalt parking lot.

They were a sight. Both of them were laying face up, spread eagled on the parking lot gasping for air. Joe Bob was bleeding some on his face and was developing some bruises. Skinny couldn't fill up his smoke-damaged lungs fast enough.

Bones Johnson walked out of the store and looked down at Joe Bob and then at Skinny.

"You boys cut this shit out right now or I'll call the cops. I've never seen the like." Bones shook his head and walked back into the store.

Joe Bob sat up. He looked at Skinny and said, "I don't think Bones is going to let us borrow his truck."

Skinny looked up at the sky and said, "No, probably not."

"I guess we'll just have to carry those wheels over to Bodittles", Joe Bob said as he began laughing.

"What are you laughing at?" Skinny replied.

"I was laughing about you and me hugging. Some people may think we are more than close friends."

"You can just put a shankle on that shit right now. I ain't gay—never have been and never will be."

Joe Bob looked fearful, "Well, I'm not neither for the record." He looked around to make sure no one had heard them talking.

Skinny sat up. "Let's go get those wheels and get over to Bodittles."

"Skinny, you're going to have to help me pay off this credit card," Joe Bob said on the way with the wheels with concern.

'I will, I will. We just got to get moving cause Bucky may have the jump on us, and we can't let him have all that treasure."

They alternated carrying the wheels and rolling them the three blocks to Bodittles. The hot weather with high humidity was taking its toll on them. Both men were not in the best physical condition and by the time they got to Bodittles, they looked like they were going to pass out.

Bodittle Carter was sitting in a padded chair in the shade of what used to be a cover for the gas pumps on a gas station from another time. He had been the second owner of the establishment. He had worked there since he was fourteen Over the years, Bodittle had pumped gas, changed oil in vehicles, greased them, put on new tires and batteries, and gave sage advice about everything. The gas business had gone away when the new EPA requirements had made it too costly for single station operators to make a living. But Bodittle had always been adaptable. He accepted it graciously and focused on all the other services he had provided in the past. He even installed three more vehicle lifts and another bay. Life was all right.

Bodittle looked at Skinny and Joe Bob. "You boys look like you've been in fight and you both lost."

Skinny replied, "Well, sumthin like that. Bodittle, we need to get some cheap tires that will handle a load. We blew these out with a load of fertilizer."

Bodittle looked at both tires suspiciously. "Must have been one helluva load."

"It was." Skinny said impatiently. "Can you put something on them?"

Bodittle knelt down and ran his hand over each tire. He shook his head and stood up.

"I think so. These tires are in pretty bad shape. It's a wonder they didn't blow out before now. I can sell you some Cooper tires that are good for about 20,000 miles. That's the cheapest I got."

"How much?" Skinny said with a worried look.

"Two hundred dollars driveout."

Joe Bob winced. Skinny looked contemplative. "Put 'em on," he said.

Chapter 19

It was late afternoon. Harry Jenkins, the chief detective of the Lyric Police Department, was concerned. He and Jesse needed to move quickly on the Breeden case, but they were afraid that it could get out of hand and someone might get hurt.

"I think we ought to call Scott," Harry said to Jesse.

"Why?" Jesse replied.

"Scott seems to have a sixth sense about this political stuff, and this may get way out of hand if the FBI and everyone else is alerted. Let's call him"

"Okay, George needs to be in on this one, also. I'll get a meeting with both of them." Jesse picked up the phone and called George Hanel.

Fifteen minutes later, all four men were meeting in a conference room at City Hall. George Hanel was an intelligent, easy going City Manager and had held the position for five years. He was liked by employees and the people of the community. Sometimes he ruffled the City Council's feathers when he either told them they needed to do something or that there were some things they could not do. However, they respected him, and he had made progress in making Lyric a safe, stable, and progressive community.

Jesse started off the meeting by telling Scott that a new development in the Amy Breeden case had come up and since it was politically sensitive, he thought they ought to know about it.

"I'm concerned about the FBI and Texas Rangers" Jesse said. "I don't want them rushing to judgment on this and running up on a dead end since we don't know the accuracy of this note. Also, I want to be sure that Buddy is protected if we do find them."

George was contemplative. "You realize if you leave them out of the loop, they could get nasty with us." he replied.

"Yeah, I know that, but I have a feeling about this one. We could cause more problems by rushing into this situation with guns drawn."

"I know the Tanner woods fairly good. Harry and I used to do a lot of hunting and camping there when we were kids. Why don't just the two of us go see if this checks out and then we'll call Jesse and you can bring the Rangers and the Feds with you, if it's necessary", Scott interjected.

George looked at Scott. "Mayor, you're putting yourself at some risk. This is really a police matter."

"George, I've got some emotional capital in this deal. This town is devastated about this situation. I've got a friend's daughter involved and guess who knows the Tanner woods better than anyone else—me. I'll be careful, but I want to see this done right. I'm going." Scott said with passion as he drilled George with his blue eyes.

George didn't flinch. "I know you mean it. Chief, are you okay with this?"

Jesse hesitated. "Scott, I gotta say that I'm concerned, but I think you're right. I trust you and Harry more than anyone else to make this go the right way."

"Let's go." Scott said as he got up from the table and headed for the door. Harry followed him and they got in Harry's four wheel drive Ford

Explorer. Harry pulled out of City Hall in a deliberate, fast pace so that lives could be saved, and their community could overcome this hurt.

Chapter 20

The weather was getting cooler as Amy dressed Bucky's wound. The small pine saplings were swaying in time with the wind. The sun was still shining brightly as it sunk into the western horizon. Amy knew it would be cool tonight, and they had extraordinarily little to keep them warm. Bucky had an infection and the fever would get worse with the cold weather. She began thinking what she would do when Bucky got the chills.

She looked on the north side of the camp and saw a yaupon thicket. If the truck was parked over there, Bucky could stay on the south side of the pickup in a sleeping bag along with his big work jacket. Maybe he wouldn't get chilled too much. She would also build a fire next to Bucky's bed. She told her plan to Buddy. He agreed and got in the truck to move it. Then he felt a gun barrel on his cheek. Jack was pressing the shotgun against him,

"Where the hell do you think you're goin?" Jack sternly relayed to him.

"I'm going to park the truck so that it will block off some of the wind and Bucky won't get chilled tonight." Buddy replied. "Take the damn gun off my face."

"I'll do that when I get good and ready, dipshit. Now, let me tell you something. I make the decisions around here and nobody's moving this truck. Get out and go get some firewood. We'll get 'ol Bucky so hot that he won't need any warming up."

Buddy opened the door as Jack continued to point the gun at him. He walked down the logging trail that brought them to the campsite and started looking for wood.

Amy was giving Bucky some water and glowered at Jack. "You're a real piece of work, Jack Rocker. You kidnap me, force Buddy to help you, shoot Bucky and now you don't even care if he dies. When you get caught, you'll never be able to make it out of prison—too many sentences for multiple crimes."

"And you're a real smart ass." Jack growled at her as he took the gun and hit Amy on the side of the head with the butt. She slumped to the ground and lay still, still conscious.

Bucky was too delirious to notice. Jack was enraged. Things were going wrong. This was supposed to go differently. Amy Breeden was a girl. She was supposed to be afraid. He had envisioned them staying out in the woods a few days, then he would get his ransom money, lose the authorities by using his outdoors abilities and work his way to Mexico and eventually to South America. This girl was supposed to be immobilized by fear. On top of that, this turd, Taylor, shows up and she and Buddy try to help him. Jack meant to kill him but missed the shot. He didn't want to shoot him while he was defenseless but if' he ever got up to run, 'ol Buck was a dead man.

Buddy was gathering wood under a massive white oak tree that had fallen three years ago in the hurricane. He marveled at how big the tree had been. It had begun to rot and some of the limbs would make good firewood. He would use one limb sort of like a Native American travois and pile several on top of it. When he got back to the camp, he would take the axe and chop them up for firewood. As he bent down to pick up another piece, he froze. The wind had been blowing all day, but he thought he distinctly heard his name. He looked up, looked around and heard his name spoken in a whisper. The sound was coming from a briar thicket directly in front of him about thirty yards away. Buddy cautiously started walking toward it. As he got within five yards; Scott Mitchum walked out from behind the thicket with his fingers on his lips and hurriedly motioned for Buddy to move his way.

As Buddy walked behind the thicket, Scott continued to emphasize with his body language to be quiet and then he spoke.

"Buddy, we got your note," Scott whispered. Scott noticed that Buddy's eyes were wide, and he looked fearful when he saw Harry Jenkins.

"Mr. Mitchum," Buddy replied, "I'm in a mess and don't know what to do." A tear began to run down his cheek.

Scott was overwhelmed with sympathy. He had watched this boy overcome some overwhelming odds. He had personally watched him mature in a chaotic life situation. Now, he was in a test, and Scott knew he was doing everything to pass it. Scott remembered how hard it was to reach manhood.

"It's okay, Buddy," Harry whispered. "We're here to help and we have a plan. However, you have to start the execution of it. Are you ready to do it? We have to save and protect Amy and Bucky."

"Yes sir, I'm ready. I just wish none of this would've ever happened." Buddy dejectedly said.

"Put it behind, you, Buddy," Scott replied. "Remember how I told you one time that guilt will drag you down. Get rid of it. It's over with and now you can look to the future and make your life right."

Some life returned to Buddy's eyes, and he looked at Harry and said, "What do you want me to do?"

Chapter 21

Skinny couldn't believe his good luck. They finally made it to the Rice Creek woods and were digging. They had to go through an excruciating recital of the merits of saving money with tire quality with Bodittle.

"Now, you boys know that more expensive tires will last you longer than these here cheap tires. You can even have a blowout quicker as you're driving down the road with a heavy load. Makes a helluva noise. You know I was in Vietnam, and a tire blowout with tread coming off reminds me of several rifle rounds hitting metal--makes me jump every time I hear one. No flashbacks or nothin'. Just makes me jumpy."

"Now, for just a hundred and fifty more dollars, I can sell you some tires that are guaranteed for 50,000 miles and won't have the problems of these cheap tires. You'll ride smoother and won't be worried about the tread coming off. That tread coming off"—Bodittle began to make rifle shot sounds with his mouth—"will scare the ever loving horseshit out of you and could make you have a wreck."

Joe Bob had wondered how horseshit could be ever loving and how he could have any in him. He had told Bodittle they couldn't afford the expensive tires and would have to use the cheap tires.

"Suit yourself" Bodittle scornfully replied, "but I don't think you're going to be happy."

As slow as Bodittle was in life, he did have a fast worker, Piston Gillen, who could have worked in a NASCAR pit crew. They were out of there in no time and quickly loaded up the fertilizer.

As Skinny looked over at Joe Bob, he was proud of what they had accomplished. They were just about finished with this pit for the fertilizer bomb and soon they would be loading the fertilizer in it. Skinny felt like a CEO—he loved it when his plans came together. When that bomb went off, Santa Anna's gold would be raining down on them.

No matter what Joe Bob did, he still looked like Porky Pig. His nose had dirt on in it, and he looked like a wild piney wood rooter. Skinny had this image of Joe Bob not using the shovel to dig the pit but his nose and face to root it to completion. He began laughing. Joe Bob looked over at him.

"What are you laughing at?" Joe Bob whined.

"You look like a piney wood rooter," Skinny replied.

"Well you look like a praying mantis," Joe Bob growled.

"What the hell is that?" Skinny questioned with a laugh.

"It's a stick figure insect that can't get it up because it doesn't have any meat on its bones," Joe Bob retorted.

Skinny didn't like his manhood being questioned. He wrestled Joe Bob into the sandy loam and put his face in it. For a thin man, Skinny had a lot of strength. Even though Joe Bob outweighed him by seventy pounds, Skinny was able to handle him through agility, skill, and downright intimidation.

"Listen, you fat bag of gas. My pecker can get up fifteen times to your one. I've screwed every available piece of pussy in this part of the County and you've yet to hide your salami in any toaster oven. So, shut up and keep diggin' or I'll make you do it with your nose."

Skinny let Joe Bob go and got up. Joe Bob just lay there breathing hard with his face in the dirt. He hated the way Skinny treated him when he got mad. Joe Bob was trying to have some fun with him, and Skinny couldn't take any teasing. Skinny picked up his shovel and began digging. Joe Bob got up and started to work.

After an hour they had a hole big enough for the fertilizer. They took a break. Skinny sat down and Joe Bob stood beside him. Skinny realized that they had forgotten water and had nothing to drink. He looked at Joe Bob and the sweat beading up all over his pink skin.

"Why in the hell didn't you bring some water?" Skinny glared at Joe Bob.

Joe Bob said nothing. He was tired of Skinny. All of these years he had been succumbing to Skinny's psychological games and he was about to end it.

"Are you going to answer me, Porky Pig?" Skinny stated.

Joe Bob still did not answer.

Skinny put his hands to his chest and then started to flap his arms and said: "Pa pa pa pa pa pak pak" imitating a chicken. Then he continued walking around the site where he began to step high and continue his chicken sounds. Joe Bob looked at him in awe and wondered how a grown man could be that stupid. Then he thought about himself and why he was with such a person. Maturity started to settle in on Joe Bob. He began to wonder what he was doing here in the first place.

Chapter 22

Mary Jo Breeden was not getting good vibes from her husband about Amy's kidnapping. He had been distant ever since they had heard the news, and that Buddy Parker was also missing. She had tried to talk to him about it, but he would nod his head and look off into the distance, like he was thinking about something else. Mary Jo knew she had to confront him about it.

It was Saturday night and most of the time they had something to do, but this was one of those rare times when they were at home together. Romance between them had been negligible over the last several years. Having kids and running a business put enough pressure and work on both of them that they had put it aside. Occasionally, sexual encounters would happen because they still slept together when Richard was in town. Mary Jo had tried to light a fire once in a while but to no avail. She often wondered if there was something else she should be doing. She thought she was still attractive and had been told that by other people, even men. She had tried to engage Richard in some playfulness, but he refused to go along. She was beginning to wonder if he had someone else.

He was in the living room reading the newspaper and she sat on the couch next to his easy chair. After she sat down, he never moved and continued to read.

"What are you not telling me about Jack Rocker?" she boldly stated.

He put the paper down and looked at her curiously. "Excuse me," he replied with a questioning look.

"Richard, I've known you long enough to know when you are not telling the whole story. There is something else to this kidnapping and I have a feeling it has something to do with you and Jack Rocker."

"You're damn right it does. I fired that mad bastard and now he's getting even."

"I think there's more to it than that."

"And what pray tell, Miss Sleuth of the Year, did you have in mind?"

"I've been looking at the finances, and I know we are struggling. For some reason, you have been traveling a lot lately, spending a lot of money on those travels and taking a large salary for the last two years. The regular way we do business, buying timber, cutting it, and selling it is not enough to keep up with our expenditures. I want to know if you told Jack Rocker to steal that timber and if you made a deal with him."

Richard looked at her long and hard like he was trying to stare her down. Mary Jo didn't flinch. Richard replied, "That's pretty far-fetched Mary Jo. What could I possibly gain by stealing timber?"

"Richard, you are not the same person you used to be when it comes to business. Something has happened. You just seem to want more and more money. When a person is desperate for something, they'll do just about anything."

"Is someone filming this conversation? I feel like we're in the middle of a novel or a movie. Where are you going with this touchy-feely stuff?

"Are you having an affair with someone?"

"Yes." Richard replied immediately.

Mary Jo was stunned. She had mildly suspected it, but never did she think he would bluntly admit it. She didn't know what to say.

They sat in silence for several minutes. Richard was looking at her. Her head was bowed, and she began to cry.

Richard was the first to speak. "I was going to tell you before the kidnapping, but I couldn't do that to you. It's been going on for about two years. We're in love, and I want a divorce."

Mary Jo continued to weep softly. She was pretty tough but with Amy gone and this news, she couldn't handle it.

"Then you better leave right now and don't come back," she sobbed.

Richard got up and quietly left the room. He went into the bedroom, packed his suitcase, and walked out the door.

Mary Jo watched him from the couch. Neither of them said anything to each other. Mary Jo fell on her knees and wept.

Chapter 23

It was 2:00 a.m. before Mary Jo got up off the floor. After crying for about an hour, she prayed and remembered an event when she and Scott Mitchum were dating. They had gone to Robert Ward's house.

Scott and Mary Jo were freshmen in college. Both of them were home for the summer. They had never been serious about each other but did enjoy each other's company. Scott had asked her if she wanted to go with him to dinner and movie. She had agreed and he asked her if she would like to go visit Robert on their way. She had always been curious about the man and thought it would be an interesting way to spend the afternoon.

It was the one and only time that she had been in Robert's home. She had been impressed with the man's house. It certainly wasn't feminine, but it was well kept and decorated in a masculine manner. Like its owner, it had character. The couch and two easy chairs set up in a paneled living room faced a large fireplace. On the walls were pictures of nature, which looked like they were personal enlarged photographs. One of a seagull in flight, intrigued her. The sky in the background was ice blue. The seagull's wings were fully spread as if he were about to land or was hovering. His eyes were focused and intent. Mary Jo could see the markings on his beak and face.

A set of branding irons and a crosscut saw were on another wall along with what appeared to be family pictures of another time. Half the pictures had people who were well-groomed with fashionable period clothing. The other half was dressed in cowboy and laborer clothing. Mary Jo was beginning to understand a little more about Robert.

"Well, Scott, you definitely make good choices in the company you keep, good looks and good character" Robert said as he greeted both at the door.

Mary Jo had blushed. She had only met Robert Ward on one other occasion, but her father and mother knew him well.

"Thank you, Mr. Ward" she replied.

"I'm honored to have you in my house, Mary Jo. Your mother and father are fine people, and I want you to give them a hearty hello for me when you go home. And by the way, call me Robert," Robert said and smiled as he shook her hand.

"Robert, I thought you might like a visit from Mary Jo. She and I are friends and kindred spirits. She could probably use some of your sage advice. I know I could." Scott answered and laughed quietly as he shook Robert's hand.

"Sage? Now isn't that a herb? I'm not a particularly good herbalist, Scott. You've come to the wrong place." They all laughed, and Robert motioned for them to sit in the living room, asking them if he could get them something to drink. They requested some iced tea, and Robert went to the kitchen to fix it.

Mary Jo sat next to Scott on the couch. "He is such a nice man, and very interesting." Mary Jo said as she picked up an issue of Newsweek magazine on the coffee table.

Scott looked at her with appraising eyes. How could Mary Jo be that insightful about Robert without knowing him? He was impressed.

Robert came back in the living room with iced tea and they each took a sip. Scott had always been surprised with how well the man could make iced tea. It just made the day better when you sat with him and drank a glass.

"Well, what brings you two young people out to see an old coot on a fine day like today?" Robert asked.

"To tell you the truth, Robert, I really just wanted to come and see how you are doing, but I was talking to Mary Jo the other day about college, life , you know the stuff that we nineteen year olds bat around a lot and thought she might like to hear some of your wisdom—not your herbal knowledge." Scott answered as he laughed.

"Having some angst about the future, Mary Jo? Just remember, it happens to all of us." Robert said as he drilled his gentle blue eyes into her.

"Oh, I don't know Mr.—I mean, Robert. Sometimes, I wonder why I'm doing what I'm doing. It doesn't seem to have a purpose," Mary Jo replied as she turned her head

"Sure, it does—it just may not seem purposeful to you."

"What do you mean by that?"

"You're not doing what you want to do. You are doing what other people are telling you to do or what brings you the least amount of fear or what ensures your loyalty to friends and family."

"Well, I chose my major in college and I choose the things I do in college."

"Did you really do that or was that heavily suggested to you by your mother and father or your counselor at school?"

Mary Jo could not think of a time that she had given her college major or her extracurricular activities at school considerable thought. She had acted by rote from the adults in her life about what was best.

"I guess you're right, but I don't know what to do about it."

"Follow your bliss."

"What?"

"Follow your bliss. Do whatever it is that deep inside of you, motivates you to live each day. Something you would always do for free-- something that makes you whole."

Mary Jo gave this some thought. She watched Robert as he looked at her intently. Scott was sitting beside her with one leg in a scissor position on the couch, a relaxed humorous look on his face.

She had always wanted to work with disabled children. She had seen their longing looks as she dealt with them in Vacation Bible School and working at the library in the summers. She knew she could make them happy and help them to live productive lives. But she was good at math and everyone told her to be a CPA—she would have a long career and make a lot of money.

"Mary Jo," Robert said softly "this is about your faith. It's the essence of faith. The Scriptures say that 'Faith is the substance of things hoped for, the evidence of things not seen'. Only you and God can establish the relationship of faith. Pray about this. Seek his guidance. Step out on faith and begin a journey on your own. Take the risk and own the glory. It won't be easy, and you will be lonely, but you will be blissful."

Mary Jo was astounded. In a matter of minutes, this man had looked into her soul and found the key to it, unlocked it, and set her free. She was speechless.

Scott just smiled at her, like he knew, and then proceeded to talk to Robert about skeet shooting and fishing and how the Houston Rockets were going to do this season. Mary Jo sat in silence, vaguely listening to their conversation, thinking about herself, her life, and what she was going to do about it.

Eventually, Scott looked at her and said, "Are you ready to go?"

"Yes, whenever you are."

She got up and looked at the picture of the seagull again. She said to Robert, "I love that picture. It is almost perfect--the sky, the detail, the wingspread, the intensity of the gull."

With a faraway, wise look, Robert answered, "That seagull, Mary Jo, is following his bliss."

Chapter 24

Fran Mitchum was taking her kids to a youth activity at the church. It was a ritual that had become routine over the years. Elaine had to have everything just so-so before she walked out the door and was always running late. Matthew had to get in the last moves on his video game before he shut it down. She was yelling at them to come on and get in the car.

Jesse Henderson had called Scott with an emergency concerning the Breeden case, and he had gone to the police station.

As they got on the road, everyone was silent. Fran noticed how these times were reflective for her and for the kids. She looked at Elaine, sitting in front with her. She was becoming such a beautiful young woman. She looked like Fran but had her father's determined demeanor. Elaine stood back for no one.

Matthew on the other hand looked like his father but had a much more easy-going approach to life. He drove his sister crazy because he always wanted to play video games and be with his laid back friends. He didn't want the high volume of activity that his sister required with her constant entourage and things to do and places to see. Elaine never got him, but Fran knew she deeply cared for Matthew. One Saturday night, she stayed in his room playing video games with him until 1:00 a.m. when he broke his leg. Elaine hated video games, but Matthew had been abandoned by his friends and had no one around him for a week. Elaine quietly went up to his room and told him she would like to play a game. Matthew never forgot it.

Matthew showed the same love and respect for his sister. Even though he couldn't stand her favorite TV show and made fun of it, he used his allowance and money from helping the neighbor pick up tree limbs in the yard to buy her the first season's videos.

Fran was proud of her kids and her husband. She knew it was the deep love she and Scott had for each other that was transposed to their children. Her thoughts veered to 1 Corinthians 13 and how Paul the Apostle eloquently states his treatise on eternal love. It was comforting for her to know she would always love Scott, Elaine and Matthew and they would love her.

She was coming up on the intersection of State Highway 116 and FM 1313. She felt this overwhelming need to tell her kids that she loved them.

Fran looked at Matthew to the right in the rear view mirror and then at Elaine in the front seat. She smiled and said: "I love both of you".

Elaine looked up at her, puzzled but glad to hear her mother say it. In response, she said, "I love you, Mom."

Matthew looked up from his video game and said, "Yeah, love ya, Mom."

She was still looking in the rearview mirror when she lifted her foot from the brake and touched the accelerator.

She never noticed the Ford F-350 pickup truck barreling down the Farm to Market Road. It never even slowed down for the stop sign.

The truck hit the driver's side. Fran was instantly killed.

Chapter 25

Buddy Parker sauntered into the campsite with wood for the fire. He was trying to look nonchalant. He must have been overdoing it because Jack asked him what was wrong.

"Nothing," Buddy replied.

"Well, you sure are acting funny," Jack sneered.

Buddy tried to look calm. He was extremely nervous. He wasn't sure that he could carry out his role in this arrest. Mr. Mitchum and Detective Jenkins had told him they didn't want anyone to get hurt and that if Buddy could distract Jack away from Bucky and Amy, then he wouldn't be able to hold them hostage. Although they knew that Buddy would also be at risk, he was much stronger and quicker and could probably move away before Jack could act.

Buddy agreed. He looked at Jack and said, "Hey, Jack. I need to talk to you away from the others. Can you come over here with me?"

Jack was immediately suspicious. Why did this dipshit kid all of sudden want to talk to him, privately? He was cautious. "Sure, kid but you come over here," Jack replied.

Detective Jenkins and Mr. Mitchum had suspected this move by Jack. They had told him to come up with something that would make Jack want to talk to him privately.

Buddy immediately knew what it would be—his mother. Jack and Buddy had come to blows in the past over the way Jack had treated his mother. He knew that Jack wanted an opportunity to beat him up and that discussing his mother may be the provocation and justification that Jack needed to whip Buddy.

In a defiant voice with a trace of nervousness, Buddy answered, "I want to talk to you about Mom."

Jack knew he had Buddy. This was just the opening he needed to whip the shit out of the boy. Buddy couldn't control himself around Jack when it came to his mother. He walked to the edge of the woods, where Buddy was standing.

"Okay, dipshit, what do you want to say to me about that bitch you call dear old Mom?" Jack stated.

Harry Jenkins stepped out of the woods, in a shooter's stance with his .357 Magnum, and said, "Drop the gun, Rocker, it's over."

Jack Rocker in blinding speed, grabbed Buddy by the arm and wrenched it behind his back. At the same moment, Scott Mitchum jumped on Rocker's broad back putting his right forearm around Rocker's neck and holding it in a death grip with his left hand. Rocker let go of Buddy but pulled his shotgun up and shot Buddy in the leg. Scott held on as Rocker ran around the campsite like a wild bull trying to shake him. Rocker was gasping for breath and bucking like a mule, but Scott was relentless. He finally fell on his back with Scott still holding on. Scott knew something got messed up on his body when Rocker fell on him, but he would not let go. Harry ran up and stuck the gun up to Rocker's temple and said: "Let it be, Rocker or you're a dead man. Now get up slow and easy."

Jack Rocker was spent. Scott let go. Rocker rolled off Scott, gasping for air. Scott tried to roll over but found it hard to move. Harry jumped on Rocker's back and handcuffed him in two seconds. Jack Rocker began to wail and then after a few seconds, he started that insane laughing cackle.

Chapter 26

The world fell apart. A huge explosion blew through the woods. The tops of pine trees were snapping, and the concussion was laying over pin oaks all around Jack Rocker's camp site. Scott couldn't move. Buddy was bleeding profusely from his leg and Bucky was wounded. Harry, Amy, and Rocker were the only ones healthy and Rocker was handcuffed.

Even though the explosion blew them off their feet, Harry managed to hang on to Rocker and his gun. He got him back up, looked at Scott and said, "What the hell was that?"

Scott grimaced and said, "I don't know".

Harry looked around for a reason this happened. All he saw were downed trees and dirt everywhere. Then he looked to the south and coming toward him, about fifty yards away, were two balls of fire, screaming. He really couldn't believe his eyes. One was a skinny white guy and the other was a fat white guy. The fat guy was actually running faster that the skinny one.

When they got about ten yards away, Harry could see that their clothes were on fire and were gradually being extinguished by the running and lack of fuel. The skinny guy was Skinny Merritt and the fat guy was

Joe Bob Presswood. They ran directly up to Harry. Joe Bob screamed, "Mr. Jenkins, help me, help me!!

Harry couldn't let go of Rocker. He yelled at both of them to drop on the ground and roll. They immediately followed his order and the rest of the flames went out. Amy ran over and looked at them. Their clothes had been mostly burned off their bodies and they had suffered some first and second degree burns. Harry told them to lay there and be still. Amy ran and got them some water. Harry took Rocker to the patrol car and locked him in the back. He sat in the front seat and got on the radio.

Elizabeth Perry answered at dispatch. Harry was thankful for that. Elizabeth knew how to get people in the right places. Harry felt like he was back in the Gulf War.

"Elizabeth, I've got a crime scene and a major explosion out here in the Tanner Woods by Rice Ridge." He read her the GPS coordinates and continued. "We'll need an ambulance. It looks like the Mayor has been seriously hurt, Buddy Parker has been shot in the leg—maybe a severed femoral artery, Bucky Taylor has been shot in the arm, Joe Bob Presswood and Skinny Merritt have third degree burns. Tell Jesse to get out here with two detectives. We have a crime scene. Get this moving, Elizabeth. I'm out here by myself with Amy Breeden." He clicked off

Elizabeth couldn't believe it. She thought Harry was fooling with her. She tried to respond but she couldn't raise him. She put the wheels into motion.

Harry ran back to Buddy. He had passed out and there was blood everywhere. Harry knew it was serious. He looked at Scott and said, "This is triage, Scott. I've got to take care of him first." Harry took his large wide receiver hands, put them over Buddy's blue jeans at the entry wound and pressed. He just hoped he could save the boy.

Scott nodded his head and looked at the sky. The pain in his back was more than he could take. He wanted to turn over, but he couldn't.

Amy rushed up and said to Harry, "What can I do?"

Harry said, "Go get any towels, rags that you can find so that we can put on this wound and stop the bleeding."

Amy rushed off and Harry looked at Scott, "He's lost a lot of blood, Scott. He'll be lucky if he makes it."

Joe Bob and Skinny had not stopped screaming and crying. Even Bucky had woke up in his weakened state and was looking around in bewilderment.

Scott couldn't see any of it, but he knew life was about to change dramatically for him, these people, and his community.

He began to pray.

Chapter 27

The towels that Amy had found in Rocker's truck helped to staunch the flow of blood from Buddy's leg. He was still bleeding when the three ambulances arrived. Jesse had been close when he got the call from Elizabeth. When he arrived on the scene, he helped Harry with Buddy. They were still pressing on his leg when the paramedics took over.

Scott had still not moved. The paramedics asked Scott several questions and then told him he may have broken his back. They were procedurally going through the process of stabilizing his movement so that they could get him onto the stretcher without hurting him further.

As they were taking Buddy to the ambulance, Amy asked if she could ride with him. The paramedic looked at Jesse and he nodded yes. Amy got in the back with Buddy. She sat down next to him and held his hand.

Joe Bob and Skinny were up on their feet but looked like they had been in a war. They were mostly naked. Most of their hair had been singed off their body and they had bad burns in various places. As the paramedics were taking care of them, the Lyric detectives drove up. Harry walked over and looked at Joe Bob and Skinny. He motioned for the detectives, Luke Chambers and Josiah Wilridge, to come to him and then began speaking to Joe Bob.

"Joe Bob, I don't know what you two have been up to, but this doesn't look good. We're going to take care of you, but there are going to be lots of questions. Luke, you go with them in the ambulance. For right now, they are under arrest for suspicion of building and activating a bomb. Read them their rights and post a guard on them in the hospital."

Joe Bob was crying. Skinny was seething.

As the ambulance sped to the hospital, Amy thought about the time she had known Buddy. It must not have been easy having Jack Rocker as a stepfather. Not only was Jack unsupportive to Buddy, he abused Buddy's mother. Amy knew that it must have taken a lot of willpower on Buddy's part to live in such chaos and despair. He had been brave, and now he was seriously hurt. Amy wondered what motivated a kid like Buddy to overcome it.

As the paramedic continued to work on him, Amy noticed a flicker in his eyes. She got close to his face and softly said, "Buddy, can you hear me?"

He nodded his head and weakly said "Amy, come closer".

Amy got close to his mouth with her ear.

Buddy said, "I love Jesus. He lives in me. I did it for Him. T-t-tell my mo-mother." Then he went unconscious.

Chapter 28

For a town its size, the Lyric hospital was a good one. Most of the doctors lived out of town and practiced in Houston or in suburbs around it. The emergency room was contracted to a group of ER doctors and nurses who specialized in trauma care. For many years, the hospital had a poor reputation for a variety of reasons but had managed to build a level of trust with the community in recent years. This had been in no small part thanks to the efforts of Scott Mitchum and a group of his Lyric government and business contemporaries who saw the community and economic benefits from having a well-managed and functioning hospital.

Amy watched the paramedics take Buddy into the emergency room and then stepped out of the ambulance. She had to step out of the way for the other two ambulances as they pulled up. She watched as they took Skinny and Joe Bob, still whining and moaning, into the hospital. Mr. Mitchum was carefully moved out of the other vehicle, and Amy walked up to him as they were taking out Bucky Taylor.

Scott moved only his eyes as he looked at Amy from his neck and back brace. "Well, Amy I'm glad to see you're all right. Quite a day, huh?"

Tears welled up in her eyes, "Mr. Mitchum, I am so sorry this has happened to you. I'm…so grateful to you and to…Buddy."

"Amy," Scott replied in a strained voice, "please call your mother as soon as possible and ask her to call my wife, tell her about this and where I am."

Amy looked around and saw no one she knew to ask for use of a phone. She walked into the emergency room, heard Skinny and Joe Bob still moaning and Joe Bob asking for his mama. She looked down the hall and saw her pastor, Bruce Jones, walking down the hall. She immediately ran to him and cried behind his back, "Pastor Bruce, can you help me?"

Bruce Jones turned around and was astonished, hugged her and said, "Amy, where did you come from?"

"Pastor Bruce, something terrible has happened." She explained the entire story to him and then said, "Mr. Mitchum is hurt really bad, and I-I-I'm scared to think about what might happen to Buddy. I just want to call my Mama." She broke down crying.

Bruce pulled out his cell phone. He had Mary Jo Breeden's cell number. He called her. She answered on the third ring. "Mary Jo, this is Bruce. I've got someone here that wants to talk to you."

Amy had stopped most of her crying and with a few sobs answered the phone and said, "Mama, it's me. I'm at the hospital. Mr. Mitchum has also been hurt really bad rescuing me. Can you call Mrs. Mitchum and tell her and come here as soon as possible?"

"Amy, I'm coming right now, lovey. I'll be there in two minutes." Mary Jo ran out the kitchen door, got in her Lexus and tried to call Fran Mitchum on the way but got her voicemail. She left her a message. She was at the hospital in fifteen minutes, parked the car in the patient pickup area and ran in the front door. There stood Amy with Bruce Jones. She grabbed her and hugged her hard. Amy sobbed uncontrollably. Bruce watched with pastoral satisfaction, as if he had been the reason for this reunion.

After ten minutes of hugging, Mary Jo stepped back and looked at her. She was pleasantly surprised that Amy looked physically healthy, although incredibly sad.

She smiled at Bruce and whispered, "Thanks."

Bruce whispered back. "I'll leave you alone. I'll be down this hall in the waiting room when you're ready to talk."

Mary Jo directed Amy to a nearby bench and Amy told her the whole story.

Chapter 29

Bruce Jones was devastated and knew he had to find some courage and some strength. It wasn't coming. He was scared. He bowed his head and started crying, "God, how could this happen to him? He is such a good person and now all of this hurt and grief. I am the only one here who knows what has happened and I have to tell him. Please, God, give me the right words to say. I don't know what to do."

He looked up and saw Mary Jo Breeden in the doorway. She was drawn and weary. She had been weeping and was shaking her head. Bruce got up and walked over to her, hugged her and she grasped him as if she were drowning. She whispered hoarsely, " I just heard about Fran." She and Bruce both started sobbing. Their friend, Scott, had taken a major hit, and he didn't know it.

She and Bruce sat down and stared blankly into space. The room was quiet. Finally, Mary Jo spoke, "What are you going to do?"

"I don't know", he replied. "The kids are going to be okay—broken bones and lacerations. They've been sedated and don't know about their mother. Scott is going into surgery—some problem with his back. I'm not sure what happened to him, but it must have something to do with Amy's appearance."

"It does," Mary Jo sobbed. "He saved Amy's life from Jack Rocker. He had kidnapped her and was holding her hostage. Scott and Harry Jenkins found them in the Tanner woods. There was a fight and bomb explosion. Scott got injured in the fight; Buddy Parker was shot by Jack and is in critical condition; Bucky Taylor was shot in the leg and should be okay; Skinny Merritt and Joe Bob Presswood have first, second and third degree burns from a bomb they set off at the same time of the confrontation with Rocker. This is such a mess, Bruce, and I think Richard may have had something to do with it."

"Richard? What are you saying, Mary Jo?"

"I confronted Richard last night about something I've been observing over the last two years. He was gone a lot and was spending a lot of money. The business was suffering. I accused him of telling Rocker to steal that timber. He vehemently denied it—his protest was over the top. Then he admitted to me that he was having an affair and wanted a divorce. I asked him to leave. He's gone. I haven't told Amy."

Bruce was incredulous. This was a mess. He had never been in such a convoluted, awful situation. He had been told when he became a minister these things would happen, but he expected it to happen to people who never seemed to have their lives together. These people—his close friends, educated, experienced—why had it happened to them? How were they going to recover?

He was sitting in stunned silence when Mary Jo's face appeared right in front of him. "Bruce, what are you going to do?" she said.

"I don't know," he replied in a catatonic state.

"The doctor is at the door. He needs to talk to someone about Scott."

Bruce kept staring straight ahead.

Mary Jo went to the door and introduced herself to the doctor. He was a doctor who worked for the contract service that operated the emergency room for the hospital. Most of them lived in Houston. He was not aware of personal relationships in the community and was trying to find someone who was related to Scott Mitchum or knew how to get in touch with his family.

Mary Jo explained that Scott's wife was in the automobile accident right before Scott arrived. She had been brought to the hospital with her two children. The doctor knew about the case but didn't know she was his wife. He asked if there was someone else. Mary Jo told him that he was an only child, his parents were dead and that to her knowledge he had no other relatives.

The doctor looked up at the ceiling and then at Mary Jo. "We have to operate on him. His back is broken, and his pelvis is fractured. It's a serious condition. We can do it here and have a surgeon on the way. However, he says he wants to talk to his wife first. I would rather someone who knows him tell him about his wife, than me."

Mary Jo looked back at Bruce. He was still staring, immobile, no expression. She said, "I'll tell him."

Chapter 30

Scott was dreaming or at least he felt like he was dreaming. Once he got into the operating room, the sedative they gave him started kicking in. The pain had become almost unbearable. He wanted to move but he couldn't. He knew something was terribly wrong with him, with the whole atmosphere of the hospital.

Robert was talking to him. He was at Robert's house. They were sitting in his living room.

"Faith is the evidence of things not seen; the substance of things hoped for." Robert was telling him. "Not an easily understood concept but it is simple in context. Why are you asking about it, Scott?"

"How do I know I have it?" Scott replied.

"It depends on you, exclusively. It is a part of your awareness. Do you believe that life is more than the actions you take every day."

"Well, yes, I think about the past, the present and the future."

"Is it evident to you that unseen forces have an effect on your thinking, your activities, your relationships with others?"

"Yes."

"Do things happen to you which have deep meaning to you or have made your life fuller?"

"Yes."

"Are some of them things you have hoped would happen?"

"Yes."

"Then you have faith."

"But faith in what or who?"

"That's a good question." Robert retorted. "These unseen forces have been given many names over the years—God, Yahweh, Allah, Jesus, Holy Spirit, the many gods of Buddhism and Hinduism, The Force. You have to answer it yourself. No one, not even me your good friend, can tell you. Personally, I choose the Christian God because it's what my finite human brain can understand in this life."

"Then you're saying my faith in God means I agree that He is in control of this creation and that as a part of it, I know through my faith in God those things I hope for, but not see, will be evident to me?"

"Yes, but to truly walk with God and his Son, Jesus, you have to accept his grace. It is what saves you from an empty, destructive life."

"What is grace?"

"A gift."

"What kind of gift?"

"The unmerited, comprehensive, no quid pro quo favor of God.

"Why would God give me that gift?"

"Because you are God's creation. He loves you."

"This means that my faith will prevent bad things from happening to me, right?"

Robert paused. He looked down. When he raised his head, his countenance was serious but confident.

He said, "No, it doesn't prevent bad things from happening to you."

"Why not? Scott replied

"It's mostly a mystery, Scott, but it's also because you are his creation. You live in His created world along with other spiritual forces, which are also at work. Some people do not have this faith, nor do they accept this grace. They center their lives around themselves, their possessions, their jobs, their unhealthy relationships. Then they do things that are not in Creator's plan for his Creation, and it is upsetting to the dynamic."

"Why would people be inclined to be that way?"

"Primarily because of fear and guilt and self-centeredness."

"How does that cause bad things to happen to me?"

"Because God gives these people free will to make decisions and many times they base their decisions on fear and guilt and self-centeredness. Those type of decisions usually upset the created order and bad things can happen to a believer. The difference between a believer and a non-believer is that the believer knows it's going to happen and learns to deal with it, adapt, cope and falls on grace to see himself or herself through those tough times. The non-believer doesn't understand it and usually blames all of their problems on someone or something else."

"Then bad things will happen to me if I have faith?"

"Count on it." replied Robert. Robert handed him the Bible he was holding and said, "There's a story about such happenings to a guy named Job. It's at the bookmark."

The dream was dissipating, and Scott partially opened his eyes. He saw Mary Jo Breeden standing beside him, holding his hand..

"Hi, Mary Jo." Scott said with slur. He was feeling fairly good but kind of slow. He thought it must be the pain medication.

"Hi, Scott." She replied with a strained voice.

"How's Amy?"

"She's going to be okay, thanks to you."

"Good."

"Scott, they need to operate on you. It looks like your back is broken and your pelvis is fractured." She said as a tear rolled down her cheek.

"I vaguely heard a little bit about that before I went out with those drugs they gave me, and I think I asked them to get Fran here before they proceed."

Mary Jo had never been so out of control in her whole life. She loved this man. She had always loved him. She knew she had to have courage, his kind of courage, to tell him. She prayed, God, give me strength.

She gripped his right hand with her left hand, looked into his slightly glazed eyes and got close to him. She put her right hand on his left shoulder and looked him in the eyes and said, "Scott, Fran is not coming. She was killed in a car accident while you were saving Amy."

Scott shut his eyes.

Chapter 31

The Lyric hospital was a satellite hospital for the CHI (Catholic Health Initiatives) St. Luke's non-profit health care system. If health care specialties were not available in Lyric for patients then they were taken, most of the time by Life Flight, to affiliated care centers in the Greater Houston Area. The hospital was a source of pride for the Lyric community and especially for Mayor Scott Mitchum who had worked tirelessly for CHI St. Luke's to build a facility in his town. As a person entered the hospital, it was open, clean, smelled good and the people who worked there were friendly. Lyric area residents sent family and friends to the hospital with confidence something would be done for them with regard to their health care needs.

The structure was only three years old and had thirty beds, an emergency department and highly qualified medical personnel. Its décor was simple but elegant and done in a manner that made people feel comfortable when they had to spend time in the place under trying circumstances.

Skinny Merritt was looking at the patterned wallboard in the emergency room contemplating his next move. He was lying in bed with his head and shoulders propped up. He knew he was burned pretty bad in all areas of his body, but he had not viewed the most important part. As he lay naked on the bed behind the privacy curtains, he was praying that he still had a penis. The nurses had given him a bunch of drugs, but he had heard some of the conversations between them and the doctors. The "tsk tsking" had gone on forever, and Skinny just knew he had blown off his dick with that crazy bomb stunt.

He was working up the courage to look down there when a nurse he had never seen came in and looked at him, took a second glance at this crotch and begin to take his blood pressure and temperature. She asked how he was feeling, and he told her that he was fine other than being burned to a crisp. She didn't say anything else and Skinny was glad because he didn't want to talk to anybody. He felt like being a smart ass. Here he was lying in this damn hospital hurt bad and people like Harry Jenkins grilling him to the nth degree about what happened in the Tanner Woods. And now, he just knew he didn't have a dick because something was feeling funny down there. The nurse left the room.

He was going to have to look because it was driving him crazy. He decided to bend his head slowly in case it was really bad, he wouldn't have to see it all. Moving slightly, he began to see the head of his penis and felt like jumping up right there. Continuing the downward rotation of his head, he grinned from ear to ear. His penis was not injured. It was erect. He was relieved, but it didn't make any sense. He certainly had not been in a sexually arousing situation. In fact, the last time he had been with a woman, he had some trouble getting it up. This was amazing.

He looked back at the patterned wallpaper. God had answered his prayer and had given him more than he deserved. Skinny thought he may be able to get over all of this mess and had some hope he could be up and running pretty soon. His doctor, Dr. Shane Vandelay, appeared at the doorway and came up to his left side.

"How are we doing, today, Mr. Merritt?" asked the doctor.

"Just fine, if you like burnt human," Skinny retorted.

Dr. Vandelay smiled a very false smile with all teeth.

"Yes, well, you have several first and second degree burns and one third degree burn on your leg."

"So, what's the scoop, Doc? When do I get out of here?"

"Well, you'll be out of here soon, but you will be going to an adult burn unit in the Houston medical center. They will treat your first and second degree burns and will have to perform a skin graft on your third degree burn. I've already discussed this with them, and the transfer will take place in the morning.

"I can't just stay here and get patched up?"

"No, unfortunately, we do not have the expertise nor the resources to deal with your burn injuries."

Skinny looked down and forlorn. He had only been out of Lyric a few times in his life and he didn't want to go stay in Houston to get fixed up. He only had a sister and her family, and he was not friendly with them. All his buddies were here, and he knew they wouldn't come to see him.

He looked back at Dr. Vandelay and the doctor said, "There is one other medical condition you have, Mr. Merritt, that is concerning to us.

"What would that be, Doc?"

"You have priapism."

"What?"

"Priapism."

"What the hell is that."

"You have a permanent erection."

Skinny was confused. He knew he had a hard-on, but he was quite sure it was not permanent.

Dr. Vandelay looked serious, no smile, and said, "Mr. Merritt, you have been here six hours and your penis has been erect the entire time."

A six-hour erection, Skinny mused. Wait until the boys at the bar heard about it.

"Well, Doc, I wouldn't be too concerned," Skinny said with confidence, "not every man has my gifts."

Dr. Vandelay showed his false smile and teeth, "Yes, well, Mr. Merritt, you will probably not like the results of priapism. It doesn't enhance your sexual prowess and it may disfigure your penis."

That last part didn't sound too good, Skinny thought. "How can that happen?"

"Well, essentially the long term erection damages the penile tissue. It could disfigure the penis and cause erectile dysfunction. What may even be more serious is that we think this may have been caused by damage to your spinal cord."

Skinny knew he had hurt his back when the bomb blast threw him up against a pine tree. Dammit, he thought, this diagnosis is getting worse.

Skinny asked, "Does that mean I have to get my spinal cord fixed, too?"

"Well, hopefully it's not permanent damage and you will be able to walk in the future. But right now, we are cautiously optimistic that you will heal. However, a neurologist will look at your injury after you get to the burn unit at the medical center. Do you have any other questions?"

"No." Skinny replied.

"I'll check on you after you get to the burn unit." Dr. Vandelay replied with his permanent toothy smile.

Skinny considered his future and began seething about Bucky Taylor and Joe Bob Presswood for getting him into this shitstorm. It was every bit their fault.

Chapter 32

Amy looked out the window of the intensive care waiting room. She was looking at the pine trees across the street. Her Dad had told her that pine trees were not good for shade. The pine needles did not reflect the sun very well because of their shape and consequently, it was hot under a pine tree during the summer. On the other hand, hardwood trees usually had larger green leaves and they constructed a canopy which shielded the ground from the sun's rays. Amy had always liked trees, maybe because her Dad was in the timber business and she considered herself knowledgeable about them. Trees gave her some peace of mind, and God knows she needed it now.

Buddy was in intensive care along with Mr. Mitchum. Amy had been waiting to see what was going to happen to Buddy. She thought Mr. Mitchum would be okay but Buddy had lost a lot of blood. They had operated on him as soon as he came in to see if they could stop the bleeding. It appeared they had been able to stop it, and he was given a lot of blood. Now it was just a matter of time before they knew if he would overcome his injury. She had given blood to help replace some of the units used on him.

She was also depressed, not just about Buddy, but about the death of Mrs. Mitchum. She had always been such a nice person to her. She knew

Elaine and Matthew were also each in a separate room of the hospital and wanted to go see them, but she couldn't because she wanted to see Buddy when he woke up. She actually didn't know what to do. She needed her mother and didn't know where she was in the hospital. She just kept looking at the trees and prayed that something would go right.

Her mother stood at the door and looked at her. She had never seen her mother look like she did at that moment. She had been crying and her eyes were red-rimmed. Her countenance was sad. She was wearing a blue "Relay for Life" tee shirt, jeans, and sandals. Her mother always looked beautiful, no matter what she wore. But today, she looked more than beautiful and sad. She seemed to have a steely reserve in the depth of her eyes that spoke of endurance and courage. Amy knew it meant something.

"Hi, Darling. Come here and give me a hug." Mary Jo said to her daughter. Amy ran to her mother's arms and they embraced. Amy had never felt so good in her life. It was like all of this burden had fallen from her. She started crying from the relief.

"How are you doing?" Mary Jo queried.

"Much better, now that you are here." Amy replied.

"Well, I won't leave you alone like that again, today. There was something I had to do, and it was important."

"What was it?"

"I had to tell Mr. Mitchum about Mrs. Mitchum."

"Oh, Mama!" Amy put her hand to her mouth and started crying. "Why did you have to do it?"

"Because he was asking for her before he would go into surgery and I'm his oldest friend."

"How about Brother Bruce? I thought they were old friends." Amy replied with tears rolling down her cheeks.

"He couldn't do it." Mary Jo replied tersely.

Amy didn't understand. Brother Bruce was their minister. It was his job to minister to the people of his church in times of despair. Her mother's reply was said in a voice she had heard before, and Amy knew no comment was needed after it. She just continued to hug her.

Mary Jo looked down the hall and saw Bruce Jones come out of the waiting room and leave the hospital. She was not happy. There were several people in this hospital who needed him now, and he was taking a powder. So much for his sermons on ministry and service. Well, she had listened to them and had taken them to heart. She knew the people who could use her help, and she was going to do something about it.

She gently grasped Amy by the shoulders and slightly pushed her away, looking into her face. "We have to be strong for our friends, Amy. They need us right now. I know that is why you are waiting on Buddy to wake up. His doctor told me it will probably be another hour. In the meantime, let's go see Elaine and Matthew. They need us."

Matthew Mitchum was lying in the hospital bed looking up at the ceiling. He was trying to get his mind off the car accident. He knew his mother was hurt bad and that Elaine had been able to walk away. That's all he knew. He wondered why he hadn't seen his Dad, and he was beginning to get scared and angry. No one seemed to know anything. The airbag had broken his nose and his hand. He knew that much. They had taken him out of the emergency room after they had looked him over, asked him a few questions and then sent him for some X-rays. It seems that something else had happened and the emergency room was beginning to fill up. He had seen Bucky Taylor rolled in on one of those portable beds from the ambulance, and he looked unconscious. And other people were in the ambulance. He knew Bucky had not been a part of his car accident.

They put Matthew in the room with an older man who looked to be about 70 years old, skinny with a hook nose and piercing blue eyes. He was lying in the bed in a hospital gown on top of the sheets watching the TV, high upon the wall. It was some talk show with a bunch of pretty women in short skirts spending most of their time looking good, trying to pull down their skirts or crossing their legs. Matthew didn't think the man was too interested in what they were saying. Matthew listened to if for a while and tried to start up a conversation.

"Why are you in here?" Matthew asked when a commercial came on. He had sat up in the bed and looked at the old man.

"Hernie," the man answered as he continued to look at the Cialis commercial.

Matthew didn't know what a "hernie" was and it piqued his curiosity.

"What's a hernie?" He asked.

"Messed up muscle holding your guts." The man replied.

"How did you mess it up."

"Lifting sacks of fertilize."

"Is that like fertilizer?"

"That's what I said—fertilize—ya' know—cow shit."

Matthew never heard that word very much. His Dad only said it when he got angry and his mother did not like it. He quit talking to the man.

Elaine walked in the door and came next to his bed. Mrs. Breeden and Amy came in after her. The right side of Elaine's face was red and bruised. Her right arm was in a sling. She had been crying. It looked like a lot.

She controlled her emotions a little and hugged him real hard and whispered, "How ya' doing, Roadrunner?"

Elaine had not called him that in a while. When he was four he would run up and down their driveway amazingly fast, and it would make her laugh. She would call him Roadrunner, and he would do it some more. She showed him the Roadrunner cartoon on TV, and he loved it. The name stuck.

She only said it to him these days when she wanted to be affectionate with him, and Matthew knew something was wrong.

"Get out of the bed and come with me and Mrs. Breeden and Amy. We need to tell you something."

Matthew did as his big sister told him and held her hand as they walked down to a waiting room. He was getting really scared.

He sat down in one of the waiting room chairs. It was a small room with some pictures of flowers in vases on the wall. It was neat and tidy, and a TV was on high on the wall. The same pretty women with short skirts were on the screen. Mrs. Breeden found the remote and turned off the TV. Elaine sat on his right side and put her arm around him. Amy sat on his left side. Mrs. Breeden sat right in front of him and looked him in the eyes and she began talking.

Matthew traveled to another place after she told him about his parents. It was a place his mind occupied when he had trouble at school with kids who were jealous of him because his Dad was an important man. Matthew wasn't scared of them, but it was difficult to ignore their rude remarks and their taunts. This was a place that was free from these bad things but allowed him to live alongside these flawed people without becoming too sad. He was in that place now. He knew that tears were rolling down his cheeks and that he couldn't understand how he was going to go forward, but in this place he was at peace. This place was beyond description and he knew it was real because he could still hear and understand Mrs. Breeden. She finished talking to him and gently reached over and held his good hand. He could feel her energy go all the way into his place of peace. Elaine started sobbing as well as Amy, but Matthew looked at Mrs. Breeden and she looked at him. Her lovely blue-gray eyes were captivating. He knew somehow he was going to make it.

Chapter 33

Jesse Henderson had on his lights and siren. As soon as he and Harry had booked Rocker, he had jumped in his cruiser and headed to the hospital. He couldn't believe all of these horrible events had happened and the consequences were being shouldered by the best man, white or black, he had ever known. He knew he was driving too fast, but he had to do something. If there was only a way he could undo some of it, but the fact remained that Fran was dead, and Scott was hurt bad.

Jesse blamed himself. He should have never let Scott go to the Tanner woods. That fucking sonofabitch Rocker. It was all Jesse could do not to just whip his ass while he stood there smirking at the jail, looking at Jesse and telling him he wasn't going to let no nigger cop put him in a jail cell. Harry looked at Jesse while he held Rocker and said, "Easy, Jesse. Don't let this piece of shit provoke you. I'll put him back there in the cell next to Birdman and we'll see how he likes it."

Jesse thanked God Harry had been there. He would have killed Rocker and then he would have been in prison. Birdman would make Rocker even crazier. Birdman was about 6'4" tall and weighed 160 pounds. He was a schizophrenic who from time to time didn't take his medicine. Then he would take off all his clothes, go into town and start acting like a bird. He did look like a crane. Then he would walk down the sidewalks of Lyric, naked and mimic cranes, storks, and caw like a crow. The little old ladies were scared of him because he looked intimidating, but he was also weird beyond explanation. He would caw like a crow and then start explaining algorithms of computer programs he had invented. Someone would call the police and they would have to arrest Birdman because he was nude. He was harmless but since there were no mental health facilities in Lyric, and they rarely had a person in jail, Jesse would bring him to the police station until they could get his family notified. The family would take him to his doctor, Birdman would get back on his medication and continue his computer programming. They had just put him in the jail cell right before Rocker arrived. He was not only posturing in the cell but cawing all the time and today he was beginning to do the repetitive sounds of a cardinal. Jesse smiled. Rocker was going to start chewing the steel bars.

What Jesse didn't understand was Rocker's motivation for setting these events in motion. He had known Jack Rocker before he came to Lyric. They had been in the Army together twenty years ago. He was a racist then, but he was smart. Rocker knew how far to go without getting into trouble, and Jesse had watched him do it a few times in the service. They served together in the same infantry company. Rocker would take risks but never do it without some leverage. He always had an out—a way to blame somebody else or set up somebody for the fall. This kidnapping was his style, but it had some substance to it. Jesse wanted to know his leverage.

Jesse pulled his police package Dodge Charger up to the hospital and parked in the law enforcement parking space. There were a few people outside smoking in the covered area away from the hospital door. Most of them were patients looking frail and some looking like they were using their last breaths to get cigarette smoke into their lungs. A huge man on a scooter was coming up the sidewalk in front of Jesse. He had a florid face and was wearing a tam on his head. There was red triangular flag attached to the seat and waving in the air about three feet above his head. He probably weighed four hundred pounds. Other cars were coming through the three lane porte-cochere and as soon as the man came off the sidewalk via the handicapped ramp, he began to direct traffic through it. The man was very officious and stopped cars, waved some through, showed others to take the next lane. He then proceeded through parked and moving cars as if he owned the place

Jesse thought as he went through the door about what he was going to say to Scott. He didn't know if he had been told about Fran and it was eating at him about how he was going to handle it. He was hoping Bruce Jones had already told him, which would have been helpful. This was a good hospital, but Jesse hated to be in a hospital. Just the hinted smell of rubbing alcohol and Lysol reminded him of his mother and the horrible death she had died at Northwest Hospital in Houston when he was in the service. She had cancer and the family didn't know it until a big lump had come up on her chest near her collar bone. They did a biopsy on it and found the cancer had metastasized over her entire body.

The oncologist called it anaplastic. There was no hope. They put her on a ventilator. Jesse remembered the visits to the Intensive Care Unit. He would talk to his mother, and she would write him notes. Then she would start coughing and couldn't quit. The nurses would ask him to leave as she kept gasping for air even with the ventilator. She eventually just choked to death. It killed a part of him. He would never forget it.

He came to the front desk and saw Mary Jo Breeden talking to the desk clerk. Jesse came up behind her and touched her on the shoulder. Mary Jo turned, saw him, and put her arms around him.

Jesse patted her on the back and said, "It's goin' be okay, Mary Jo. We'll get through it." Jesse thought he was beginning to sound like his mother.

"Oh, Jesse. I wish this would all go away." Mary Jo replied.

"It will eventually, but it's going to take some time. Have you seen Scott?"

Mary Jo let go of him, stepped back, and looked down, then raised her beautiful eyes and said, "Yes".

"Well?"

"He's in surgery right now. He broke his back."

"What about the others?"

"Buddy Parker and Bucky Taylor are also in surgery. Skinny Merritt and Joe Bob Presswood are still in emergency room beds. Amy's okay. Just traumatized."

"Has anyone told Scott about Fran?"

"Yes. I told him and the kids."

"You did it? Where's Bruce Jones? I thought he was here."

"He was. He left." Mary Jo chewed her bottom lip to keep from crying.

"He left? Why?" Jesse said incredulously.

"I don't know. Scott would not let them operate until he talked to Fran. The doctor wanted someone who knew him to tell him about her because they needed to do something immediately. They were afraid he might have permanent damage to his spine. I did what I could."

Jesse looked at her. He had never known her very well, even though they had gone to high school together. She was always quiet and reserved in an elegant way. He was marveling at her strength.

"Okay. Well thanks for your courage. I guess we can just sit down and wait."

"What happened to Jack Rocker? She asked."

"Harry and I put his sorry ass in jail and if it were up to me, I'd go bury the key in the Tanner Woods where he started all this shit. Pardon my language."

Mary Jo looked at him and then looked away.

"I'm sorry, Mary Jo. I hope I didn't offend you." Jesse implored.

"No. It's not that," she said with her head bowed. "Jesse, I need to talk to you, privately."

"Okay. Let's go into this small waiting room down the hall. We often use it to interrogate people, and the hospital knows we use it for official business."

"That sounds good. Let's go."

Jesse looked around to see if anyone had been eavesdropping on their conversation. He didn't see anyone. His sixth sense was that Mary Jo was about to reveal something to him that might shed some light on this crime. He was ready for it. He needed something.

They walked in the room and Mary Jo sat down. Jesse sat across from her. She told her story.

Chapter 34

Mary Jo and Amy walked out of the hospital. They had been there six hours. It was 11:00 pm and both of them were exhausted. They went home. While they were in Mary Jo's car, Mary Jo thought about what to say to Amy about her Dad. She knew they were not at their best and it would be better to tell her in the morning after they had some sleep. She hoped that Amy would not ask about Richard before she went to sleep, and it would solve some problems. She turned on some soothing music and didn't say anything to her.

Amy was beginning to come down from her adrenaline high and started to doze off as they drove through Lyric. The Breedens actually lived outside the city limits of Lyric, about ten miles from the hospital. Mary Jo had some time to think and she begin to put pieces together about what caused these sordid matters to happen. She looked out the window at the fog beginning to appear on the road, condensing from the water in the ditches after the rain started when she had gone to the hospital. The tall pine trees intermingled with oak and gum trees looked eerie in the foreground of the full moon spotlighting the vehicle as she made the solitary drive. However, it was comforting to her. The trees, the moon, the drive was part of her inner being. She had never had the deep spiritual commitment she had seen in Scott or at least she didn't think she did until today. She had reached deep to reconcile the truth of her marriage, her relationship with her daughter and her connection to people in Lyric. She had cared for people today and had forgotten about herself. Not that she didn't think she was important, but she saw a need and did what she could to meet it. She also had insight about injustice when she confronted Richard, and she was determined to get to the bottom of it.

They lived on a two hundred-acre farm with a palatial five thousand square foot, two story home built in a modern ranch style with big open rooms and custom-made furnishings. Behind the house was a three thousand square foot barn. The farm was her home. Her parents had been the previous owners. She had always loved the place growing up and when her parents got older and started talking about downsizing, she had convinced Richard they should buy it from them. Her parents bought a smaller, newer house in a nice subdivision in Lyric and were much happier not having to maintain the farm and being close to their friends. As she turned in the drive, everything was dark at the house, the barn, and the outbuildings. She was at peace and found it remarkable. She stopped the car at the front door because it would be easier for Amy to get to her bedroom and go straight to bed. She went around to the passenger side, opened the door, and looked at her beautiful sleeping daughter. She stood there pensive for a moment, enjoying it. Of all the maddening things that happened today, her daughter was still whole and safe. She bowed her head and said, "Thank you, God".

Mary Jo rubbed her hand from Amy's cheek to tousle her hair.

"Hey, Rambo, time to go to bed," she said as she used her nickname that Amy liked when she was little.

Amy woke up, looked around and unbuckled her seat belt. She got out of the car and stood, looked at her mother and said, "God, it's great to be home."

"I agree. Come on, let's go to bed. I think we're ready for it. We can talk in the morning."

"Sounds good to me," said Amy as she walked down the sidewalk.

Mary Jo hit the remote, locked the Lexus and walked behind Amy, hoping she would not notice the dark house.

Mary Jo unlocked the front door, looked at her sleepy daughter and said, "Go to your room, take a shower, put on your nightgown and I'll be there in a minute with some milk. It will help you sleep."

"Where's Dad?"

Mary Jo didn't hesitate, "He's gone."

"Gone where?"

"On a trip."

It was enough. Amy nodded. Richard had traveled a lot in business, and this is a conversation they had had before.

They both walked through the door, Amy going right, and Mary Jo went left. Eric came out of his room and saw his mother. She told him that Amy was home. He went toward her room, and Mary Jo grabbed his arm.

"Wait, Eric," Mary Jo said, "let her get ready for bed. I'm going to bring her some milk, and we can both go in together and see her."

"Where's Dad?" Erie replied.

"On a trip."

"On a trip? At a time like this? What is wrong with that man?"

"Calm down. Let's all talk about it in the morning"

Amy got ready for bed and Mary Jo came to her room with the milk.

Eric was close behind his mother. He walked around her and held Amy like he hadn't seen her in years.

"God, I'm glad you're okay. I was worried sick about you."

"Thanks, Eric," Amy replied as a tear rolled down her cheek. "I'm grateful to be here. I never knew how much all of you meant to me until all this happened."

Mary Jo gave Amy the milk. As Amy drank it, Mary Jo looked at her and said, "We'll get up in the morning and talk, and we'll also go back to the hospital to see how everyone is doing. I know you're concerned about Buddy. If you have any trouble sleeping, come into my room and we'll get through the night together."

Amy nodded, handed the glass to her mother and was asleep before her head hit the pillow.

After they left the room, Mary Jo told Eric she wanted him to be a part of the conversation in the morning. He put his arms around her, and they held each other for a while. Eric went to his room.

Mary Jo took the glass to the kitchen and went to her bedroom. It was a beautiful room. Richard wanted the big house with its ranch design, but she insisted on designing the interior. They had moved her mother and father's block and beam house to town, set it up on lot, rehabilitated it and added to their other rental properties. She loved the house, but she loved this bedroom the most. It was comfortable and had a nice bathroom/dressing area. She walked into the bathroom and took off her clothes. She turned to the closet to get her nightgown and then saw herself naked in the full length mirror. She walked over to the mirror. As she turned from one side to the other, she wondered what Richard had seen in the other woman. She thought she looked good. Her breasts had stayed reasonably firm. She tried to keep her muscles toned by working on the farm with horses and doing yoga on a consistent basis. Once a week, she ran at least two miles. Maybe someday she would know why Richard had strayed. Right now, she needed to be strong.

She walked out of the bedroom door to the adjacent patio door and looked at the full moon as it cascaded over the pasture and reflected off the four-acre pond about 200 yards from the house. She liked being naked. It made her feel free. Looking at this beautiful scene and thinking about God's creation, she felt as if she could walk straight to heaven on the path of light presented by the moon. She would like to go to heaven. She opened the door, left it open and walked out on the patio. It was pleasant out here and she stood in the path of light, raised her hands and said, "Thank you God for this peace. I know you are walking with me."

She stayed there another moment, turned, and went to her bedroom, laid her nightgown on the floor beside her and slipped under the covers. She went to sleep immediately.

Chapter 35

Buddy Parker heard someone calling his name. He vaguely remembered Amy speaking to him earlier. He could tell she was sad, and she wanted him to do something. He couldn't quite remember what it was she asked him to do. Everything was slow and foggy, and he couldn't think very well.

He felt at peace, though. He had heard Brother Bruce talk about God's grace one time and it made him feel the same way. The person calling his name was peaceful, certainly not insistent. The bed he was lying in was wonderfully comfortable. It felt like how he imagined one of those pillow top beds must feel. He almost thought he was floating. The voice was becoming clearer, and Buddy thought he recognized it—a voice from his past. He looked up toward the ceiling. He thought the light was incredibly bright, not harsh but inviting. The voice was in the light.

Buddy couldn't see anyone, but he was hearing a trumpet playing and the pleasant voice calling his name. He knew that voice. He closed his eyes to think. It had something to do with baseball in the yard when he was growing up. This voice in the past had called his name and was laughing with him and having a good time. He looked at the light again and heard the trumpet playing and someone was in the light looking down on him. The person was motioning to him to come toward him. Buddy wanted to do it. He had never felt this good in his short life. He knew he was moving out of the bed but also felt like he was staying. It was like he was two persons, but the one going toward the light was the one he wanted to be right now. Another figure appeared in the light, and he could hear the voice much stronger now. It was a male voice, deep with resonance, and it felt comforting as if he were home again. Buddy moved toward figures, as the voice called his name again. The voice belonged to his dad.

Scott was vaguely aware of needles and small tubes running into this body. He wanted to move. He was sore all over and laying on his back. He could detect the antiseptic smell of the hospital. He opened his eyes and through the haze of post-surgery awakening, the room looked small with plain wallboard in front of him, a television mounted on it close to the ceiling. He couldn't see outside but could detect that no light was coming through the window. He assumed it was night. He reflected on why he was here and began to remember the day's events. He just couldn't believe all of it. It was surreal, but down deep, he knew this disjointed, jumbled mess of events affecting the very core of his life had happened. He began to consider his future and what it would be like without Fran. He had lost Robert not more than two weeks ago and now Fran. He had two children still to raise and his body was broken. His business was dependent on him being healthy and God only knew what would happen to the politics in Lyric without him being Mayor. The thoughts began to tumble on and on and he couldn't get control of them. He felt the anxiety attack coming on before it happened. He knew this one would be a whopper. His heart began to race, and the monitors began to respond. A nurse stepped in and saw that he was awake. She walked to the side of the bed and asked him how he was doing.

Scott said in a weak voice, "Not good, I'm having an anxiety attack."

The nurse looked at the monitors, looked at him and said, "Well now, we can't have that with you being all laid up. I'll be right back."

Scott used some of the techniques he had learned to quell the attack. The nurse's matter of fact demeanor had helped, and he noticed that she moved quickly.

She returned with a syringe. She gave the shot to him in his arm and within a couple of minutes, Scott felt better.

She looked at him in the eyes and said, "How are you doing, now?"

"Much better, thank you." Scott replied.

She responded, "Mr. Mitchum, there are very many concerned people waiting to see you. It's 3:00 a.m. and they have stayed here to make sure you are going to make it. Your Doctor has said you can see two of them when you wake up and after that you will need to rest some more. Who do you want to see?"

"My kids." He replied.

"I'll be back with them in a few minutes. I think they're asleep."

Elaine was laying on the couch with Matthew beside her. She had dozed fitfully but for some reason she awakened and knew down deep something had happened. Matthew was sleeping peacefully next to her. It reminded her of family camping trips when they were in the tent. Matthew always slept through the storms, but she stayed awake until they went away. They would lay next to each other while Mom and Dad were in the other tent.

She saw the nurse standing over her saying, "Elaine, your Father is awake. He wants to see you and Matthew."

Elaine nudged Matthew and said, "Hey Roadrunner, come on. Dad's awake and he wants to see us."

Matthew was groggy and looked her and said, "What?"

"Dad wants to see us."

Matthew immediately sat up, looked around and said, "Where?"

The nurse looked at both of them and said, "Follow me."

Elaine and Matthew got up and walked down the hall, as all of the other people waiting to see Scott Mitchum watched them. The nurse had already briefed all of them on Scott's wishes, and they were reverent as the two children made their way to his hospital room.

Scott thought about what he would say to his kids. Right now, he was not in a praying mood. He was angry, but something kept him from going full bore on releasing it. He still had to sort some things out and the first thing was to hold his kids. He was just going to let this play itself out. Robert had once told him that anger is a tool and if you abuse it, it hurts you and can ultimately destroy you. Love on the other hand, Robert told him, is like water. It is absolutely necessary, and a person needs it every day. Scott needed some love right now, and he knew his kids needed it.

Matthew and Elaine came through the door. Matthew ran to his side and laid his head down on his shoulder. Scott embraced him. Matthew started sobbing and Scott felt a tear roll down his cheek. Elaine hesitated at the door. She wanted to be strong. Her mother was gone and now she, well she didn't know what to do. She looked at her Dad and he motioned her to him with his left hand as he looked at her.

She ran to the other side of the bed and cried, "Oh, Daddy!"

Scott embraced her as she lay her head on him and started sobbing. He could feel the wetness on his own cheeks.

He looked at both of them and then looked up at the ceiling and quietly said to God in a non-demanding but desperate manner, "You've got to help me. I can't do this by myself."

PART II

Faith by its very nature must be tested and tried. And the real trial of faith is not that we find it difficult to trust God, but that God's character must be proven as trustworthy in our own minds. Faith being worked out into reality must experience times of unbroken isolation. Never confuse the trial of faith with the ordinary discipline of life, because a great deal of what we call the trial of faith is the inevitable result of being alive.

Oswald Chambers

Chapter 36

The dust from the road was covering everything—his truck, the vegetation on the side, houses when he passed them. It was a hot August day in East Texas in the middle of a drought. The pine trees were getting some brown needles and the pin oaks were beginning to show some root distress. A wet hurricane would destroy them. The shallow root system would be weakened by drought and the water would soften up the dirt foundation. Hurricane winds would blow down these one hundred foot tall, beautiful trees. Unlike red oaks, the sturdiest and most resilient oak tree, pin oaks couldn't survive lack of water, too much water and too much wind.

Scott Mitchum had an affinity for the red oak tree. He liked its toughness and its shade. That's why he planted them in all of his timber stands and in his yard because of their character. He was headed to one of his fifty acre timber stands right now to see how it was faring in this dry time. The drought had been going on for three years. It started right after Fran died. Scott thought it would pass and the area would get some rain, but the average rainfall had gone from 50 inches per year to 40 inches over the drought period and he was getting concerned about his timber. He may have to cut it prematurely and sell it at a lower price than he would get for mature trees. He was going to meet his forester and look it over today to determine if he needed to make some decisions.

He had three hundred acres of timber scattered in different spots around Lyric. They were in various stages of development. Scott liked land as an investment. The timber helped pay the taxes and maintenance while the land appreciated in value. He tried to buy tracts in good locations so that when a tract sold, its appreciated value would give him a good return on his investment.

He also liked to walk on his tracts and be out in nature. The walks had helped heal him after Fran's death. His love for her was deep, and he missed her greatly. There was a hole in his soul that would probably never be healed, but the faith he had in God and His grace had sustained him. When he walked, God would reveal real and mysterious truths to him that had given him peace and understanding. It was unexplainable, but he gradually got better. It sounded trite when he talked about it, but he had found a presence with God every second of every day, giving him encouragement, love, strength, and courage.

He had shared his experience with other people who were in similarly desperate situations. Otherwise, he kept quiet about it. There had been too much gratuitous, superficial caring after Fran had died. He understood how people wanted to help him feel better, but it was way too much, and he had quietly begun to keep people away from him and the kids after it had gone on some time.

Both kids had suffered, but Elaine had suffered the most. She had lost her role model and her confidant. Matthew missed his mother but in a way much like his father. He missed the nurturing atmosphere when he was around her and the "Matthew can do no wrong" attitude she projected to him. Elaine had gone to college and had to drop out because she couldn't focus. She got a job as an office assistant in an engineering firm in Caddo and had gradually become surprisingly good at computer aided drafting (CAD). Scott had encouraged her to keep herself busy with work so that she could focus.

It was day to day with him. At first, it was moment by moment. He had no idea what to do with himself. He would think about his business and the work he needed to do to keep it going. Then he would think about his kids and what he needed to do for them. Then he got an overwhelming feeling and anxiety would set in. He had always been a high achiever and anxiousness was a part of his makeup. He had coped with it growing up and going to college, but Fran had been the person who could calm him down and help him to focus. Now, she was gone.

Scott's Aunt Wanda, his mother's sister, was childless and had always been one of his biggest cheerleaders before Fran. He had turned to her after Fran died. He often thought what he would have done if she had not been around. She helped with the kids—provided some of the nurturing they needed and took them places that Scott could not fit into his schedule. It helped that Elaine was driving now, but she needed mothering still.

Wanda was seventy-two years old and still had a lot of energy. Scott confided in her about his anxiety and depression over Fran's death. Wanda had been a rock and encouraged him to reach deep and rely on his faith in God to make the moments seem real and give him courage, strength, peace, and joy. She also recommended that he see a counselor so that he could discuss his turmoil with someone objective.

Scott listened to her. Each night after Fran died, he cried before he started a fitful sleep. On the night he came home from the hospital, he cried out to God before he went to bed and said again, "I don't know what to do, please help me." His mind became still for the first time since Fran died, and he had a peace he had never known. He slept and when he woke up during the night, the peace was with him. His mind was working with some of the same harried, good, and evil thoughts but underneath it all was the peace. It was like a cloud where he could float and know that he would live forever, regardless of what happened. It reminded him of the description of grace he had read in the Bible and in a book by a prominent Christian psychiatrist. He nurtured it because it was all he had individually to make it through each moment.

Friends and family had varying degrees of sympathy and empathy. A lot were superficial, some didn't know what to do but a few were surprising by their ability to actually make him feel better just by their presence. Ben Smith, his firm's surveyor and longest serving employee, was one of them. Ben had come to see Scott in the hospital and didn't just sympathize with him but told Scott things were under control at the firm and outlined some things he had done to make sure projects were kept on track. There was another engineer in the firm, an older man name Frank Jones, who was very capable but wanted nothing to do with leading the firm's activities. He was strictly a designer and project manager and made it clear to Scott that's what he wanted to do.

Ben had been outstanding and comforting. Scott often wondered why it had happened. He had never seen Ben use these abilities. Scott kept going back to this underlying peace in his life now. He still had the same problems, in fact they were worse, but he wasn't at the abyss. He knew he would get through them and grace had given Ben to him.

Another surprising person was Mary Jo Breeden. At first, Mary Jo expressed her deep gratitude to Scott for helping in the rescue of Amy. A few tears came to her eyes when she talked to him in private. It was an emotional time for both of them. Scott didn't cry but he stood up from his chair in his living room, walked over to her and motioned for her to get up. He put his arms around her, and she did likewise with him. It was more than a friendly hug. They needed each other at the moment and held each other tight for what seemed to be a long time. Scott let go of some of his grief and Mary Jo sobbed out her relief. They had been friends a long time and it was like returning home after you had been gone a long time. He and Mary Jo then spent about two hours talking to each other about their futures. She, discussing her pending divorce from Richard and the whole sordid affair with the Crazy Jack, and he, discussing being without Fran and moving on with life.

That wasn't the end of it, though. Three years had passed after Fran's funeral and Scott would see Mary Jo in Lyric more often than not. They would bump into each other at the school, Walmart, restaurants, and church. She had never been a regular churchgoer, but Scott noticed her increased attendance in the worship service. Scott had to go back to church. He needed the intangible power of fellow believers. He prayed a lot and he knew that he was not alone when he prayed. God, of course, was listening to him and Scott was listening to God. However, he knew other people were praying with him—some in heaven—"a cloud of witnesses". He never felt truly lonely. He felt alone in the physical sense but never spiritually. His faith was being tested and he knew it, but it was comforting knowing that the Holy Spirit was with him. After he had seen Mary Jo sitting by herself for several Sundays, he sat down with her one Sunday morning. He knew this action would create a stir in the community, but it didn't bother him, as long as she was okay with it.

Since Fran had died, he had had his share of romantic interest from single ladies, widows and even a few married women. Scott had been polite but told them he needed some time. None of them were absolutely overt when they approached him, with one exception. They would ask him to social functions or over to their house for dinner or some other subtle hint. The one exception was Cassie Loren who caught him late one night when he had to go get some milk at a convenience store. They were the only two people in the parking lot. Scott knew Cassie from high school. She had just been divorced for the second time and was on the rebound. Beautiful woman and Scott got nervous when she walked up to him and started a conversation. She put her hand on his arm and expressed her sympathy about his loss, moved closer so that her mouth was about five inches from him.

She looked great, smelled wonderful and then she said "Scott, I've always wondered what it would be like to sleep with you."

It woke him up and he said politely, "Well, Cassie, I consider that a compliment, but I'm not ready to get involved with anyone right now."

She was gracious, smiled and said, "Just keep it in mind."

Scott smiled and said, "See you later, Cassie." He got in his car and left.

When he sat down next to Mary Jo, she smiled and said hello. They engaged in some small talk and the service began. Elaine had moved out into her own apartment in Caddo after she got her job and sporadically attended church when she was visiting in Lyric for the weekend. Matthew was sitting with his friends. Scott enjoyed sitting next to Mary Jo that morning. There was something familiar about it that was reminiscent of Fran but also his long time friendship with Mary Jo. When the service was over, Mary Jo told him she liked his company this morning and laughed and said she hoped it wouldn't hurt his reputation. Scott laughed and said he was thinking the same thing about her. They had been in Lyric long enough to know the talk had already started. Scott asked her how her life was going now that Amy was away at school and she was on her own. She told him it was difficult getting used to it, but she had her interior decorating business that was keeping her busy and she was also dealing with the aftermath of Richard's involvement in the timber theft. Lawsuits had been filed and the business was operating but waiting for some resolution in court. Mary Jo was part of the lawsuits based on her divorce filing. It would probably take another year. Meanwhile, Jack Rocker had been charged with the murder of his stepson, Buddy Parker, and there was some indication that the District Attorney may charge Richard as an accessory to Buddy's murder, although the case was weak.

Mary Jo didn't go into any of those details although Scott knew about it through the City of Lyric. Though he had thought seriously about it, he had not resigned his mayoral position. He had gradually gotten back to full speed and had run for re-election with no opponent. He was a hero to the people of Lyric. He didn't want to be one, but he knew it by the way people in the town treated him. He knew all earthly glory was fleeting, but it was nice not to have to defend every political thing he did for the community. It was coming to an end and he knew it, but all the same, it had been a peaceful period.

Scott wanted to continue the conversation with Mary Jo when she asked what he was doing for lunch. Scott told her he was going home to fix some soup. She asked about Matthew's plans and Scott told her he was going to a friend's house this afternoon.

"Look, Scott," Mary Jo looked him in the eyes, "I'm not ready to get involved with anyone but ever since you saved Amy, I've wanted to spend more time talking to you because you're my friend, and we've been through a lot together. Would you come eat lunch with me today? I was thinking about going to Village Mills and eating at Kelley's because I like the buffet."

"Sure, I'd like to go. Why don't we go separately, and I'll meet you there in thirty minutes?"

"Great idea," she replied. "At least it will tamp down some of the gossip."

That had been five days ago. They sat and talked at the table for three hours. Scott was thinking about it as he walked through the timber tract.

What was it about some people where you had an immediate deep connection, some were only partial, and all the rest were mostly superficial. Scott had made that deep connection with Mary Jo on Sunday.

He looked at the timber and noticed that the brown needles were more extensive than last time he observed them. The needles on the forest floor were brittle, dry and a major fire hazard. He noticed that the pine bark beetle had been doing its damage as some of the trees had that ghostly look from the standing death it was now portraying. The pine bark beetle usually worked in about a five to ten tree area and would bore into the bark getting to the sap of the tree in many places along the trunk. The tree was unable to fight this predator and would eventually succumb to it. Then the beetles would jump to the next tree. The only way to combat this threat was to cut all the timber in and around the "bug area."

Scott got his cell phone and called Andy Travis, his forester. When Andy answered, Scott said, "Andy, Scott Mitchum. How are you?"

"Doing pretty good, Scott, how are you?" Andy replied.

"Hey, what happened to the Lumberjacks last night in Huntsville?

Scott had to rib Andy who was a huge Stephen F. Austin Lumberjack basketball fan. The Lumberjacks had been ranked Number 23 in the nation and their major rival Sam Houston State, which was unranked, had beaten them in an overtime game last night.

"Let's not talk about it. Suffice it to say that I almost got thrown out of the gym over giving my loud opinion about the 'youth' basketball league officiating."

"I'll not mention it again. I'm out here on my fifty acre tract off of County Road 2011 and the drought is seriously hurting these trees and it looks like a tinder box. I'm also seeing some bug damage."

"You and everybody, else. The only way to do anything about it is to cut the timber and the mills are stacked up right now. None of them are taking pulpwood."

"What do you recommend that I do?" Scott replied.

"Hold it. I really believe we are going to get some rain this month or a hurricane because it's been so dry. By the time you cut it, pay my fee, prep it for replanting and plant, you'll lose money."

"What if it burns up?" Scott asked.

"Well you've got your insurance and that will net more than what a cut will net. The bugs will just do their five to ten tree damage in spots and that will be somewhat limited."

"Okay, you're the expert. I still want to look at this tract in the near future for cutting because it does need to be thinned."

"Yeah, I know and that one hundred acre tract on County Road 4321 is in the same condition. As soon as we get some rain, I'll go take a look at them and see if we can't set some kind of schedule for marking and cutting."

"Okay, thanks, Andy. Calm down, those Lumberjacks will be back."

"Thanks, Scott. I'll do my best, but they better get their ass in gear if they want to make the NCAA tournament and quit getting beat by teams like the Bumbling Bearkats."

"Bye, Andy."

"Bye, Scott."

Chapter 37

Joe Bob Presswood was sweating like a racehorse. He and Skinny Merritt had been working on demolishing a trailer for the last two days. They had gotten good at metal scrapping and were actually making a little money so that they could pay bills. Joe Bob had lost some weight and was putting on some muscle. He was proud of himself. After Skinny had had his surgery to get rid of his permanent hard-on, he seemed a little calmer. Joe Bob thought about it and surmised that it was the hard-on that made Skinny crazy. Joe Bob had had hard-ons before, especially when he used to see Carol Hartley in her bikini at the City pool. Hard-ons drove him crazy. He couldn't imagine what permanent one would do to him. He had reluctantly forgiven Skinny for his insults about him. He did like the fact they had a thriving business together.

"Joe Bob, when we finish here, we'll have about $500 and when we split it, it'll be $250 each" said Skinny.

"I reckon I'm going take that money with what I've saved and buy that new assault rifle I was showing you at Academy." Skinny said.

"I thought you were going to invest in Bucky Taylor's business to find Santa Anna's gold?" Joe Bob replied.

"Now don't go trying to convince me to follow Bucky's bullshit pipe dreams. I nearly got blowed all the way to Austin, the last time I had anything to do with that fuckin' Santa Anna treasure."

"Yeah, but now Bucky is using science and technology. He's got some kind of machine where he can look about twenty feet into the dirt and determine what's down there, you know kinda like an X-Ray machine."

"Joe Bob, I wish you would get some damn sense. Bucky bought that Rube Goldberg machine from a shyster in Fostoria. I've watched it work and I think it's all fake. It sure as hell don't look like it's seeing through the dirt."

"I saw it work, too. Bucky buried a fork in the ground then the machine found it."

Skinny threw the last piece of metal on the trailer. He was still thin, but he looked much healthier than he had four years ago when the nitrogen bomb had exploded.

Skinny's deep set blue eyes bored into Joe Bob's, "I ain't goin' look for gold no more. I've made up my mind to work and make my money. Now if you want to go following Bucky with his head in the clouds about some bullshit gold stash, then go right ahead. I'm going to invest in an assault rifle. You never know when it might come in handy."

Joe Bob was looking at Skinny when a white recent model Ford F250 Diesel drove up the driveway. Joe Bob was proud of his ability to identify pickups by the way they looked and sounded. He could almost tell who the owner of the vehicle was by the way it was driven. He wasn't really sure, but he suspected this one was Scott Mitchum. He had seen him a few times in a truck similar to this one, and he was right. Scott got out of the truck.

Skinny, because he suffered some hearing loss after the explosion, looked more intently at Joe Bob and said, "Are you listenin' to me dipwad?

You tell Bucky Taylor that I'm not going to go down that armadillo hole with him again and furthermore, I'm not going to lose some hard-earned money on pansy-ass theory about Santa Anna's gold."

Joe Bob started pointing toward Scott as he made his way toward them and Skinny said, "What, asshole?" and then turned after Joe Bob pointed a second time.

Skinny's other personality went into gear. Joe Bob always marveled at the change he could make in his demeanor. One minute he's cussing you out and the next his honey voice starts soothing another person like he's a preacher ready to baptize you. Joe Bob thought it was just a natural inclination of East Texas talkers and knew that there were many of his other acquaintances who had similar abilities.

"Why, Hi, Scott. It's good to see you." Skinny relayed with about a cup full of syrup.

"Hello, Skinny. Hello, Joe Bob. How are y'all, today?" replied Scott.

"We're reeeeal good, Scott. We're just finishing up this trailer. We're ready to get paid and get onto the next job. Is everything going your way?"

"Can't complain."

"Well, if you did nobody would listen." Skinny guffawed as if he had said something original.

Scott looked intently at Skinny. Joe Bob noticed it immediately and Skinny finally did.

Skinny started his apology. "Scott, I-I-I didn't mean anything by it. It's just something I say from time to time. I'm really sorry about your wife and all."

"It's all right, Skinny. You don't need to apologize. I was just looking at you because something's changed about you. You've gained some weight, got some gray hair and looks like it's getting a little thin on top."

Joe Bob laughed. Scott was right but Skinny hated going bald. He just knew it was going to hurt his chances with women.

"Yeah, Scott. It happens to all of us," Skinny looked down at his navel.

"You're right about that" and Scott took off his hat. Not only was he going bald. He had shaved his head since the last time they had seen him.

Skinny and Joe Bob were stunned. Scott Mitchum, "Most Handsome, Mr. Everything" in school was bald. They couldn't believe it.

"Time does catch up with us." Scott said. "Anyway, I know you guys are busy and I wanted to see if I could get you to tear down a couple of mobile homes for me over on Jordan Bottom Road. I bought some property over there and I can't even give those mobile homes away. I need to get them down in thirty days because I want to build some houses on the property."

"Is that across the street from Deward Malone?" replied Joe Bob.

"Sure is," said Scott. "The address is 2347 Jordan Bottom Road, Pumpkin."

"That's a Pumpkin address instead of a Lyric address?" asked Skinny.

"Yeah, it confuses a lot of people because Lyric addresses are only about 200 yards away." replied Scott.

"Could've fooled me," said Joe Bob. Skinny sneered at him.

"Sure, Scott. We can tear down those suckers and get started next Monday," Skinny said.

"How much money are we talking about to get the job done?" asked Scott.

Skinny puffed out his chest. "For me, it's twelve dollars an hour and for Joe Bob, it's ten dollars and hour, seeins I have the technical skill and all, and I'm the boss. Plus, we get all the metal and the money they pay us when we take it to the metal recycler over in Hampshire." Joe Bob sneered at Skinny.

"Sounds good. I'm going to trust you guys to be square with me on the hours. Also, I'll have to send you a 1099 IRS form if I pay you over $500.00."

Skinny hated those damn things. Now he'd have to pay taxes on what he made. He was seething, mostly at the government but some at Scott for not keeping it under the table.

"Okay, Scott. We'll get on it next Monday," said Joe Bob.

"Thanks, Joe Bob and Skinny. I'll be out there to see how it's going next week some time. Can I get your phone numbers, in case I need to call you?" He took out his mobile phone and looked at him. They recited each of their phone numbers to him. He put them in his contacts.

"See you guys, later. Don't work too hard." He shook hands with both of them. Skinny and Joe Bob watched Scott walk away. It was a confident, unhurried walk and it unnerved Skinny.

"What do you think Scott has up his sleeve?" growled Skinny.

"What do ya' mean?" replied Joe Bob.

"Well, first of all dumbass, why is he tearing down those mobile homes when they could be remodeled and secondly why is he reporting our wages to the IRS? Guy is a socialist if you ask me."

Joe Bob was stunned. He always thought he had better sense than Skinny but now he doubted if his friend would ever have any.

Joe Bob looked up at the clear sky and the bright sunshine. He could smell the pine trees and the damp moist earth. He had been a lot more grateful for the beauty of nature since he had almost died in that explosion. He had begun to believe in himself. It was a good feeling, and he didn't want to lose it. He had known Skinny for a long time and knew he was moving away from Joe Bob's way of living. His insults, greediness, his patronizing, his disrespect for women and now he was trying to make it look like Scott Mitchum was an evil man just because he wanted to give them some work. He had to say something.

"I've seen those mobile homes and, just like these, they were in bad shape. He's probably going to tear them down and build some nice rent houses like he did over on Ballard Road. This community needs more nice rental property that's affordable. And as far as reporting our wages, that's the law. He has to do it."

"Well, Mr. Affordable Smartass, I think he's too much of a goody-two-shoes and is making too much money on all of us by pretending he's helping people."

"He helped my momma one time, and nobody ever knew about it, except me."

"Is that right. Well whaddaya know, your old lady is beholdin' to Scott Mitchum."

"No, and he's never asked anything from either one of us."

"Well, I don't believe it and you're a damn liar."

Joe Bob was seething, and it was just a natural reaction. He didn't even think about it. He hit Skinny with a right hook below his left eye and lifted him up in the air. Blood shot out of his mouth. He fell to the ground and was out cold.

Joe Bob wasn't even shocked. It had been a long time coming. He walked over and checked Skinny's pulse. His heartbeat was strong, and he was still alive. He put Skinny on his shoulder and took him over to his truck, laid him in the back seat and took off for Skinny's house.

As he drove, Joe Bob thought about what he had done and why he had done it. He had changed. Skinny was always making decisions for him, and it was as if Joe Bob didn't have a mind of his own. Now he knew he did. This incident had been the proverbial straw that broke the camel's back. He was not sorry he did it, and he really didn't care what Skinny thought.

Joe Bob pulled up to Skinny's rattletrap trailer, put the truck in park and turned off the engine. He looked at the trailer and the logic from Skinny escaped him about what Scott "had up his sleeve." If Skinny wanted to live this way, which Joe Bob abhorred, that was his business. However, a lot of people wanted to have a good place to live with a family. Why shouldn't Scott be encouraged to do what he was doing? And as far as abiding by the law, that's what Joe Bob liked about Scott. He was a good man and he did things that were right.

Joe Bob opened the back door, put Skinny on his shoulder and crept up the dilapidated porch looking for places he might fall through with this extra weight. He opened the door (it was never locked), entered the living room with its smelly, matted carpet. He walked down the narrow hall past the bathroom and to the bedroom at the back of the trailer. He noticed a light on in the bathroom when he walked by and made a note of it. He laid Skinny on his back on the filthy, unmade twenty-year old broken down mattress with a couple of sheets and a bedspread.

He looked at him and decided to leave him there and turned to leave. He walked into the hall and came face to face with a naked Dora Prescott coming out of the bathroom.

"What the hell are you doing here, Joe Bob?" she screamed as she covered her crotch and breasts with her hands.

"Sorry, Dora, I didn't know you were here. Skinny got hit and I brought him home to sleep it off."

"Got hit? Who hit him?"

"I did. I was trying to reason with him, and he got angry. Then he started putting me down like he always does and called me a liar. I had had enough."

Dora was staring at him in awe. She didn't even seem to care about her nudity.

"You know what's going to happen when he wakes up, don't ya'?"

"Yeah and I'm prepared for it. I'm not going to take it anymore. He's a bully and has been doing it to people all his life and you know what I'm talking about."

She was pensive, not knowing what to say.

"Look, Dora, I need to go home. I don't want to offend you by brushing up against you in this hallway. If you'll just step back into the bathroom, I'll be on my way."

"Yeah, sure, Joe Bob." She stepped back into the bathroom, still thinking. Joe Bob walked down the hallway and went out the front door.

He stood on the plywood porch with the exposed joists underneath. The plywood had rotted in various places and it was dangerous walking on it. It was actually the first time he had noticed it. He walked down the untreated wooden steps that looked like they were going to fall apart and knew he had changed. Something happened to him after that encounter with Scott Mitchum, and he knew it was for the better.

Chapter 38

Mary Jo was aching. It was a good kind of ache. She was at the end of her yoga class, but it had taken a lot of effort at her age to make it all the way through the class. It was her first time to go that far. After the debacle with Richard and Amy, getting up and getting moving had helped her anxiety and depression. She had started walking in her neighborhood and noticed a lot of nice things she had not been aware of previously in her hurried life. The weather changing had not been an annoyance but had actually begun to interest her. At night, she would go outside and look at the night sky, even if it were cloudy. At a full moon, the fluffy cumulus clouds in the night sky floating in the sea of dark with pinpoints of starlight was better than a movie. She had begun to like her own company.

Simple things had begun to please her. Exercising and enjoying the self-awareness of her body. Eating good meals and not stuffing herself. Listening to the music she had loved growing up and even some new music that interested her. She had volunteered to help at the church's food pantry once a week and had started to see how she had taken so much for granted in her life by seeing the lives of people in poverty and despair. It had been eye-opening. Some of the people had even taught her a few things—like being grateful for food. It had never occurred to her that simple basic things like food were extremely important. She had always had it whenever she wanted it.

One man had even taught her how to change her tire. He came to the pantry with his wife and two small daughters. They had been living from paycheck to paycheck, and then he had been laid off from his job. She could tell it was hard on him to ask for food, but he was determined to feed his family. After she and the other workers gave them some milk, bread, cereal, canned meats and canned vegetables, he mentioned to Mary Jo that someone had a flat on their vehicle. He described the vehicle and Mary Jo told him it belonged to her.

"Well ma'am, I'd be glad to put on your spare if you wouldn't mind" said the man.

"No, of course not, let me get my keys, and I'll meet you at the car" Mary Jo replied.

She got her keys and went to her car. She introduced herself and found out his name was Michael, and his wife's name was Heidi. The five year old girl was Courtney and the three year old girl was Scout.

"I'm so glad that you offered to do this for me. I've never changed a flat in my life," Mary Jo stated.

Michael was about six foot tall, in his mid-thirties, blonde hair and piercing blue eyes with a thin face and a muscular build. Heidi was about the same age with dark brown hair, green eyes, around five foot four inches. She was a beautiful woman and together they were a handsome couple.

Michael responded, "Well ma'am, every person should know how to change a tire. We Texans love our vehicles and we use them a lot and a flat is inevitable. When those little girls turn sixteen, it will be a requirement before they get a driver's license that they show me they can change a tire."

Mary Jo looked at him, stunned, at this very practical idea coming from this man. Why should he do it. Here she was with a grown child and she had no idea how to change a tire.

Michael went on, "If you would like, I'll teach you how to do it right now and the next time you won't need a man to do it for you. I'm a mechanic by trade and firmly believe women should know everything they can about vehicles."

"I'd love for you to do that for me," Mary Jo responded.

Heidi laughed and said, "I knew that was coming."

Michael smiled at his wife and asked Mary Jo if she knew where the spare was located on the SUV. She didn't know but Michael had no trouble finding it. He proceeded to extract it from the vehicle and carried it over to the flat tire. Meticulously, he taught her each step of changing a tire properly. He let her loosen the lug nuts and showed her how to keep the car from rolling as she used the jack to elevate the car. After the flat tire was off, he showed her how to pick up the spare and place it on the lugs and then seat the lug nuts properly. She then let the car down and tightened each lug nut once again.

Mary Jo was elated. She had learned how to do something every driver should know how to do and this man had taken the time to show her how to do it.

"Thank you very much," she said as she shook his hand and Amy's hand.

"No ma'am, thank you," he said as he hesitated after he said it.

"Why are you thanking me?" Mary Jo replied.

He kept his head down and she realized he couldn't talk because he was overcome with emotion. He lifted up the sack of groceries and then looked at her.

With a quivering voice, he said, "We haven't eaten very much for two days. Changing that tire was the least I could do for you helping me to feed my family. I'll be forever grateful."

Michael and his family walked away. Mary Jo watched them as they walked down the street. Her stomach roiled as she thought about their predicament and how ungrateful she had been for the abundance she had known all her life.

Chapter 39

They were on their first date since they were twenty years old. As Scott sat across from Mary Jo at Bodittle's Steakhouse and Grill, Scott thought about the times they had shared together back then. They had never been serious about each other, at least he felt that way, and didn't go too far in their physical relationship. Some fairly heavy kissing but beyond that it was mostly just fun. They liked to dance and that was one reason they had decided to come to Bodittle's. Not only could you get a good steak but there was live band and a lot of people would actually get up and dance. Mary Jo had always been easy to be around, but he had not been in love with her. When he met Fran, it didn't take him long until he knew she was the one he loved and wanted to marry. After they were married, Mary Jo met Richard, and they soon tied the knot. Scott was wistful about how he had come back to this familiar setting in his life—eating and dancing with Mary Jo.

The evening had not been the same as when they were younger. They had eaten a good meal and danced until they couldn't dance anymore. However, since their younger days, their lives had been filled with achievements and disappointments but on very separate journeys. The rhythm of their dancing and the way they held each other manifested past and present living. The need for companionship was driving their feet and their touching.

Scott took Mary Jo back to her house and she asked him if he wanted to come in. He thought about it and decided it was time for him to spend some quiet time with her, nothing more. He told her he would be delighted but he couldn't stay too long. As they entered the house, Scott realized he had never been here, and Mary Jo must have known it.

"You've never been here have you?" Mary Jo asked.

"No." he replied.

It was huge and magnificent. The entry hall was eight feet wide with a gradual vaulted ceiling, which fit quite nicely into the twenty foot ceiling of the living room and floor to ceiling fireplace. Mounted deer heads flanked the fireplace wall along with a javelina head and elk head. Richard had been an avid hunter. The living room dovetailed with style into the kitchen which had open windows on the west side looking at their ten-acre private lake. It was quite a sight. The staircase wound up from the living room to a substantial landing that had walkways and hallways going east and west to bedrooms and bathrooms on the second floor. Scott could also see that there were a couple of bedrooms on the lower floor along with an office/den. He guessed that there was about five thousand square feet in the house.

Mary Jo watched Scott. She could tell he was taking in all of the details in his engineer's mind. She had wanted this house, but she and Richard had disagreed on its size. She wanted a lot of children, but two was his limit. He had wanted a big showplace and a place to entertain. That's what they had done. Richard had shown off, and Mary Jo only got two children. Now she was in this large abode all by herself.

She walked into the kitchen and asked him if he wanted something to drink. Scott followed behind her and told her he would like a glass of unsweetened tea, if she had any. She thought it unusual that a man would make that request. Richard always had to have it sweetened but like Scott, she liked it unsweetened. She had plenty.

"Here you go." Mary Jo poured the tea in a large glass.

"Thanks." Scott took a sip.

"This is really good. Did you stick your finger in it?" He smiled.

"What do you mean?" she said.

"I just mean it's probably so good because you stuck your finger in it."

She laughed and loved the remark. It had been a long time since she had had some fun with a man. The night had been delightful, and Mary Jo hadn't felt this good in years being with the opposite sex. Richard had always been extremely jealous and wouldn't tolerate her even talking to other men in a one-on-one conversation. It had restricted her life considerably.

"Let's go in the living room and sit." Mary Jo offered.

Scott led the way and sat down on the leather couch at one end. Mary Jo made a note of it and sat on the couch with him about two feet away.

"I heard you're volunteering with the food pantry at the church." Scott said as he sat down.

"Yes," she said. "I have really liked working with the people there, the volunteers and the people we are helping. It is such a wonderful thing to do."

"I agree," he replied. "I was on the ground floor helping to get it started. In my mayoral job, I see so much need and it occurred to me that the church should be practicing its faith."

Mary Jo looked straight at him and realized this was not the boy she had known years ago. Not only was he still handsome and sweet, but he had become so much more than men like her former husband. His life was full of….something she couldn't put her finger on.

"Scott, something happened to me the other day, that I can't explain, after we gave some food to a family. You're the only person I know with whom I can share it."

"Did it have anything to do with changing a tire?"

"Yes. How did you know?"

"I watched it."

"The entire thing?" She asked with her eyes growing wide.

"Yes."

"Oh, no. I'm so embarrassed. I didn't know anyone was around." She looked down.

"Don't be and it was only me. I was coming out of the church alone, and I saw you with them. I was curious."

She looked up at him solemnly.

"I don't know what happened to me. The man was so nice, and he was grateful, and he taught me how to change a tire and then he thanked me and I…I… She began to cry.

Scott scooted close to her and put his arm around her. She put her head into his shoulder and sobbed.

He held her for a long time until she stopped sobbing. She looked up at him and said, "I am so sorry for ruining this wonderful evening." she said.

"You haven't" he replied. "You just made it richer."

She got up and went to the bathroom and Scott went back to his place on the couch.

Composed, Mary Jo came back and sat on the couch noticing that Scott had moved back to his original position.

She had her head down and there was a long silence between them. Finally, she raised her head, looked at him with piercing blue-gray eyes and said, "How do you do it?".

"That's a pretty open-ended question, Mary Jo. It could range from my worldview to choosing what deodorant to use."

She smiled and Scott noticed. "I'm talking about how you become who you are—your stability, your intelligence, your confidence, your compassion?"

He looked out the windows in this large room at the vast expanse of the Breeden ranch and its panoramic view of trees, lake, grass with a full moon and sky full of stars shining over it. He got up from the couch, moved close to the bank of windows and looked at the beautiful night.

He looked back at her and said, "Come here and stand by me."

She complied and without looking at her, Scott with a sweeping arm from right to left said, "How do you explain this?"

With a knitted brow, Mary Jo asked "What do you mean—this ranch and how Richard and I got it to this point?"

"No, look again. Take everything into consideration."

Mary Jo looked again at the beautiful scene before her and a faint realization came to her, but she still didn't know how to answer his question.

"I don't know how to explain it," she replied.

"Exactly, we make these places for ourselves, puff out our chests and the first thing that comes to mind is that we did it. Sure, we spent some time on it but the natural part of this scene, the most beautiful part, belongs to a mysterious and ultimately unexplainable God."

Mary Jo looked outside, and it looked different. The moon and stars were brighter as they accentuated the oak and pine trees making long shadows across the pasture and the yard. The reflection of the moon and stars off the lake were indescribable in their beauty. There was a light pathway all the way up to the moon. Starting on the water it was smooth and white as it came upon the opposite bank and showed the tall trees in the background. Then it went straight to the moon. Mary Jo could imagine walking out to the lake and taking that pathway to the moon. She felt like she could walk into the heavens seeing much more of the earth and all its beauty as she made her way to this celestial midnight light.

Scott put his hand on her shoulders and gently encouraged her to move around and face him. His brown eyes met her studied gaze. "Now I need to answer your question. I only know that I'm a part of the scene outside—indescribable, unexplainable. I know God loves me and I give my life to serving God. It's the only thing that makes any sense to me. In turn, God gives me the grace to move through this life in a way that interacts with the ongoing process of creation. I get an inkling of the direction to go through prayer, meditation, and lessons from the Bible. I can't live any other way."

Mary Jo was enthralled and consumed with this man. He was not like any other person she had known--even the young Scott she had dated. She wanted to take him in her arms and hold onto him forever. His hands felt good on her shoulders.

He interrupted her thoughts by stepping forward and hugging her. She could feel his strong hands grip her back and the closeness to him was comforting, exciting and downright passionate. She wanted to kiss him and looked up. He put his index finger on her lips.

"Let's take this easy. Each of us has a lot of psychological baggage we need to understand before we go much further. I want you to know, this has been my best evening since before Fran died, and I want to thank you for it."

She looked at him passionately. "I know you're right and I'll do my best, but Scott I-I-I." She hesitated, "Let's do this again."

"We will. I need some time, and I'll call you in a couple of days."

With that, he let go of her and walked out the front door without saying a word.

Chapter 40

Bucky Taylor was determined to succeed. He had healed from being shot by Jack Rocker and although he had a little trouble with his left arm functioning correctly, he was adapting to it. He had become something of a hero in Lyric, but Bucky was an introvert and he didn't like all of the publicity. The County Commissioner had looked him up and asked him if he wanted a job driving a truck and for the first time in his life, Bucky started to think he was amounting to something. He took the job and had become good at it. He even was beginning to learn how to operate some of the equipment. The Commissioner received a lot of political kudos for his decision to hire Bucky and it was a win-win for both of them. Bucky had a steady job, health insurance and retirement benefits and got to work close to home.

It was Friday morning and he was out in the woods near his treasure site that had been blown up by Skinny and Joe Bob. It was still damp from the three weeks of intermittent rain. He had noticed, since he was a small boy, that the woods of East Texas had a pungent smell in the wintertime. It was unique not a horrible smell but all of the leaves from oak, sycamore, ash, ironwood, and tallow added to the soup of water, bacteria, wildlife dung and fungus to make this rich, dense smell that was like no other in the world. He loved it. This was his home and being out here this morning, especially with the sun shining and a light north breeze was comforting and inspirational to him.

He looked at the scar caused by the explosion from the nitrogen bomb detonated by Skinny and Joe Bob. He mused about it now and wished he had seen them running and screaming after the explosion. Fortunately, they had not been burned as bad as it looked at first. The fire retardant in their clothes had helped with staunching the fire but their pants had somehow come off during the explosion and because neither one of them had any underwear on, they had been exposed when Harry and Amy had been helping them. He was sure Amy was probably still laughing.

The damp forest floor made of the natural soup had covered the scar. It was only visible in a few places. The earth had begun to heal itself. Bucky had learned a lesson about looking for treasure—don't tell anyone about it. He was going to do this on his own. He still believed in the story. After they had healed, Skinny and Joe Bob got in trouble and had to spend a little jail time because of the bomb. First of all, they were trespassing. No one had given them permission to look on private land for treasure. Secondly, after Oklahoma City and 9/11, making explosives out of fertilizer was a huge no-no and if the incident had not been in the vast woods of East Texas, it would have been considered a terrorist act. As it was, they had been fortunate because they had hurt no one but themselves and had not violated any federal laws. Additionally, local officials had given them a break. It was not likely to happen again.

Bucky had met with the landowner and after a long discussion regarding safety and not destroying his property, he agreed to split the treasure with Bucky, if he found any of the loot. They had an attorney draw up the agreement in writing. Bucky felt like a grownup. He had a good job and now he was pursuing his dream. The job had happened because Scott Mitchum had talked to Bucky while they were both in the hospital.

They discussed the incident with Jack Rocker and Scott had told him he had been brave to try and run for help. Bucky had received very few compliments in his life and that one had come from a man like Scott. He decided right there that he was going to be somebody. His only male role model in his childhood was his father who was indifferent to him and his mother. He left when Bucky was ten and it was just him and his mother. He hadn't seen or heard from his father since. His mother died on his eighteenth birthday. He had no siblings or other close family and had been alone in the world since that time. His mother taught him how to work and made sure he got his high school diploma He had always had good work habits and was able to get cowboy jobs, construction jobs and logging jobs that paid his bills, but they had not been permanent.

After Scott complimented him, Bucky told him that he wanted to be somebody—like Scott.

Scott looked at him and said, "What do you mean, Bucky?"

"Well," Bucky replied, "I know I can't be you, but I would like to have a life like yours, Scott. I've always admired you. I'd like to have a good, steady job, have a family, a nice place to live and be respected for the person I am—not just some goofball drinking hick."

"Thanks, Bucky for saying that about me but you know I'm not a perfect person."

"Yeah, I know but you make an effort to be good and to help other people. I'd like to be that way."

Scott looked pensive, and Bucky thought he might have said the wrong thing.

With his intense, brown-eyed stare, Scott looked at Bucky and stated, "Bucky, I have a friend who's a supervisor at Lubrisol in Baytown. He asked me to be on the lookout for reliable workers who could make good plant operators. Would you be interested in working at Lubrisol?"

Bucky couldn't believe it. He had tried for years to get one of the good-paying jobs in one of the petrochemical plants along the Houston Ship Channel. He had never been able to break into it because he didn't have the right connections, and he didn't have any training and experience.

"You bet," he exclaimed, "I'd love to work at Lubrisol".

"I'll call him today and see if he can interview you soon."

The rest was history. He got the Lubrisol job after he had worked six months at the County. He had already received his first raise and commendation for the work he had done. He had to work shift work, but that didn't bother him, and it also gave him some time to fish and work on the Santa Anna treasure.

After Skinny and Joe Bob got out of the hospital and jail, Skinny had called him and asked if he wanted to go bar-hopping with them. Bucky turned him down and told Skinny he wasn't drinking any more.

"Well, well, well, aren't we getting high and mighty," Skinny said on the phone.

"First of all, Skinny," Bucky replied, "I didn't show any disrespect toward you and if you want to go bar-hopping, go ahead. Secondly, I've got to go to work tonight at Lubrisol, and I need some rest before I get on the road."

There was silence on the other end of the phone, as if Skinny hadn't heard him. "YOU got a job at Lubrisol? How did that happen?" Skinny said in a loud voice.

"Yeah, I've been working there for about seven months. Scott Mitchum helped me get it."

"Well, how do like that shit. Are you Scott's butt boy now?" Skinny snarled.

Bucky seethed and paused but he couldn't help himself, "Skinny, you are a low class, jealous sonofabitch who couldn't get a job shining Scott

Mitchum's shoes. Scott helped me because he's a good person, something your pea brain could never understand because it's floating in alcohol."

"FUCK YOU, BUCKY." Skinny screamed and he hung up.

Bucky didn't know what had made him say what he did to Skinny. They had been friends for years. But now he was beginning to understand something about friendship, and it didn't come in the form of Skinny Merritt.

Chapter 41

Spring in Lyric had a fascinating way of providing a diverse sensual experience. To summarize it, a person could call it lush. Flowers were blooming, trees were budding, and gardens were being planted everywhere. Geese were flying north in large numbers. It was fascinating to watch the V formation of each group as they proceeded back to cooler weather. In a clear sky you could see some that were slow or fast causing one or both sides of the V line to have a curve. It was clearly a V though from the perspective of a person on the ground. John Marsh was watching them as he stood outside enjoying the spring day. He wondered what natural instinct made the lead goose know that he was to be at the apex of the V. John had known he was a leader from the time he was seven years old. He took risks that the other kids did not want to take. He understood patterns of human relationships and how to motivate groups, even at that young age. Although he couldn't explain it in words, he believed he understood the lead goose.

That didn't mean he had always wanted to be a leader, especially now. Politics in America was difficult. There was a tremendous diversity in ideas about effective leadership. John thought once he got into politics, he could solve every problem that faced his constituents within six months. His first elected office was the Mayor of Lyric. He knew the City government was not moving forward with proper community and economic development. It also had some budgetary problems. John had been a successful attorney for ten years. He thought he would be able to take that experience and translate it into success as Mayor. He knew he had an uphill battle when the City Council voted on the budget presented by the City Manager. It was fair, cut some expenditures and didn't raise taxes. It was also balanced with projected revenues and not dipping into the City's slim cash reserves. Two of the City Council members saw it vociferously different. He was cutting services to the citizens.

The budget passed on a 3-2 vote. As Mayor, he could only vote to break a tie. The night of the budget vote, one of the Council members with a reputation for never taking a stand was conveniently absent. The vote was tied, and he voted to pass the budget. He immediately made his first two political enemies and one of them, Evelyn Hare, ran against him in the next race. He easily defeated her but had found out one of the cardinal rules in politics—it's not logical. The very parts of the budget most affected by Evelyn's constituents, John had fought to protect and increase. He had just not seen the thirst for power the Council member exhibited until the election was almost over. Both of them were at a community event and he had walked up to her to ask her what motivated her to run against him.

"You're running all over the people of this town, John, by not giving them the services they need," said Evelyn.

"Evelyn, we increased the budget amounts for all of the people you claim to represent, so what gives?" replied John.

"I represent everyone in this town, John, and you think it belongs to you. Well, it doesn't and I'm going to see to it that you stop running over them."

"You still didn't answer my question."

"I don't have to answer your question. I answer to the people of this community."

"This makes no sense, Evelyn. What are you trying to accomplish?"

"I'm trying to get some good leadership for the people and you only think about yourself and the good 'ole boys." And Evelyn walked away.

John had been flummoxed. He and Evelyn had worked together to do some much needed improvements in Lyric, and she had become his political opponent. That conversation had enlightened him. It was what she didn't say that was important. She knew he paid attention to her during the budget process. She just didn't want him to be Mayor again because she wanted to be Mayor. She ran against him in the next election, and he won by a comfortable margin. The downside was that Evelyn never worked with him again to do anything for the community.

He was now facing another one of those moments. He had a strong opponent from the other political party facing him in the November election. He had done a good job, in his opinion, representing his District. He accomplished a lot locally and nationally with his leadership. He was scandal free and made it a point to visit his District often to get the "pulse of the people". Legislation sponsored by him had made a difference in education, energy, and transportation.

He understood he was going to have people who had political differences with him in his District. But illogic had once again crept into his political life. He could not seem to connect with some people over simple matters. His friends and neighbors had been affected by divisive national politics. Everyone had a platform with social media and the internet. He felt like a whirling dervish trying to understand his constituents when it seemed like they couldn't understand themselves. He hadn't had but one or two decent conversations with people over policy matters and the rest of them had blown up over one or two issues that were really minor or irrelevant and had no direct effect on the people in his district. To him, it was a new political world and for the first time in his political career, he thought he might lose an election.

The geese were small specks in the sky, and he began to take in the other sights, smells and sounds of spring. As a boy he loved this time of year and now at this age he was sorry that he had not taken more time to appreciate it in his adult life. Why had he ignored those special moments of childhood? The daily grind of his business and political life, the excitement of having money and power and the always constant care he had to give to political relationships had exhausted him. He had forgotten about himself. Most of all he had forgotten about his faith, which he had tried to nurture but found his tangible pursuits were always in the way. He needed to change his life. He needed to talk to Scott Mitchum.

Chapter 42

Ashley Wilson was in the produce section of HEB, and she didn't notice Joe Bob Presswood right down the aisle from her putting some tomatoes in a plastic bag. Joe Bob was noticing her, though. He knew she was about five years younger than him and he had only been around her a few times. She lived just a couple of blocks from his mother's house and hadn't been an outgoing person, much like himself. However, their mothers knew each other, and Joe Bob had been in Ashley's house on occasion. The last time he remembered talking to her was about five years ago when his mother asked him to go pick something up from Mrs. Wilson and Ashley answered the door. Mrs. Wilson wasn't at home, but Ashley knew what Joe Bob was supposed to pick up. She went to the kitchen table and brought a bag to him. Joe Bob had noticed that she was pretty—a little overweight—but unimportant to him. He was overweight himself. He didn't realize she had grown up that much and tried to make some small talk as he was taking the bag from her. She looked him in the eyes and smiled but didn't say much. He remembered she had a great smile and some very outstanding blue eyes.

Here she was again, and Joe Bob was astounded not only with how much prettier she had become but something was different about her—

more confidence? He wanted to say hello to her but really didn't want to get a brush-off. He had never been really good with girls. He knew that Ashley had liked Buddy Parker from what his mother had told him after Buddy was killed, and that she had been devastated by the loss. Joe Bob had somewhat felt responsible, even though it was ridiculous, since he and Skinny had set off that bomb during that whole sordid affair. She would probably not want to talk to him. and he started sacking more produce so that he could get out of the store.

He jumped when he heard, "Hey, Joe Bob. I haven't seen you in a while." It was Ashley. She had come to within about three feet of him and was looking at him with that radiant smile and beautiful eyes.

"Oh, hey Ashley. Yeah it has been a while." Joe Bob couldn't think of anything to say.

"What have you been doing with yourself?" she responded and Joe Bob could not believe how this timid girl had all of this confidence. He was dumbstruck.

"Well-well I've been working and doing some hunting and fishing." He was ready to kick himself for giving such a redneck answer.

"Sounds like you're keeping busy," she said with that great smile and with no appearance of walking away. Joe Bob thought she might be looking at somebody else and turned slightly behind him to see if there was some good-looking guy back there. There was nobody and then he remembered something about what his mother told him about Ashley. He turned and faced her. He felt like he was drowning in those great big, blue eyes.

"I heard you were going to college at Lone Star. How is that going for you?"

"Great, I've had to work and go to school. It's taken longer but I'll be graduating in a year. I want to be a teacher"

"Oh, wow. I'm impressed. I think you would be a great teacher. I know you're really smart." Joe Bob didn't know it and wondered why he said it. He just thought it, and he was ready to kick himself again.

"Thanks for the compliment." she said, blushing a little bit. "It looks like you must have been doing some hard work. I mean your shoulders have become pretty broad, and it looks like you've lost some weight." Ashley thought: I can't believe I said that. Why would I say such a thing?

Joe Bob was turning red and it was noticeable. Nobody had ever complimented him like that. He was bewildered.

"Well, uh-uh-uh, thanks, Ashley. It's nice of you to uh-uh tell me that. It looks like you've lost some weight, too." Now he was going to leave the store and beat his head on top of the car. He had really stepped in it.

They both looked each other in the eyes and laughed and laughed and laughed.

"I apologize, Ashley," Joe Bob said, still laughing. "I'm just not very good when it comes to talking to girls."

"And I'm not very good when it comes to talking to boys." Ashley responded. "Hey, why don't you come to my house on Friday night and I'll cook you some supper, and we can catch up. It might not be so awkward talking to each other like that."

Joe Bob couldn't believe it. A girl had actually asked him on a date.

"I'd love to come."

"Okay, then, how about 6:00 pm?"

"I'll be there. Thanks, Ashley."

"See you then." And she walked toward the register.

Joe Bob had no idea how that had all happened, but he was grateful it did. He needed a new friend and Ashley Wilson was a good start. He walked through the rest of the store in dream world looking at the grocery list on his smartphone. The aisles were pretty small in this HEB. It was hard for him to think after his encounter with Ashley. He finally got the list finished.

Chapter 43

As Bruce Jones sat in the Worship Center of Whispering Hope Church, he reflected on his success. The Church had grown in numbers under his leadership, was healthy financially and his stature among the Southern Baptist hierarchy had never been better. He looked at the stained glass and the size of the sanctuary and knew that God had blessed him because of his attention to doing the right things to grow the Church attendance and making the Church richer. It was about time for things to change at Whispering Hope. He needed to start a new building campaign so that there would be enough room for all of the new people who wanted to come to Whispering Hope.

He also needed to develop more relationships with the right people in the Southern Baptist Convention so that he could obtain some important positions in the future and then reach his goal of becoming President of the Convention. He was at the right age to begin that journey and as he sat there, he prayed that God would give him those opportunities.

He had to cut his ties with John Marsh, though. John was a friend, but he was in the wrong political party for Bruce to make any headway in the Convention. He knew John was a Christian, but his political party stood for the godlessness of America. Voting for people in that party was a vote against God. His association with John would prevent him from moving up and knowing the right people. Bruce had been ignoring John's phone calls and had been subtly but deliberately undermining his standing in the community and with his constituents. Bruce was doing it for the good of the nation and for the glory of God, and therefore knew he had justification. He just couldn't abide John and his ilk. They were against God, and he had to take action to stop them, even if it meant telling some half-truths or insinuating things that might not be true. This was war and what was the old saying? "All's fair in love and war".

The feel and the smell of the sanctuary consumed him. He loved to preach, and he knew he had power in his sermons. People responded to what he said, and he had influence in their lives. He had been blessed by God and he was going to use the blessing to further his influence. He had thought about running for political office but knew he had to overcome the distaste people had for preachers in politics. He was certain that his best route was to use his influence in religious organizations and deliver votes by manipulating the thinking of voters through the pulpit. Although he would not directly ask them to vote for a particular person, he could make it appear that there was no other choice than the candidate he was endorsing. Of course, he would make sure that the candidate granted him access with his advice and recommendations. And if he didn't act on them, he would choose another worthy office holder.

As he was looking at the stained glass, praying to his god and wallowing in the aphrodisiac of his power, John Marsh walked up behind him.

"Bruce," John said. "I'm sorry to disturb you but I need to talk to you."

Bruce looked around at John and replied, "Well, John, I'm in the middle of my prayer time and it's a particularly important part of my day. Can it wait?"

John gave him a fixed stare and sternly replied. "No, it can't, Bruce. I need to talk to you now."

"Okay, you don't have to get angry about it."

"It's interesting that you said that, Bruce. I haven't told you I'm angry nor have I raised my voice. Should I have a reason to be angry with you?"

Bruce looked at him then looked down and stood up from the pew he had been sitting in and smiled, every tooth pearly white. "No, you shouldn't be angry with me. I'm humbly trying to do the Lord's will."

"Tell me Bruce, is it the Lord's will when a friend and a member of your church confides in you confidentially and seeks your advice and then you break that confidentiality to reveal it to that friend's political opponent?"

Bruce's eye twitched and he looked away. He looked back at John and said, "What are you talking about John."

"When my daughter Megan was raped, I came to you devastated. I didn't know what to do for her and on top of that, she was pregnant and sixteen years old. I told you my wife and I were considering an abortion but wanted to be sure we were doing the right thing for Megan. I told no one else in this community but you. Now it's out there in the wind during this campaign and not only do I have a tight race, I have to battle this problem. The whole story has been manipulated to make it look like Megan was a slut and she was flippant about the abortion."

Bruce was silent.

John looked at him and recognized the allure of power in his face and stature. He had seen it in his political colleagues and now it had overtaken his old friend.

"Okay, I get it. I know you've been sidling up to that bunch for years and now that you're a popular preacher, they have convinced you that you are moving up the ladder to power and glory." He shook his head and looked up at the ceiling.

"I remember after playing a football game in high school, when Scott and I came out of the fieldhouse, we looked over at a dark recess of the main building and saw a fight. We walked over toward it and there were three Allison brothers beating you to a pulp, calling you a queer and a pussy preacher boy. We waded in and whipped their asses and took you to the hospital. We vowed that we would protect you from them the rest of the time we were in high school, and we did. I've even kept that vow extending it to your career and family. You don't know how many times I've defended you, and it has been plenty."

Bruce kept silent and didn't say anything.

John looked at him intently and said, "Goodbye, Bruce. That power you are seeking and probably will eventually get, is not worth it."

John turned around and walked out of the Worship Center. He walked through the huge lobby with its high ceilings, inspirational sayings on the wall, expensive wall coverings, stained glass, and the smell of a high rise corporate building. He walked outside and looked at the town of Lyric, his hometown. He was still proud of his community, but it had lost its way. He couldn't put his finger on it, but this meeting with Bruce was getting him closer to the reasons.

He looked up and over the trees. The sun was shining, and the clouds were moving in a graceful floating motion through an azure blue sky. His mood immediately became better and he knew why. This was the God he knew. Not the definition given to God by humans through their religion and politics and in their quest for power over other humans. God was the Creator and Sustainer. It was through God where power ultimately flowed. Bruce had forgotten his Sunday School lessons when he was a child. Now John had to go talk to his oldest friend and hopefully he could shed some light on what he needed to do.

Chapter 44

The skies were ominous looking around Lyric. Black clouds were gathering on the western horizon. Weather reports about Hurricane Harvey had been dominating the news for five days. Harvey had wrecked communities on the southern coast of Texas—Corpus Christi, Rockport, Ingleside, Calhoun County—and it had gone back out into the Gulf of Mexico.

Residents of Lyric breathed a sigh of relief when Harvey hit the southern coast but began to get concerned when it went back into the Gulf and regained a lot of its strength. It had recently moved toward Galveston, and Houston but its winds were just barely hurricane strength at 80 miles per hour. There was hope that when it came inland, Harvey would be weak and pass on through with just some local flooding.

Southeast Texas was hurricane weary. Hurricanes Rita and Ike had come through the same area just a few years before and now they were about to suffer through another one. It was afternoon when the rain warnings had become reality and everyone in Lyric knew they could expect a good soaking. But fortunately, the winds were not too strong and being used to huge windstorms, they were counting their lucky stars.

The rain started around 7:00 pm that evening and continued through the night. At times, the thunder sounded like repetitive shots from loud cannons in the distance. Then lightning strikes accentuated the thunder with a sharpness like the crack of a baseball bat. It was hard for folks to sleep. Many stayed up all night wondering if the rain would ever stop. The next morning it was still raining, not hard but steady. It never quit during the night. Within twenty-four hours there had been twenty inches of rain. Low lying places through Lyric were flooding substantially. Water was already in some houses and businesses.

The rain did not stop. The next evening it continued through the night with rolling thunder and lightning again. Another sleepless night for many but not only because of the noise but fear of the rising water. More houses were getting water in them and people needing to be rescued by first responders who were having problems getting to them.

Mary Jo Breeden was beginning to get concerned about herself and what she needed to do about her current status. She and Richard knew to build their house on high ground in Lyric because of potential flooding problems in the flat terrain of the Lyric area. However, Richard had insisted that they build a lake that was fed by Lum Creek. The lake was close to the house and Lum Creek was a major drainageway for the area watershed. Water had accumulated in its upper watershed and was now coming into the lake and overflowing the spillway. It was on the porch of the house. She could see the water coming so fast into the lake that she was certain it would get in the house. She was by herself. She actually had stayed in the house during Rita and Ike with Amy. Richard had been out of town. They had weathered both hurricanes quite well. This was different.

Mary Jo called 911 and the dispatcher was very professional. Mary Jo explained to her that she was surrounded by water and about the potential for water to get into the house. The dispatcher stated that they were overwhelmed and were assisting only families who may be in life threatening situations. The dispatcher asked her if she had a second story on the house and Mary Jo confirmed that she did. The dispatcher suggested that she try to take her valuable things to the second story and elevate her higher, heavier items on the first floor. Mary Jo thanked her and got off the phone.

She was scared. Not a paralyzing scared but a helpless scared. She could do all the things the dispatcher told her to do, but she was alone. She had talked to Amy but had told her not to come to Lyric—it would be dangerous for her. Her mother had passed on a lot of fortitude to her, and she told herself she could make it through this situation. That did not completely take away her fear, though. She began taking things upstairs to one of the larger bedrooms. She began to think about insurance and if it would pay for the flood damage. Then she remembered that she didn't have flood insurance because Richard was confident it would never flood. I was just another one of those false yet imperceptible parts of his personality. He was so good at projecting his ability to make events go his way, and she had been fooled by it for years.

As she worked, she began to see water come through the back porch door and wall. She looked at some of her expensive furniture and she knew she was probably going to suffer some damage to it. Then the phone rang. On the readout, she could see it was Scott. She answered it immediately. Scott said, "Are you all right?".

Mary Jo tried to keep her emotions in check but knew her voice was high when she said, "Not really. Water is coming through the back door and back wall from the lake. I'm surrounded by water."

Scott replied, "Matthew and I are coming over to help you."

"No, Scott. Don't put yourself in any danger. I'm going up to the second floor, now."

"Mary Jo. I only live two miles away. I have a four wheel drive Ford F250 pickup. I can make it on the roads to your house. Fortunately, they are at the highest part of the community. We are high and dry here and we can help you move your stuff and keep you company."

Mary Jo didn't want to say anything to him because she was about to cry. She got out, "I would be so grateful."

"See you in a about thirty minutes. We'll have to go slow." And he got off the phone.

Mary Jo was overwhelmed with emotion. She was determined not to cry. She sat on the couch as the water swirled under her feet. She could not believe that she deserved this kind of attention from Scott.

She was taking things upstairs when she heard the knock on the front door. She sat them down on the landing and quickly went back to the front door. There stood Scott and Matthew in slicker suits and rubber boots and looking like they had not had any sleep.

Mary Jo hugged Matthew and then hugged Scott in a death grip. Scott kept his arms around her and told her everything was going to be okay. He finally said, "Let's get to work. If we cry, it's just going to cause the water to get higher." Mary Jo started laughing, let go of him and walked back into the living room explaining what she was trying to save, she pointed to several items and said she just considered the furniture as a loss. They all went to work and when the water got to the top of their rubber boots, Mary Jo told them it was enough. Scott asked her if she had food and water upstairs. She said that was the first things she put up there. They all went upstairs, took off their boots and sat on the floor leaning up against the bed.

It was 7:00 pm and it was still raining. Water was rising on the lower floor and some of the furniture was floating. The water was dirty and was beginning to stain the walls a grayish black. It also smelled putrid. Not only was there mud stirred into the water but septic tanks throughout the area had been invaded by flood water, and some tanks were floating out of the ground. It was about four feet in Mary Jo's house. Fortunately, the water system was still working thanks to good planning on the part of the City of Lyric. Emergency generators had kicked in when the power went off at the plants. The drinking water was still working in the upstairs bathroom and they were able to clean up. Mary Jo had brought her clothes upstairs and found some of Richard's old clothes in a storage closet that she gave to Scott and Matthew. They all took showers and then went into the other bedroom without all the stuff in it. Mary Jo had set up a small table with two chairs and the bed for them to sit on. She had some cold fried chicken, iced tea, potato chips, jalapeno peppers and left over peach pie she had made herself. When Scott got dressed after his shower and went into the bedroom, the food was a site for sore eyes.

"I did not know we would be having a king's feast when we came over here tonight," he exclaimed.

Matthew laughed loudly, and Mary Jo had a quizzical look on her face.

Matthew was still laughing and said, "You have to understand, Mrs. Breeden, that my Dad has always said the things you have on that table are a king's feast. He likes them that much."

Scott smiled at Mary Jo and replied, "Let's pray and thank God for this good food and for giving us the courage to get through the devastation of this hurricane."

They prayed and Mary Jo was overwhelmed with a deep sense of gratitude. This had been a humbling experience for her. She wiped her eyes before the prayer was over and looked at Scott and Matthew.

She said, before it looked obvious that she had been crying, "You two look like you haven't had any sleep in a while."

"Yeah," Scott replied, "We've been doing this same sort of thing all night—mostly helping people get out of lower lying areas. The first responders have been overwhelmed. When that happens, the rest of the community has to step up."

Mary Jo looked pensive, "I never thought of it that way".

Matthew said, "Well, it's mostly Dad and a few other people, but that's the way Dad is built. I'm proud of him, and he's taught me to do it."

Mary Jo watched the two men eat hungrily and down the food quickly. "When is the last time both of you had a meal?"

Scott looked up as if he were calculating. "About 36 hours."

Mary Jo was aghast. "You mean you have had nothing to eat for that long."

Scott laughed. "You said a meal. We've been drinking water, tea, Gatorade, and I had a couple of protein bars but not a meal. This is wonderful."

"I've got plenty of chicken. Would you like some more?"

Scott looked at Matthew and said, "Well Mary Jo, if you are offering, we'll take you up on it. I'm not sure when we'll eat again."

"Here," she said, and handed them a family size bucket of Hartz fried chicken. They ate two more pieces each.

They sat in silence for a few more minutes and enjoyed the quiet steady sound of the rain. Scott and Matthew were in recovery mode and Mary Jo was contemplative. Scott laid down on the carpeted floor and Matthew did the same. Scott looked at Mary Jo and asked her to wake them up in a couple of hours. They needed to try and get back to the Emergency Operation Center if they could, to see if anyone else needed some help.

Mary Jo sat in the bedroom chair and watched the two sleeping men. She went to the closet and pulled out a couple of blankets and put one on each of them. She looked at Scott and how peaceful and content he seemed to be. She wanted to lay right next to him and put her arm around him and hug him again. She knew she couldn't, especially with Matthew in the room and for some reason she also knew he needed the space. His contentment was genuine. He didn't need anyone bothering him.

She decided that she may need to rest some and went to the other bedroom. She set her alarm for thirty minutes later and laid on the bed. She thought about the evening's events and then drifted off to sleep.

Chapter 45

The wind began to shift slightly, and the rain was taking a southward slant. There was a barely noticeable chill in the air as the north air began tumbling toward southeast Texas. It was dark and not visible from the ground but in the upper reaches of the atmosphere, autumn was coming. The dry air was beginning to have its effect on the dampness close to the ground. The rain began to subside, and there was a stillness that was a result of a perceptible shift in the humidity that had inundated the area.

Mary Jo woke up from her nap, looked at her phone and realized she had slept through the alarm. She had been asleep for an hour and half. She sat up in bed, feeling much better and went to the bathroom. After she and came back to the bedroom, she realized it was very still. She looked out the window in the dark night sky and realized it had stopped raining. She went out to the landing and it appeared that the water had stopped coming into the house. She felt excited. Could this nightmare be over?

She went into the other bedroom. Scott and Matthew were still asleep and hadn't moved. It was hard for her to imagine these two men taking their time to help other people without expecting anything in return. She was just not used to it. She had some sense of it herself working at the church food pantry but the men in her life, her father and especially

Richard, were always looking for something in return if they did something for anyone. She knew they would probably want something to eat and drink when they got up and she began to look for something to give them. She had also remembered to bring the coffee pot upstairs. She got some beef jerky, some sourdough bread, put it on some paper plates and brewed some coffee. She also had some bottled iced tea and set it beside the pot.

She went into their bedroom and gently nudged Scott on the shoulder. He was sleeping hard. She finally put her hand on his hair and pushed him on the shoulder. She noticed how his hair was thick and felt good on her hand. She quickly set that thought aside for later. He woke up and looked at her.

"You sure that was two hours?" he said with a sleepy smile.

"Yes, to the minute."

"Can you wake up Matthew while I get this old body moving?"

"Yes." Mary Jo wanted to tell him she'd like to see that body without any clothes on it, and she would decide if it was old. She also couldn't believe she was thinking these thoughts.

She walked over to Matthew and shoved him firmly on the shoulder, and he woke up immediately. He looked at her bleary-eyed and said, "That sure was a short two hours."

Mary Jo replied, "I heard the same thing from your Dad."

Matthew smiled and sat up.

Mary Jo said. "I got you some food, coffee and tea on the table over there. I thought you might want something to eat and drink."

Scott looked at her, "That's very considerate of you Mary Jo. I do need some coffee."

Both men went to the table and started eating the food and while Scott drank coffee, Matthew was drinking the bottled tea.

Scott looked at Mary Jo. She had on a slicker suit and rubber boots.

"Going somewhere?" he asked.

"I'm going with you when you leave. I want to help."

Scott looked at Matthew, and Matthew looked back at him.

"Mary Jo, this is not like working at the food pantry. We could be in some dangerous situations, and it's extremely messy and dirty. I expect we'll have to go to the doctor after this over and may have to get some antibiotics along with whatever else to keep us from getting some disease. I don't think you will like it."

"Do you like it?"

"Not really, but people need the help and that overrides the problems associated with giving it."

"I feel the same way, Scott. Don't deny me this opportunity to get out of my comfort zone and use my God-given abilities and blessings to help someone."

Scott stopped eating and looked intently at her. He nodded his head slightly and said, "Okay. Let's get going. I looked downstairs, and it looks like the water is receding. If we can get the truck started, we'll head back to the EOC and see what is going on. I'm sure we can find something to do."

They got their gear together and Mary Jo picked up a storage bin. She said, "I've got several flashlights, lots of batteries that fit them and some MREs from the last hurricane. I want to use them tonight."

Scott looked at her again, "You're serious about this aren't you?"

"As serious as a heart attack." She looked at him with a hard stare.

Scott laughed, "I'll never question your motives, again, Mary Jo. Thanks for pitching in with us."

Chapter 46

The Jim Bowie subdivision on the Trinity River had always had flooding problems. It wasn't the river overflowing its banks as much as it was the tributaries feeding the river. Water would come from the north, fill up the river and any rain water falling in the immediate area would back up into the tributaries, go outside their banks and flatten out in to the alluvial plain making the subdivision look like a lake with a strong current.

Hurricane Harvey had not reached much beyond a few miles north of Jim Bowie, but the rainwater had come so fast, fifty-six inches in seventy-two hours, that it had the same effect. It was unusual because of the amount of rainwater in such a short period of time. The average annual rainfall was between 50-60 inches in southeast Texas. A year's worth of rain had fallen in three days. Jim Bowie looked like some of the major swamps in Louisiana and Florida, except occasionally you could see the upper half of a mobile home or possibly see one struggling to float on the current.

Skinny Merritt had been confident when he had heard the news on television that he could "hunker down" and survive this one just like he did all the other storms coming through here. He wasn't scared and thought all the weather people were full of shit and just trying to put on a show.

That bitch, Dora, had left him when she got scared that it was going to be so bad that they would be swimming out of the subdivision.

Skinny thought about it as he held on to his jon boat walking in water up to his chest. He was mad. People had abandoned him. He couldn't get any help from his neighbors when the water started coming into his mobile home. They were looking out for themselves. When the water got to the point of starting to move the mobile home, he decided he probably should leave. He didn't want to be floating down the Trinity in a half-submerged mobile home.

It's not like he hadn't been in this situation on other occasions. He had survived other floods. Hell, he thought, I even stayed when we had that major flood fifteen years ago. Skinny had been living in a house on stilts at that time. The water got so high that it was above the top of the stilts and about one foot of water was covering the first floor. Skinny had gone up to the second floor and after the water had breached the lower floor, he began to hear some groaning and cracking. It scared him a little, but he figured out how to solve the problem. Part of the porch attached to the first floor was coming undone and wanted to go with the current. Skinny grabbed his chainsaw and waded through the water to the support attachments from the porch to the house. He cut through the wood two by fours and two by sixes in critical places and stood back as a major portion of the porch began to be taken by the current away from the house. There was no more creaking and groaning. Skinny had been the only one to stay on the river during that flood.

Of course, the house was no good after that storm. He didn't have any insurance. The County wanted to buy the property, demolish the house, and not let anyone build on it again. Skinny didn't want to do it and he kept the property. A friend of his who had a mobile home on higher ground wanted to get out of the subdivision and just needed some money to move. The mobile home had suffered minor damage and Skinny bought it for $1,000 dollars cash money. He had been in it ever since. Occasionally, he would go down to his old house and pick up some lumber to use on his new place.

Skinny knew he could survive this one, and he would do it on his own. Joe Bob, that fucking pussy, had gone soft on him and was hanging around with his girlfriend all the time. Skinny just knew he was with her now, and they were probably eating and drinking and having a good old time with nary a thought about Skinny. And where were the emergency people and those famous first responders? Why hadn't they come down here to help? The more he thought about it, the madder he got. Then he heard something that sounded like an airplane coming toward him. He figured it was some kind of watercraft but couldn't make out the sound. As he looked to the west, he could see that there were some ripples in the water and right after them he saw a huge air boat come around a red oak tree and head toward a pine tree to the north of him. It had about five people in the boat. He started yelling and realized that they couldn't hear him. He started walking as fast as he could toward them and then remembered he had a red towel in the jon boat. He found it and waved it over his head at the same time. Just then they cut the motor on the air boat. They all turned in his direction. They must have been about fifty yards away. The air boat motor was cranked up and they headed in his direction. At the bow of the boat was Scott Mitchum and driving the boat was Joe Bob.

After they got back to land, Scott looked Skinny in the eye and said, "Skinny, Joe Bob came to me and told me you might try to ride out this storm in your mobile home just like you have in other floods."

Skinny look back at him with intense bloodshot eyes, "That's right, Scott, and I survived. I don't need anybody's help."

"You realize you were heading right into Lum Creek, which has as strong as current as the Trinity right now. A few more steps and it would have sucked you under. We've already had three people drown in Jim Bowie. We came at the right time."

"I know that creek better than anybody, and I don't need no lecture from you about what I can do or can't do."

"Suit yourself. There's a shelter with food and drink and there are some vehicles up the road ready to take people to them" Scott pointed to them and looked at Skinny one more time. He walked away to the air boat.

Skinny walked over to Joe Bob. Joe Bob was putting gas into the air boat engine. Skinny looked at him for a minute and said, "Well it's about time you thought of your old buddy. Where have you been?"

Joe Bob looked at Skinny and said. "As soon as this storm looked like it was going to cause some problems, I volunteered to help."

"You mean you've been doing this for a while, and you're just now coming to get me."

Joe Bob looked at Skinny with a blank stare and turned away. Scott looked over at Skinny and said, "Skinny, I thought you told me you can take care of yourself. I'm sure that's what Joe Bob thought himself. We had law enforcement down here going house to house to tell people to evacuate and we even checked to see if you had gotten the notice. You did. If Joe Bob hadn't persisted, no one would have come to get you. You should show some gratitude toward him."

Skinny walked around the air boat and got about two inches from Scott's nose. Scott could smell his unwashed body and the tobacco, alcohol stale breath that emanated in clouds of putridness as he said, "You don't tell me what to do Scott Mitchum. I've got better sense than the two of you together."

Scott kept looking at Skinny in the eyes. He knew he was dangerous, but he couldn't back down. It was bullies like him who made people lose their joy. He replied, "If you're looking for a fight, Skinny, you won't get one from me. But I'd be careful if I were you, there's a Sheriff's Deputy about fifty feet behind you."

Skinny would not take his eyes off him. He was insanely angry and said, "I've heard that shit before, Scott, and I'm not going to fall for it." He stepped back and then hit Scott right in the nose.

Immediately, he was pulled back and the Sheriff's Deputy cuffed him. He told him he was under arrest and read him his rights.

Skinny went ballistic and started trying to jerk away from him. The Deputy was a big man but not as agile as Skinny. Skinny got away from him and began running, tripping over cypress tree roots, and trying to get away. The Deputy may not have been as agile as Skinny, but he was quick on the draw with his taser. When Skinny fell over a yaupon bush, the Deputy got close enough to taser him. His body started jerking and Skinny was yelling to beat the band. The Deputy hauled him up to his feet and pulled him over to his car. He pushed him in the back seat and then stood at the open driver's door as he reported the incident to dispatch. As soon as he was finished he looked at Scott and said: "I'm not going to ask you if you are going to press charges. I'm going to state on the arrest report that he assaulted you and then resisted arrest." The Deputy hesitated and then said, "and we may be able to attach not obeying an evacuation order. I'm tired of fooling with this guy. I've had enough of him over the years."

Scott looked at the deputy as he started the car and drove away. He was holding a handkerchief to his nose to stop the bleeding. Joe Bob hung his head and didn't say anything. Scott looked at Joe Bob. He realized that Joe Bob was going through a dilemma. Here was a lifelong friend that had belittled him for a long time, bullied him to submission and now this friend was being arrested because Joe Bob had tried to help him, and he had no gratitude for what Joe Bob had done.

"I guess we should have just left him alone," Joe Bob said.

"No, Joe Bob, this is more about you than it is Skinny," Scott replied. "You did something today that showed how you've changed your life. You've been volunteering to help people, and you didn't leave your lifelong friend out of it, even though he hasn't treated you very well in the past and certainly not today."

"Yeah, well, I didn't like what Skinny said to me, but I certainly didn't like what he did to you. He had no call to do it."

"That's true. But I'll get over this bloody nose. You learned a lesson about people. Just because you help them or they may be friends with you, they are going to take advantage of you. It doesn't mean you stop doing it. In fact, if you don't continue doing it, you miss what God has created you to do."

"I really don't understand what you're saying, Scott."

Scott thought a moment and then he said, "Joe Bob, what does it do to you when you help people that have been hurt by this disaster."

"Wuul, I go home every night and I feel like I've done something that day—not just fooling around like a stupid ass."

"Would you rather feel like you've done something than fool around like a stupid ass?'

"Yes."

"That's what I mean. When your life has purpose, you are usually doing something to nurture God's creation. It's like gardening."

Joe Bob looked at Scott. He was looking at him with understanding eyes and a light in them Scott had never seen. Joe Bob said, "Thanks, Scott, I needed to hear that."

Without saying another word, they tied up the airboat and went back to their respective vehicles. They left the area to return to the Emergency Operation Center in downtown Lyric.

Chapter 47

After Scott returned to the EOC, he asked Joe Bob if he wanted to go to the shelter with him. As Mayor, he was trying to keep a general eye on how the disaster response efforts were going, and he also wanted to see Mary Jo, who was helping in the kitchen. Joe Bob told him yes but didn't tell him he wanted to see Ashley who was also working in the kitchen. They jumped in Scott's truck and took off.

Scott had never seen this amount of water in the Lyric area. It definitely was going to set a record. He could tell the water was receding, but it was still going to take a while, and he could tell that the recovery efforts were going to take years. Many houses had flooded that never remotely had water in them before Harvey. Scott from his engineering perspective knew the area was behind the curve on providing proper flood detention and drainage with regard to all the new development. He had warned the County Judge and Commissioners Court that they were going to experience the disaster they were seeing right before their eyes. Fortunately, in the City limits of Lyric, there was not much of a problem. Through careful planning and financial management with grants and loans the City of Lyric had identified its detention and drainage needs and had fared well through this storm. The majority of the flood damage was outside the City limits, like at MaryJo's house. However, Scott never drew lines when it came to helping people. All of these folks were his friends and neighbors. He had gone to school and church with them. He had played with them. He had rejoiced with them and felt their sorrow. He was going to do what he could to get them through this disaster.

When he went in the shelter, some folks he didn't know were sitting outside smoking cigarettes. Scott stopped and introduced himself and Jo Bob. He found out that they had been stranded on the highway and had no place to go. First responders had brought them to the shelter. Two were from Mississippi, one was from Ohio and one was from New York. One of the ladies from Mississippi was quite a talker. Her name was Christie. She was about 50 years old with long disheveled brunette hair, a thin face but had a curvy body and Scott thought she probably had been a beauty when she was younger. She had kept some of it, but the smoking had taken a toll on her skin and her face.

"This is the nicest community. I've been in lots of places in my life and have never seen such friendly people. They have helped us with everything--food, clothing, a place to sleep. I don't know when I'll be able to leave, but it certainly has not been a hardship."

Scott replied, "Well thank you, we hope your stay in Lyric is suitable especially under the circumstances. You'll need to come back and spend some quality time with us."

"You must be with the Chamber of Commerce," Christie replied.

"Well, I am a member, but actually I'm the Mayor," Scott said.

Christie looked at him from head to toe. Scott was muddy from his waist down. He had a blue nose with some blood at the bottom of it. His shirt had blood and dirt on it and his eyes were sunken from not enough sleep. His slicker was torn and in general he looked like someone who needed rescuing.

Christie was astounded. She said, "You're the Mayor? The Mayor of my town wouldn't get his Rockport dress shoes dirty to help an old lady across the street. No wonder the people in this town are nice." She looked at the other out-of-towners. "This is the kind of Mayor every town needs, helping people in trouble, making sure everybody in his town is all right. I may just have to move here!"

They all laughed, even Scott. He thanked her once again and went through the front door. Joe Bob followed him and quietly considered what Christie had said about Scott.

Scott found Mary Jo and the first thing she said to him was, "What happened to you?"

"Oh, just part of the job." He looked at her and said, "I've been through worse."

"I know you have, but why don't you take a shower, get some clean clothes and let me take a look at your nose."

"I'll just get dirty again. I'll wash my face and come back. You can give my nose some tender loving care then."

Joe Bob found Ashley. She was cooking a lot of biscuits for supper. She looked up from the oven and saw him. She smiled and said, "Hey, Joe Bob. Did you find Skinny?"

"Yeah, but he's in trouble."

"Why?," she asked.

"Wuul, Skinny was giving me a hard time for not coming to look for him sooner, and Scott took up for me. Skinny didn't like Scott taking up for me, and he hit him. The Sheriff's Deputy was right behind him and pulled him back and then cuffed him. Skinny got away but he tripped and the Deputy tased him. He arrested Skinny and took him to jail."

Ashley was listening intently, focused on Joe Bob with her wonderful eyes that looked incredibly angry to Joe Bob.

"Skinny Merritt is a low life and always will be. Joe Bob, I don't like to talk about people like that, but he is not someone you should be around. I'm sorry, but you were concerned about him and made a special effort to go find him. He is a mean and ungrateful loser."

Of course, Joe Bob had already come to that conclusion, but he couldn't believe the passion shown by Ashley and how she really cared about him. They had only had that one dinner date and it was great but this, this statement she made about Skinny and him was like someone fighting for him. In fact, he wouldn't want to cross her.

"Yeah, I think Skinny needs to cool off in jail for a while and don't worry, I've cut my ties with him."

She smiled and put her arm through his, kissed him on the cheek and said, "I'm so glad that you're all right. Do you want something to eat?"

Joe Bob thought he had died and gone to heaven.

Chapter 48

Seven days after the last raindrop fell, looking at the fields and forests, one wouldn't know that the Lyric area had experienced its greatest inundation of rainwater on record. Fifty-six inches fell in a period of seventy-two hours—the equivalent of a full year's average rainfall. However, if one were to travel up and down the streets of Lyric but especially nearby county roads, the evidence was quite clear. Piles of sheetrock debris, ruined furniture, clothes, lumber, insulation and electrical wiring were out on the edge of roads waiting to be picked up. Volunteers and contractors were either demolishing ruined structure interiors or beginning reconstruction on some houses. Debris piles averaged ten to twenty feet in height and special debris collection sites had been set up all over the county. It was a mess.

The amount of cooperation and sheer energy exhibited by the people of Lyric to restore their community and help their neighbors was beyond admirable. It had caught the attention of the entire nation. People who were complete strangers were volunteering their time to pull sheetrock off of walls, tear out electrical wiring, pick up ruined furniture, bring food, water, and clothing. Nothing in the recorded history of the area had been like it. People had helped each other in disasters, but the magnitude of help this time was overwhelming. In fact, many of the shelters had to start refusing clothes and would only take water and food. That was not a problem. People began bringing more water and food and very few clothes.

John Marsh was exhausted. He had been working in three shelters making sure that they had everything they needed. He worked beside his constituents, got filthy rescuing many of them and helping to feed them. Then he would go and interview with the regional news media. They were wanting to know how the government was responding to the disaster. John had stayed in touch with his staff and federal agencies. The response had been slow at first and then had picked up with resources arriving from the Federal Emergency Management Agency. John made sure through his staff and with the White House that people in his District were at the top of the federal government response because they had been hit the hardest by the storm—so far so good. His interviews with the news media had gone well.

He hadn't slept in thirty-six hours and knew he needed to clean up and get some rest, but he hadn't felt this alive since he had first entered Congress. This was better. He felt useful again and not bickering about the nebulous policy ideas that never seemed to accomplish anything. He walked out of the shelter and went to his car. He was going home, take a shower and get some rest. But as he was walking toward his car, he saw Scott Mitchum talking to Bruce Jones. They were standing right behind his car.

He had not had a chance to catch Scott after his discussion with Bruce. The storm had hit and neither he nor Scott could have taken the time to talk because of the emergency. He didn't want to talk to Bruce, and he was too tired to talk to Scott. Scott saw him coming and smiled at him. He said, "Hey, John, I haven't seen you that dirty since we went camping about thirty years ago and you fell in the mud. How are you doing?"

"As well as can be expected," he replied to Scott. "I wouldn't have looked that bad back then if you would've slowed down on that four wheeler. I actually didn't fall, if you remember, I got thrown off the four wheeler"

Scott laughed, "Caught. I confess, but I am proud of you for the 'legitimate dirt' you have on you now."

"Yeah, this has been quite an adventure," he replied.

Scott glanced at Bruce, who had his head down, and noticed he had not said a word. He looked at John and said, "Do you need me or Bruce for something?"

"No, actually, you're standing behind my car. I need to get home and rest for a while. However, I do need to talk to you pretty soon."

As Scott and Bruce moved away from the car, Scott replied, "No problem. Just call me on my cell phone and we'll get together."

John got in the car and noticed his legs were trembling. He knew most of it was from exhaustion but some of it was from seeing Bruce. He was still angry at him. He had so-called political friends stab him in the back, and he knew it went with the territory. But Bruce had been one of his oldest friends. He had confided in him about details regarding his personal life, and he had betrayed him. John had developed a pretty hard shell on his emotions, but this betrayal would take some time to get over. He put his head on the steering wheel and started the car. He said a prayer and put the car in gear. He didn't want Bruce to see he had a weakness— he would just exploit it.

Meanwhile, as they watched John leave, Scott looked at Bruce directly in the eyes and said, "What was that about?"

"What do you mean, Scott?", replied Bruce.

"For God's sake, Bruce, you didn't say anything to John."

"Well, he didn't say anything to me."

Scott kept looking at Bruce. "Is that what it takes for one of your congregation to get a hello out of you—for them to talk to you first?'

"No, but I didn't have anything to say to John."

"That's a duplicitous answer."

Bruce looked at Scott angrily and said, "I'll tell you what's duplicitous, Scott. It's for you to support that baby-killing politician and then tell the world you're a Christian"

"Whoa, Whoa, Whoa," Scott said. "He's our friend. He's a member of our church congregation. He's our congressman. He's a human being. Are you telling me I'm not a Christian because of the way I vote?"

"Yes, and if you don't vote the way that Christ would vote, you are not one of his followers."

"Do you have some scripture to back that up, Bruce?"

"Yes, it's throughout the Bible and it's called the sanctity of life."

"What's that got to do with voting?"

"If you don't vote for sanctity of life candidates, then you are voting against God."

"Well, I don't agree with you since I generally look at the competence and the character of anyone I vote for. Anybody can say they are a sanctity of life candidate and be incompetent and a horrible person otherwise."

"Are you questioning my position to tell you what is for or against God?"

"Well, if you are going to tell me you are my priest and that what you say is the only authority for me to interpret my relationship with God, then yes, I am questioning it."

"Then, we don't have anything else to talk about."

Bruce abruptly turned and walked off. Scott was aghast. He had never seen him act that way.

Chapter 49

Bucky Taylor was getting gas for his pickup on his way home from work and noticed Tracey King pull up to the opposite pump from him. He watched as she got out of the car. He and Tracey had been in the same class together in high school. Bucky had always secretly admired her but never had the guts to ask her on a date. He would speak to her occasionally in school but just out of necessity or in a group. She always was nice to him and smiled whenever he spoke to her. She had a boyfriend, though, Allen Griffin, who was a popular athlete and well known to everyone in Lyric. Bucky knew to keep his distance because he didn't want any trouble and couldn't afford it. He had a good job back when he was a junior in high school. He worked for Allen's uncle. He didn't want lose the job over getting into a conflict with Allen.

As Tracey got out of the car, Bucky remembered a story someone had told him about Tracey and Allen. They were married about two years after high school. Both of them were in college. and it had made big news in Lyric. Allen was playing football for Texas A & M and Tracey was going to Sam Houston State. Tracey's family didn't have much more wealth than Bucky's family, and Bucky had heard her Dad had a drinking problem like his Dad. In fact, Bucky remembered his Dad talking about drinking a few beers with Tracey's Dad at a local redneck dive called Trigger's. Tracey had worked a lot like Bucky and evidently found a way to get into college. After she and Allen were married, she moved to College Station and finished her degree. She had her first child almost immediately after she graduated and then had another one nearly two years later. The story Bucky heard was that Allen had left her when their youngest child had turned two. He had run off with a wealthy woman ten years older than Tracey. He was living in New York. Tracey had moved back home to Lyric to live with her mother. Her Dad had died about a year ago.

This was the first time Bucky had seen her since they graduated from high school. She looked more mature but was still attractive, and he even thought she was prettier than when she was in school. Her brunette hair was long and came down to the middle of her back. It was full and rested easily on her shoulders. Those blue gray eyes of hers were still highlighted by the soft white perfect skin on her face. She was wearing jeans that accentuated her figure and a pullover tight pink blouse that further showed her beauty. Bucky was staring but he couldn't help it. He actually didn't know what else to do. As if she knew someone was looking at her, she turned and looked at him. No smile at first and then it widened when a look of recognition came over her.

"Bucky Taylor!!" she exclaimed as she walked over to him.

"Hi, Tracey." Bucky said as his hand was frozen to the pump and didn't know what to do with it.

"I haven't seen you in forever," she said as she stood about two feet away from him.

"Yeah, well it's sure good to see you. I heard you were back in town."

"I've been back for about two years. I haven't seen you, but I've heard a lot about the local hometown hero you became a few years ago."

"Well, I've definitely been tagged with it and it's more publicity than I need or want. Scott Mitchum was the real hero in that incident."

"I was proud of you when I heard that you found the bad guy and tried to run for help. Not everyone would have been that brave."

Bucky thought to himself how this story had gotten out of control. He was actually out in the woods looking for Santa Anna's gold. He had told that several times to people, and they dismissed it. He was their hero. He had done his best to be humble and honest about it.

"Thanks, Tracey. What's keeping you busy these days?" He was trying to change the subject.

"I'm teaching at the high school and raising two children. I guess you heard that Allen and I are divorced."

"Yeah, I'm sorry to hear it. I understand that divorce can be hard on people."

"Well, that's true, but it really has been the best thing for me. Allen really didn't love me, and the kids just bothered him."

The gas pump stopped, and Bucky took the handle out of his gas tank. For some reason, he was fumbling it and got embarrassed. The pump handle landed on the ground and some gas came out of it. Bucky turned red and immediately picked it up. He knew he was nervous around Tracey, and he couldn't believe she was still smiling. In fact, he saw a glint in her eye like she knew he was nervous.

As he was putting the pump handle back in the pump, Tracey said, "Those things are always getting away from me."

"It's the first time it happened to me. I guess it was slippery or something," Bucky responded.

Tracey couldn't help but notice how the red was creeping up Bucky's neck to his face. She just thought he was the cutest thing. She had always thought it, and now she was making him nervous. It made him even cuter.

Her smile broadened as she looked at him as he was putting on the gas cap to his truck. He couldn't seem to get it on straight. There was a pause in their conversation and Tracey waited for him to finish.

Bucky finally got the gas cap on and thought he was going to die of embarrassment. Tracey kept looking at him. He turned and looked at her.

Bucky stared at her and said, "Well, I-I-I gotta go. It was sure good seeing ya." He averted his eyes and grabbed the driver's side door handle.

Tracey touched his arm and said, "Bucky, we're having a get together for my church Sunday School class—you know barbecue, etc—tomorrow night at Michael Kinsley's house. It's a group of people our age. In fact, you'll know a lot of them. Would you like to come with me?"

Bucky's eyes got wide. He had never had anything to do with church. The only time he had even heard a preacher was at his mother's funeral. He had been invited to church by other people, but he had no idea what to do. He liked Tracey but this was something totally out of his wheelhouse.

"I-I don't know Tracey. I'm not a churchgoer. I'll really be a duck out of water with people like that."

"I understand, and I felt the same way, especially after my divorce. But it's been good for me, and I really can't explain it. I just have a lot more hope than I used to have."

Bucky thought he could use some more hope in his life.

Tracey continued, "Anyway you would be with me and afterwards maybe just you and I can spend some time with each other and catch up."

Bucky could not believe it. Tracey King the most beautiful girl in high school was asking him on a date. He had to do it even though it would probably be a struggle the entire time with the church people.

"I'd love to be with you," Bucky said and realized what he said, how it sounded, and the red started running up his neck again.

Tracey laughed as she put her hand on his arm calming him down. "Well, Bucky Taylor that's a compliment, but let's not take it too far on the first date."

Bucky looked down at his boots and replied. "I'm sorry Tracey. What I meant is…."

She squeezed his arm as she looked him in the eyes and said sincerely, "I know what you meant, Bucky, and I'm flattered. Can you pick me up at 6:30 pm in that nice looking truck of yours?"

"Sure," Bucky replied.

"Do you know where my mother's house is on Claypool Street?"

"Yes."

She let go of his arm and started walking away. "I'll see you tomorrow night and just dress casual like you are right now. I love those jeans and boots. You wear them with style."

Bucky said, "Thanks, Tracey. I'll see you tomorrow night."

He got back in his truck, started the engine, looked out the windshield and wondered what just happened to him.

Chapter 50

Winter had arrived in Lyric. A norther had blown in the previous evening. It was the kind of weather most people in Lyric really liked. The air was crisp and cool. Although it was usually wet during wintertime, this was one of those perfect days. The sun was shining, and it made a person feel good just to experience the natural part of it.

Scott Mitchum felt it. He was going to buy tires from Bodittle Carter, and he knew it would take some time. Bodittle not only had to tell him in detail about every kind of tire deal, but he did it slowly. Scott was determined to enjoy the day as he listened to Bodittle drone on. Scott also needed a simple distraction so that he wouldn't think too much about his meeting with John Marsh this afternoon.

As he pulled into Bodittle's, Scott saw him get out of his chair in the office and generate a smile as he walked out to Scott's truck.

"Well, I didn't expect the Mayor of Lyric to be here, today," said Bodittle as he shook Scott's hand.

"Douse the Mayor bit, Bodittle. I've come here so that you can shake me down for a bunch of money on some new tires," Scott replied, smiling at Bodittle.

They had known each other since first grade. They had camped, hunted, and fished together until high school. Then they both seemed to drift toward different interests. They remained friends but not as close as they had been. Scott had always wondered about it. Bodittle had seemed to be content with continuing to do outdoor activities and remain in Lyric to ultimately own a tire business. Scott had pursued sports and academics, went to college, and got into leadership positions in the community with his business and local politics. Bodittle never had those kinds of leanings. Both of them had the utmost respect for each other and knew that their lives were different for a mysterious reason.

"Yeah, I'll relieve that thick billfold of its cash or its credit card. Some people have enough money that they don't have to ask the cost of anything. But I'm not going to treat you thataway. I'm going to assure you that this is the best tire deal in the area," Bodittle said confidently.

Beau was his legal first name, but it just didn't fit him. His Dad had been a funny guy. He always told people that Beau was always dittling and piddling with things to make them work, and he began calling him Bodittle. It stuck and that is what everyone called him. He didn't mind it. In fact, he got a lot of mileage out of it. It was such an unusual name that it helped make him a successful businessman. He married soon after he graduated from high school. He had worked at the only tire place in town, High's Tire. When old man High retired, he sold the place to Bodittle along with five acres of land he owned on State Highway 116. Bodittle changed the name to Bodittle's Tire and Car Service, worked hard and modernized the shop and started providing other services such as oil changes, alignments, tire rotation and brakes. He hired competent people and paid them well. He stood behind his work and his customer base doubled and tripled over the years.

Bodittle was also a good cook. He would barbecue brisket and chicken, grill steaks and invite people to his house. Scott had been a couple of times. Then he got the idea to turn his five acres on State Highway 116 into a steakhouse and barbecue restaurant because it was in such a good location with easy access. It was the most popular steakhouse in the area. He never spent much time there. His wife ran the steakhouse along with his five children who worked there as long as they were living at home. He stayed at the tire shop, and the steakhouse used his recipes. Every once in a while he would show up just to talk to the customers.

After Scott paid for the tires and said goodbye to Bodittle, he thought about the differences between his friend Bodittle and his friend John Marsh whom he was going to see now. What a contrast in the way their lives had been lived. One was not better or even more desirable than the other. It was just mysterious.

Scott drove up the circle driveway after going through the security gate to the spacious home of John Marsh. The house was not ostentatious but certainly had more square footage than the average middle class home in Lyric. Scott understood the reasoning behind John having such a home— meetings with important people, entertaining dignitaries and trying to put the best foot forward for the people of Lyric. But recently John had been criticized a lot more for such a "fancy" place and Scott had to defend him on occasion. Scott knew it was part of the political battles John had to face. Politics had changed since both of them started running for office. It was no longer the exchange of ideas and challenging each other with doing a better job while in office. It had become mean, bullying, and underhanded almost exclusively. Oftentimes, policy decisions were superficial having very little substance. Even Scott was seeing some of it on his local City Council, an all-volunteer group of people.

John was waiting at the door for him when he parked in the driveway. His wife, Paula, was standing next to him. Scott thought that this was an unusual greeting for him. He was not a stranger to either of them but usually when he came to visit, he rang the doorbell and either one of the household staff or congressional staff would open the door.

Paula, beautiful as always, looked like she had put on some weight. She seemed to be healthier looking than she had a few years ago. Her blonde dyed hair was expertly coiffed, and she wore a blue knee length dress that matched her piercing blue eyes and showed off her lithe figure. She had a radiant smile and one thing that Scott always liked about Paula was her sincerity. The smile showed it. She was glad to see him. Scott held out his left arm and she moved underneath it and gave him a strong hug.

"I'm glad to see you, Scott," she said. "I worry about you being by yourself and your kids grown doing their own thing."

Scott laughed, "Well, I really don't have much time to be lonely, Paula, and as far as the kids are concerned, for some reason they seem to be there quite a bit."

John smiled and said, "Happening to us, too. Come on in and let's sit in the living room."

They moved into the house. It was well-designed with an open concept. As soon as Scott walked through the front door, he was virtually in the living room with its sixteen foot vaulted ceiling that gracefully came down on one side to the kitchen. Scott thought it was Paula's touch that made it welcoming and have the comforting feeling that would lead to good conversations.

Scott sat on the couch. John sat in an easy chair across from Scott.

Paula asked, "Would you like something to drink, Scott? I know you don't drink alcohol. Some unsweetened iced tea, maybe?"

"That would be great. Thanks, Paula," Scott replied.

She brought him the iced tea and took a long look at his face. She sat in an easy chair next to John.

"It looks like Skinny Merritt has a pretty good right hook," John said.

Scott looked down at his iced tea and smiled. He looked at John and said, "I actually knew it was coming, and I did nothing to defend myself. I think that's the first time in my life that has actually happened. It didn't turn out too well for Skinny."

"I heard," John smiled and continued, "I'm curious about why you didn't defend yourself?"

"Good question. I think part of it was I saw the deputy behind him, but I think the other part was spiritual."

"Spiritual, what do you mean, Scott?" Paula said.

"Since Fran died, I have been on this spiritual journey of strengthening my faith in God. I know that sounds trite in this day of television and social media preachers, as well as some practicing politics from the pulpit." He looked at John who was intently listening to him.

Scott continued, "I spend some time in prayer every morning when I get up. It helps me to get centered during the day. I handle confrontations and problems much better. I'm convinced the Holy Spirit speaks to me during the day as I live my life. My actions are directed by that connection."

"How did that work before Skinny hit you?" John asked.

"I knew he was mad and frustrated, but I also know Skinny is a bully and he's arrogant and narcissistic. I've watched him be that way toward his best friend, Joe Bob Presswood for years. Skinny blames his failures on other people. He never makes a mistake. In fact, he probably thinks he's a genius."

John laughed, "Yeah, I bet he does think it."

"Unfortunately, it's not just him. I believe there are a lot of Skinnys out there. It's a cultural psychological problem that is only exacerbated by easy communication in our world. These folks get their confidence bolstered by other people who think the same way, and it grows. It's nothing new, it's just easier to do."

John was looking at him intently. "Keep talking, this is interesting."

"Well, right before he hit me, something reminded me of the scripture about turning the other cheek. We had gone overboard to help Skinny out of a dangerous situation, and he had done everything to blame everyone from the government to Joe Bob for his problem. It had to end. I could've told the deputy to arrest him. He had already made threatening remarks, but something was needed to show the real Skinny. That happened when he decked the Mayor of Lyric."

John and Paula were silent, contemplative.

John broke the silence. "Scott, I wanted to talk to you today before I made a pretty big decision. I'm thinking about getting out of the race."

Scott looked at both of them. Tears were welling up in Paula's eyes and John looked sad. He knew he had been taking a lot in the campaign, especially over his support for abortion rights.

"Of course, that is your decision, but frankly you are the most competent person for the job and have the best character of the two candidates."

"Thanks, Scott. You know that I can take a lot being in politics all of these years. However, it's not been in the campaign but is out there in the wind about Megan's abortion and the lies that go along with it."

"Yes, I've heard and I'm angry about it."

"I am too, but what good is the anger when you can't do anything about it?"

"You can tell the story."

Tears were streaming down Paula's face and she was shaking her head.

"No, I can't. It would be too much for Megan and for Paula."

"Have you talked to Megan about it?"

"No, but she has such a nice family now with such a nice husband and two young daughters. I just wouldn't want to subject them to it."

"I understand, but I think at least you should tell Megan and let her decide if she wants to address it."

John looked at Paula. She had stopped crying and was wiping her face with a tissue. They both looked at each other and then looked at Scott.

"Well, we really have never considered such a move, but we'll talk about it. If we do talk to Megan, we'll leave it up to her."

"You know our kids have a lot to say about their future, and you may be surprised at Megan's response. Matthew has been invaluable to me during this disaster. I was surprised at his good ideas and his initiative. I think we underestimate our children when they're grown."

"There's something else. Bruce and I had words over this matter. " John said.

"Ditto, " Scott replied.

John and Paula looked surprised.

Scott continued. "I won't tell you about the conversation, but it was strained to say the least. Bruce is losing his way and stepping over some lines. Power is the ultimate aphrodisiac, and he has been getting a good dose of it, lately."

Scott stood up and said, "I really hate to rush off, but this disaster has not only expanded my mayoral duties but has given the firm a great deal of business. We are heavily involved with some of the Harvey recovery and mitigation design for new construction. Unless you had something else to discuss with me, I'd better go."

John and Paula stood up. John extended his hand and said, "I knew you could help me, Scott, and you did. Thank you for being a good friend."

Paula walked over and gave him a bear hug and put her face on his shoulder and cried. Scott held her. After she was finished, she wiped the tears from her face and held him by his arms. She looked at him and said, "You are such a good man."

PART III

Now faith is the assurance of things hoped for, the conviction of things not seen.

Hebrews 11:1

Chapter 51

Richard Breeden was sitting on his bunk watching a roach crawl from the back of his prison cell to the bars and then go over the base of the bars out into the cell block. He looked up and out of the cell to see the glassed in guard station and the two male guards and one female guard as they monitored the activity in the block. He was in a Texas pre-release facility that specialized in housing prisoners waiting to be released back into society. This prison was not as bad as the one he had first experienced. Texas had completely overhauled its prison system in the 1980s and 1990s on the orders of federal judge, William Wayne Justice. A prisoner, David Ruiz, had sued the State for the inhumane conditions in the prisons and argued that those conditions violated his constitutional rights of not being subjected to "cruel and unusual punishment." Judge Justice had ruled in his favor and the prison system, under his supervision underwent a vast change. Richard had certainly not enjoyed his time in prison, but it was not the hellhole he thought it would be. However, the first prison was pretty tough, and he had to be tough to survive. This prison housed all the guys who were going to get out. They were usually on their best behavior because they wanted to get back into society.

Richard kept watching the roach as it made its way toward the guard station. That would be him soon. He would be free, walking to the guard station and then out in the real world. He was ready for it. He had some matters to clear up. He had always been a survivor, and he had done it by being ruthless and reminding people that he had power over them. He had lost his power but not his ruthlessness. He felt like that roach, probably the oldest living thing on earth. They survived and that's because they would do anything to survive. He had gotten down to that level these years in prison, and when he got out he was going to survive and thrive through his cunning and his ruthlessness. But survival was not the only thing he had in mind. He was going to administer some of his own justice. He had plenty of time to plan it and the plan was coming together. He watched the roach as it went past the guard station and was hoping to see it exit the facility through some innate ability it had to find its way out. The female guard was about to make some rounds and she came out of the guard station door right behind the roach. The roach skittered away from her, but the guard saw it, took two quick steps, and stepped on it.

"Gotcha," the guard said. She went back to the guard station, got a paper towel, picked up the dead roach and threw it in the trash. She then started her rounds.

Richard whispered, "Damn!" under his breath. Women, he thought, they are always getting in the way of things. That was another part of his justice plan when he got out. He was going to administer it to some women who needed it.

As he sat there on his bunk, Skinny Merritt passed by his cell escorted by a guard. Skinny was three cells down from him. When he was in business, one of Richard's supervisors had hired Skinny once to work on one of Richard's logging crews. Richard had a cursory meeting with him right after he was hired. Skinny only worked about six weeks and then left—something about another job that paid better. Richard had not known much about him except his work for him and Skinny's crazy ideas about Santa Anna's gold. However, he had got to know Skinny a lot better here in prison. Richard had admired his ability to navigate the prison population, and some of the ideas he had for what he was going to do when he got out. It was a part of Richard's justice plan. He remembered his first encounter with him in the recreation area. He had recognized him but couldn't remember his name. Skinny approached him and Richard thought about how thin the guy looked and that's when he knew his name.

"Hey, Mr. Breeden," Skinny said, "You 'member me?"

"I do, Skinny. You did a little work for me one time," Richard replied.

"Yeah, I shoulda stuck with it. It was the only job I ever had that paid regular."

"Why'd you quit?" Richard asked.

"That damn fool Bucky Taylor convinced me and Joe Bob Presswood we could get filthy rich helping him find Santa Anna's gold and I think you know what happened there."

Richard smiled. He knew the story although it was about the same time his life was unraveling.

Skinny went on, "Yeah, when I get out of here, Bucky and Joe Bob got some payback coming from me."

Richard mused, "What do you mean by that?"

"Wuul, the way I see it, Bucky nearly got me killed with that hair brained scheme of his and besides, he's got a good job now that should belong to me. Joe Bob, he decked me one day for no reason, then saw my woman naked and didn't even come looking for me when I needed him during that big rainstorm."

"Sounds like you've got some work to do when you get out."

"Yeah but that's not the mainest one. I'm going to do something real permanent to Scott Mitchum. He's the one who got me in this place, and I'll never forget it. Besides that, I just don't like his uppity ways and all.

Richard perked up. The mention of Scott Mitchum now had him interested in this simple redneck man.

"What did Scott Mitchum do to you?"

"Well, that sumbitch just dared me to hit him, and he knew a cop was behind me when he did it. So, I hit him and because he's the fucking Mayor I got extra time put on me because he's a public official or some such shit."

"Is that so? I didn't know about it," Richard replied. Ideas were beginning to sprout in Richard's mind about his justice plan. He engaged Skinny some more.

"What do you plan to do to Scott?" Richard asked.

"I ain't figured it out yet, but it's going to be good and it's going to be permanent."

Richard had been looking for a partner in his justice plan. Someone to do the dirty work so that he could keep his hands clean. A new Jack Rocker. Skinny didn't appear to have the intelligence of Rocker, but he wasn't batshit crazy either. He knew that with enough money and instructions, Skinny could be his ally in his justice plan.

Richard asked Skinny, "When do you get out?"

"Six months," Skinny replied.

Richard got out in three months. This was perfect, Richard thought as the announcement came about the end of recreation time.

He looked at Skinny and said, "Let's talk some more. I may have something for you to do when you get out."

Chapter 52

It was the regular meeting night of the Lyric City Council. Joe Bob Presswood was in attendance, and he was nervous. He had never been to a City Council meeting. He had heard about them and read some things in the local news about them, but he was not prepared to do what he needed to do at the meeting. He and Ashley Wilson were going to get married, and they wanted to buy four lots in the Oak Shade subdivision. The lots had been subdivided a long time ago and had a fifty foot frontage and a one hundred foot depth. They both really liked the area and hoped to build a house someday soon after they were married. An older couple, Edd and Lily Foy, had owned them and their heirs wanted to sell the lots to Joe Bob's mother who had been friends with the Foys all their lives. She didn't want them because they were on the other side of town, and she was too old to buy any real estate. She mentioned it to Joe Bob, and he told her he was interested.

He looked them over, did his research and decided the frontage was too small to build a nice enough home and have a good yard. According to the zoning ordinance, the lot dimensions could not be changed unless he asked for a variance. He talked to the City staff about it. They told him a developer had bought several of these lots in Oak Shade and had received variances to combine two lots into one lot, giving the resulting lot a one hundred foot frontage. Joe Bob had gone to the Zoning Board of Adjustments and Appeals meeting and had made his request. It wasn't as hard as he thought it was going to be. He knew one of the guys on the five member Board. He sat with them at a table, and they granted the variance. He was at the City Council tonight because, even though the variance had been granted by the Board, it had to be approved by the Council. If he could get one large lot with a one hundred foot frontage for what he considered a considerably discounted price, he would be ecstatic.

Joe Bob arrived early and saw Scott Mitchum talking to some people when he came through the door. He knew Scott was busy and didn't want to bother him. He had a lot of admiration for Scott. After that incident with Skinny in Hurricane Harvey, he knew Scott was hurt, but you never would have known it. He put some ice on his nose and face and kept helping people. When they came to a lull in their rescue efforts, Scott sat down next to Joe Bob.

"How are you making it, Joe Bob?" Scott asked.

"I'm tired, but I still got something left in me," Joe Bob answered.

"Hey, I've got to say it. Watching you do work for me in the past, I've always liked your work ethic. I've watched you then and I've watched you now. You seem to have a knack for organizing and for building structures. I have a friend who is a home builder, and he's been looking for a good hand to help him. His name is Dan Robertson, and he owns Empire Homes. Do you know who I'm talking about?"

Did he ever, Joe Bob thought. Empire Homes was the best homebuilder in the county. Joe Bob had loved the design and the quality of their houses. He had often gone by some of the homes they were building, just to watch the construction.

"Yes, I know about Empire Homes, " he replied. He didn't want to sound too eager.

"I'm about to go see Dan and ask him about bidding on building new homes for people who lost their houses to damage during Harvey. Do you mind if I tell him about you and that you might be interested in going to work for him?

"Wuul, yes Mr. Mitchum, I sure would like a job with them."

Joe Bob had started to work for Dan Robertson two weeks later, mostly doing hurricane reconstruction work but getting paid for it. Scott had helped him get on the right track. His relationship with Ashley had blossomed and turned into more than just a friendship. He had never had this deep feeling of self-worth in his entire life. He still had his problems but felt more confident every day. Scott Mitchum was not only a good man; he was an inspiration.

Scott walked over to Joe Bob and was smiling. Joe Bob stood up and shook his hand.

"What are you doing here, Joe Bob?" Scott asked.

"I'm here about the variances on the Oak Shade subdivision, " Joe Bob replied.

"I saw that on the agenda. Are you purchasing those lots?"

"Yes, Edd and Lily Foy's heirs want to sell them to me, but I wanted to get the frontage wide enough to build a nice home. The Zoning Board agreed with me, and I just wanted to make sure it got City Council approval."

"I don't think that's going to be a problem," he smiled and continued. "However, it's on the consent agenda and there is probably going to be some fireworks on another item. You might want to stick around and see the action." Scott raised his left eyebrow and looked at Joe Bob and winked.

Joe Bob thought that was a problem. Surely they would approve his request after the Zoning Board had approved it. After having prayer and the pledges of allegiance, the City Council got down to work. Joe Bob listened to the financial report and the City Manager's report. He was amazed at the amount of money spent by the City and the number of things they did for the citizens of Lyric. He really never had any idea it was that extensive. Next came the consent agenda and he listened intently. One councilman, Lucius Wyatt, a black man with a booming voice, asked that item four on the consent agenda be taken off for discussion and action. He also moved that all other items on the consent agenda be approved. Scott restated the motion and asked for a second. Kelly Johnson, a pretty and well-dressed fifty-year-old attorney seconded the motion and the motion passed unanimously. Joe Bob wondered if that meant his matter had been approved. It seemed like it, but he wasn't sure.

Scott read the item taken off the consent agenda. Joe Bob understood it to be that mobile home parks had to have more distance between the mobile homes or install eight foot privacy fences between them. Scott called on Lucius to explain why he wanted to discuss this item. Lucius stated that this was a major financial burden to existing current mobile home park owners. If the Zoning Commission wanted to make the rule apply to future mobile home parks, he would have no objection. Scott said that he had a citizen who lives in a mobile home park who requested to give public comment on the item. He called on him, Odell Harrison, to go to the podium and speak and told him he had three minutes.

Joe Bob could see Lucius and Odell staring at each other as Odell walked to the podium. Odell was about six feet four inches, 250 pounds, all muscle and had some red in his large and very noticeable eyes on his black face. His hair was not buzzed close to his head but was about one-half inch high above his forehead. He wore a long sleeve button down shirt with blue jeans and casual shoes. His voice was a lot like Lucius' voice.

"Thank you Omnipotent Mayor, and Voluptuous Council for hearin' me on this matter," he said with a booming voice. "I represent the peoples in the Red Oak mobile home park. My name is Odell Harrison. All of us in the park are part of a community that live close to one another and look after each other. We do not generally have a problem with each other as we live day to day. Our complaint is that our private lives are well known to each other because these mobile homes are too close," Joe Bob could tell he was starting to roll as his voice gathered strength. "Every time there's an argument in a home, their neighbors know who won the argument and who is going to be in the doghouse. I once had one of my neighbors ask me if I ever got my checking account straightened out at the bank for overdrawing it and to top it off, my other neighbor asked my wife if she could calm down a little bit when she was watching Family Feud on TV. Every time somebody farts or takes a shit, their neighbor hears it. Every time someone is making love with his or her partner, their neighbors know every move they make, every grunt they make and every scream they scream....."

Joe Bob's mouth was wide open. He had never heard anyone talk like that in a public forum. He looked at Lucius and he could tell he was ready to fight. Lucius looked at Scott who was looking at Odell and then said.

"Mr. Mayor, this needs to stop, " said Lucius.

Odell looked at Lucius and said, "I'll stop when my three minutes are up."

Lucius said under his breath, which was still loud enough to hear, "Not if I stop you first," he said.

Odell looked at Lucius and the red in his eyes was more noticeable and said, "What did you say?"

Scott hammered the gavel down twice and said, "Gentlemen, we'll have order, or I will get our police chief to establish order." Joe Bob could see Jesse Henderson at the back of the room taking a few steps toward Odell.

"Mr. Harrison, your three minutes are up," Scott said. Odell took one last angry look at Lucius and then strode powerfully over to his seat to sit next to his wife.

"Now to the matter at hand, "Scott immediately said as he took charge of the meeting, "what is the Council's pleasure?"

Blackie Wasik, a white man who was incredibly quiet, but was purposeful in his actions said, "I move that we table this matter until the City Manager can give us a further report on the cost implications for mobile home park owners."

"I second the motion," said Carrie Bilnoski, an elderly woman who was known for taking her civic responsibilities seriously and was the longest serving councilperson in the history of the City of Lyric.

Scott said, "We have a motion to table this item and a second. All of those in favor raise your hand." Four hands were raised. "All of those opposed, raise your hand." Lucius Wyatt stared hard at Odell Harrison and raised his hand.

"The motion passes," Scott stated and looked at the City Manager. "Mr. Hanel, please take the directive of this motion and have a report for us by the next meeting."

"Yes, sir, Mayor. We'll get right on it and have a recommendation for you by that time, " responded George.

The rest of the meeting was rather routine and when it was over, Joe Bob hung around until Scott was not occupied by City business. He wanted to ask him what he should do about his lots, since he didn't really know if his request had been approved.

Scott turned after he finished what looked like his last conversation, smiled at Joe Bob, and said, "What did you think about your first City Council meeting, Joe Bob?"

"You were right about the fireworks. I never knew people could get that mad with each other in a public meeting."

Scott laughed, "Yeah, that was a hot one, but I've seen worse."

"Really?" Joe Bob queried, and then looked around and saw that he and Scott were the only ones in the room. "I didn't think black people got angry with each other over such things. I just always thought they got angry with white people."

Scott looked thoughtfully at Joe Bob and said, "Black people are just like you and me, Joe Bob. They get angry at each other, they hurt each other, they share joy with each other, and they help each other. They do have something in common that you and I do not have, and it's not just the color of their skin. Their ancestors, primarily African Americans, were officially enslaved in this country starting in 1619. That went on for 244 years and even after they were no longer slaves, their freedom was oppressed by the white establishment with unequal laws and regulations at least for another 100 years. That is why you see them being wary of white people. However, black people, and some like to be called African Americans, are among my most trusted friends."

"Yeah, well I guess I knew that about them and all, studying history in school but what you just said made it a lot more clear and..and"

"Personal?"

"Yeah, that."

"You probably know a lot of black people and may even have some black friends. I'd encourage you to get to know them more in a personal way, not just as a group of people. You'll be glad you did."

"Thanks, Scott. You always give me something to think about. I need to get home, but did my request get approved tonight."

Scott laughed again, "Yeah, right before the fireworks. Get those lots re-platted and build you a house."

Joe Bob smiled and said, "Thanks. I'll see you later"

Scott looked at him as he walked out of the City Council Chambers. His posture was erect, his shoulders were pulled back and he had the purposeful stride of a man on a mission. Scott was proud of him.

Chapter 53

Spring had come to Lyric. Pine trees were growing and were covering the area with pollen. Growth stems were long and very obvious with their light green extensions off existing limbs and their tan ends. Ponds and cars showed the most pollen, but it was everywhere. Most people around Lyric took the pollen in stride with their sneezing and coughing and many trips to the pharmacies for over-the-counter allergy medicine. It was just the way of life around east Texas forests. The lush landscape grew just about everything well except cactus and even in some spots you could see it growing naturally.

Natural flowers were everywhere representing all colors and the air smelled wonderful. Honeysuckle and gardenias perfumed the air with their distinctive odors. The white flowers of gardenia bushes were prolific and adorned the consoles of many cars as people would pick them and put them in their cars as air fresheners. Yellow jasmine in the deep woods could be seen on their vines crawling high about the ground into hardwood trees and then spreading their unique smell to anyone walking in the forest. Birds were singing everywhere, and life was abundantly shown as it grew and manifested itself once again in a creative and miraculous yet mysterious way.

Bucky Taylor was walking through the woods to the Mill Pond with his rod and reel and his cooler. He had some minnows in a bucket and was going to do some fishing and some thinking. The Lubrisol plant was about to have a turnaround, a time where the plant caught up on its maintenance and re-tooled to manufacture new products or higher quantities of the same product. Bucky was a plant operator and would still be working but the turnaround was mostly done by a contractor. He had a few days off while they started the turnaround and he just wanted to relax.

He had always come to the Mill Pond when he needed to relax and think. He even had a couple of spots where he could sit all day and fish, eat snacks and drink beer. It was such a fine day, and he was grateful for it. He had become a lot more grateful since he had started dating Tracey. Since that first day when she asked him to go with her to a party with her church friends, their relationship had gone nowhere but up. Bucky had never been really shy around girls. He had dated many and most of them told him he was good looking and cute. He had even slept with a few of them. He didn't want to get too serious about them because he didn't want to get married. Although his parents were not mean to him, he never did see the point of why they got married in the first place. They didn't seem to love one another, and they just seemed to exist. There was not inspiration from them about how to live his life and what he should do with it. When he got exasperated with school, they even told him he could quit when he was eligible to do it. The only reason Bucky had some drive was because of Robert Ward and Scott Mitchum.

This thing with Tracey though was different. He had finally figured it out that she was leading him, and it was not him leading her, like in his limited education and experience with women he had understood all of his life that the man should lead. She had directed a lot of their activities together—where they would go and what they would do. She had even helped him change his wardrobe some. Even when they were intimate—

kissing and exploring each other's bodies, she seemed to be in charge. He liked it, and it made him feel wonderful. And she was always so damn nice about anything they did together and asked him what he thought—even the kissing.

He was reminded of an old rhythm and blues song "Use Me" by Bill Withers he had on his phone. The lyrics seemed to describe their relationship. Bucky had gotten to the point where he didn't want to be anywhere for any long period of time without her, and he knew that he was going somewhere he had never been. He didn't know much about love. He was an only child and his parents didn't show a lot of love toward each other, and consequently they didn't share much love with him. His dad taught him how to fish and hunt and told him he had to go to school, but he never seemed to care too much for Bucky. His mother in her own shy way would do special things for him from time to time but never showed any outward affection. He just thought that kind of behavior was normal until he started dating girls. He began to figure out that girls liked him because he was cute, and he did everything he could to play it up. He liked being with them because they were pretty, smelled and felt good. It was hard for him to keep his hands off of them. His first girlfriend, Courtney Steen, had taught him a lot. By their third date, they were doing some serious kissing and exploring each other's bodies in his truck. She stopped it, though, and told him she couldn't go all the way because it was important to her that she was a virgin when she got married. Bucky was like his mother in that he wasn't going to ask someone to do something they didn't want to do. It was hard for him to stop. He respected her wishes, although he found out later she wasn't a virgin when she got married.

Women were confusing and hard to understand. That's why Bucky was fishing today. He was a grown man, living by himself and he needed the time to sort all of this out with Tracey. He didn't mind being alone, but he did mind being lonely. And loneliness had bitten him a lot harder in the last few years since his mother had died. He inherited the house and continued to live there. He was proud of the place and had fixed it up to be a pretty nice abode. He spent many nights by himself, and he could handle it, but those nights were always better when he had been around Tracey.

A bass hit his line and Bucky started reeling him in. It was a nice one, about three pounds. He put it on the stringer and threw it back into the murky water near the bank. Bucky thought he might do pretty well today and if he could catch a few more like this one, he could have a fish fry with Tracey and her kids.

It was happening again. He couldn't get her and her kids off his mind. That was something else. He had never paid much attention to kids, but Tracey's kids were just like her. One boy and one girl and they were very polite and nice around him. Oh, he had seen them having some conflict with Tracey, but they worked it out very quickly. Tracey was fair but she was stern when she needed to be. Bucky had gotten close to both of them, but especially her little boy, Jacob. He was always hanging around Bucky and wanted to know everything about him. He liked to ride in Bucky's truck, and he liked going in the woods with him. Tracey had allowed Bucky to take him fishing a couple of times, and Bucky had been overjoyed showing him how to fish and was even more elated than Jacob when Jacob caught his first fish. The little girl, Savannah, was the spitting image of Tracey. She was very pretty, but she wasn't a girly girl like her mother. She liked to ride in Bucky's truck. She was not happy when Jacob got to go fishing with Bucky two times and she never got to go. Tracey asked Bucky if he would mind taking Savannah fishing. Bucky told her he didn't mind at all, but he was little nervous being around a little girl without the presence of a grown woman. Tracey said she would go with them. Bucky had already set a date when they were all going fishing together.

He was smiling as he thought about it when another bass hit his line. Yeah, he was consumed by Tracey, her kids and wanted to be a part of their life. He couldn't explain it. He guessed it was love, but he had never experienced anything like it. He had been hanging around Tracey and some of her church friends from time to time. He knew some of them from high school. Most of them were sincere when they told Bucky they were glad he came to be with them. There were a few insincere ones. Several times when they got together, they would pray not just for the food but for their friends or acquaintances who were going through some struggles. From time to time, they would talk about Jesus, and Bucky was becoming more intrigued about what made these people the way they were. For the most part, they seemed to be content, whatever might happen to them. And they seemed to be concerned for each other. He knew it had something to do with what they believed but he didn't understand it. He asked Tracey about it.

"Well," she smiled at him, "I can only tell you that it's an amazingly simple but mysterious thing called faith."

Bucky had heard the word but didn't understand what she meant.

"It's the evidence of things not seen, the substance of things hoped for," Tracey continued.

"I'm not sure I understand," Bucky replied.

"I know how you feel. I didn't understand it in the beginning, and sometimes I still marvel at its power and my lack of understanding it. The best way I know how to explain it is using a pine tree."

"A pine tree?"

"Yes, I've watched pine trees grow all my life, they start from a small seed from a pine cone."

"Yeah, I know all about pine trees, Tracey."

"Well you know that the seed can become a mighty tree in fifty or sixty years, but you don't know it when it is just a seed. However, you know that it has the potential to become a mighty tree, the evidence that is not seen by you and the substance of what you are hoping for."

"Okay."

"Well, that's our lives too. We start as seeds and God, with care and blessings, will grow our lives if we have faith in God to navigate us through our life like he does that pine tree seed. We live out our faith every day."

Bucky was quiet and he had no more questions. He had been in nature enough to know it was mysterious. He couldn't explain it. He did know that it was astounding.

Chapter 54

John Marsh was sitting with his family in their backyard at the end of the day. All of them were there. His wife, Megan, his oldest daughter and her husband, Chris McClelland, and his youngest daughter, Rachel. Megan and Chris were living in Los Angeles and had to fly here for the family meeting. Their two young daughters were staying with Paula's sister. It was a beautiful spring late afternoon. The shade from the trees was filtering the sun and the shadows dappled the patio. The air was full of the smell of spring flowers. Paula's roses were full of blooms and looked perfect with the petal array on each stem. John was glad it was such a nice evening because he was about to bring up an unpleasant subject, but he knew he needed to do it for Megan's sake and for the entire family.

"I've wanted all of you to know I have been thinking of quitting the race," he said as he looked at each of their faces. "Some very personal and hurtful rumors are being circulated about Megan and I don't want it to go any further. I've had a good run in office, but this is beyond what I signed up for when I ran for this seat several years ago."

Megan spoke up, "Dad, Rachel has been telling me about the rumors and quite frankly, I'm angry and I want to do something about it. I've discussed it with Chris, and he thinks I should go on the offense against these lies."

"What do you mean, Megan?" John replied.

"I didn't spend four years in the military learning how to lay down and die. I learned to fight and not just physically but in a visceral way that includes body, mind, emotion, and spirit. I couldn't fight to win when I was raped, but I can now and that's what I want to do."

Megan joined the Army after she graduated from high school. She had excelled in all phases of it. She was in an intelligence battalion and had seen combat in Afghanistan. She had received a purple heart and an Army commendation medal. She had also gone to college while she was in the service. She finished her degree in business after she got out of the service and had just been accepted to Yale Law School. She and her family were about to move to Connecticut. Chris was already a lawyer. They had met in the Army. He was JAG officer. She met him at Fort Benning when she got back from Afghanistan. He had found a position with a law firm after his honorable discharge.

"Are you ready for this, Megan? Politics are a nasty business and it's hard to deal with some of this nonsense for extended periods of time."

"Yes, you've taught me well, Dad, and I have seen what people have done to you. I've also seen that deep well of character you've established and your ability to keep yourself centered during the worst of it. That man raped me, and I was too nice and too trusting to do anything about it. I kept thinking if I protested enough and kept pushing him off that he would stop but it didn't happen."

"I know that darling. They may give you that point. Now, they'll ask why it wasn't reported to the police and why you didn't just have the baby and put it up for adoption."

"I've got an answer for them. Just let me tell them at one of your televised rallies. I want to fight this evil. I'm ready to stand up for women who have been abused and controlled just because they are women. I'm not that nice and trusting teenager anymore."

"I don't know, Megan. I need to see if your mother and Rachel are okay with you making this public."

John looked at his Rachel who had a determined but solemn face and was looking at Megan, nodding her head.

Rachel said, "I'm all in with Megan, Dad. These people around here spreading these rumors are arrogant. The real people in this community know what our family has done for them, and they just need to hear the entire truth from one of us. It will reassure them and establish their trust in the Marsh name. It'll be best if it comes from Megan."

Paula was looking at both of her daughters and smiling. She couldn't have been prouder of them. She looked at John and said, "Let's do it."

"Okay, then we'll make a place for you at the next rally and I'll inform my campaign manager. I'll need to clear it with him and my marketing strategist. They had some inkling of this possibility after my discussion with Scott Mitchum. He advised me to let you tell your story. I just didn't think you would want to do it and that you would respond in such an assertive way. I'm proud of you Megan and I'm proud of you, Rachel. I would have been proud even if you didn't want to do it."

He paused and he said, "I'd like to pray and ask God to be with us during this entire ordeal."

They all held hands in a circle as John led them in prayer, praising God for his magnificence and his grace, asking him to forgive their sins, thanking Him for watching over them now and in the future with his blessings and asking Him to help those who were sick and less fortunate than them. He also asked a blessing on the food they were about to eat.

After he said amen, everyone moved inside to the dining room. John stayed behind and looked at what was now a colorful, beyond description sunset; the blue was a mixed integration with the yellow and orange and infused with wispy white clouds throughout. The trees in front of the sunset provided a foreground silhouette that could never be painted or photographed by a human. John knew he had done the right thing. He had to thank Scott and then he said, "Thank you, Lord."

Chapter 55

Scott sat in the beach chair watching the ocean. The vastness of it took him to another place. While he listened to the waves and felt the wind, he was calm. This was bigger than him and anything he could imagine. He felt the same way when he was in mountain ranges. He knew why songwriters wrote music about the ocean and the mountains because about the only way you could describe them was with music. Sea gulls were everywhere, and it didn't bother him. He liked watching them soar and also exhibit their herd mentality behavior, which reminded him of his fellow human beings. Hold a piece of bread up and the seagulls flew immediately to you. They would fight over the bread when you threw it in the air—sort of like the human pursuit of power and control.

Mary Jo was sitting beside him. It was their fifth date. They had decided to take a break. They were in Galveston. They came early to go to the beach, sit and watch the waves and get in the water before it got too hot. Then they were going to eat lunch at The Spot. Tonight, they were going to have dinner at Waterman's and watch the sunset over the bay. Then to a Willie Nelson concert at The Grand. The Grand was the restored Galveston Opera House, built in the 19th century. Scott and Fran liked to come to concerts at The Grand because it was a relatively small venue and had great acoustics. Scott was a Willie Nelson fan. He liked his concerts because he played a lot of music and didn't talk very much. He also liked Willie's outlaw style.

Mary Jo had not been much of a beach goer. She told Scott that Richard didn't like the beach, and she never wanted to come here on her own. Occasionally some girl friends would invite her and Amy to come with them, and she had made a few trips like that. She had always liked it and had good memories of the times she had been on the Texas coast.

They reserved two rooms at the San Luis Hotel. It was a bit awkward when Scott asked her about taking the trip. They had become somewhat intimate on their third date—hand holding, kissing good night. They both knew it was going further, but Scott was hesitant. The loss of Fran was still a scar he bore, and he couldn't get her love for him and her beautiful face and body out of his mind. Mary Jo was beautiful, too and the more he was around her, the less he thought about Fran. He wondered if he was being disloyal to his departed wife. Mary Jo had readily agreed to the trip and thought having the two rooms was a good idea. She, too, was still wounded from the hurt caused by Richard in their marriage. She remembered what Scott had said on their first date about taking it easy, and she now knew how important that decision had been. They had renewed their friendship in a deeper manner, and it was growing into a more sensuous desire to be with each other.

"What are you thinking?" Mary Jo asked as she ran her fingers up and down the cold Michelob Light beer in the cup holder of her canvas chair.

"I'm thinking about what is beyond the horizon," Scott replied as he pointed to the ocean.

"Why are you thinking about what is beyond the horizon?"

"Well, it's an exercise I have always done when I come here. I spent some time cruising the ocean with the Texas A&M campus here in Galveston. We went to Europe one summer. It was a training session and college credits for me. I had to work on the ship, and we went to several ports of call. The ocean has always fascinated me with its vastness. My parents brought me here when I was a kid and we always had a good time. I feel a kinship with what is out there—it's really a philosophical experience for me."

"I can see that from the way you seem mesmerized by looking at it."

"That obvious , huh?"

"Yep, I definitely wasn't getting your attention and I bought a new bathing suit just for this occasion."

Scott smiled. He had noticed the revealing but in good taste bikini Mary Jo had beneath her cover up. He had not seen everything, but he was sure it was something to behold.

"Sorry," he said as he took her hand, "the ocean is just an incredibly special part of my life, and it has been awhile since I've been here."

He stood up, pulled her up with him and said, "Let's go for a dip and let me look at that beautiful body of yours, scantily covered with your new purchase."

"Now, you're embarrassing me."

Scott pulled off his shirt and revealed a masculine build with some jacked guns, noticeably firm pecs, and a toned abdomen.

Mary Jo looked at him and stared for a moment. She had never seen him with his shirt off and really couldn't speak. She imagined he might be like that but was at a loss for words.

Scott grabbed her hand and started pulling her toward the water.

"Wait, wait, let me put this stuff in the chair," Mary Jo said.

She took off her hat, undid her ponytail, and let her hair fall around her shoulders. Then she kicked off her sandals and slowly removed her coverup.

Scott watched and was amazed. She couldn't have been more stunning.

He said, "Mary Jo, the bikini is really nice, but you are really the star in this picture I'm seeing. You're beautiful."

"Enough said," she replied as she reached up, put her hand behind his neck and kissed him, laughed, and said. "We're both happy with each other's pictures."

They walked hand in hand to the water.

After a lunch of fish tacos, they went to sit underneath the shade at a beach pocket park on West Beach. The sun was not too hot, but they didn't want to get burned. Once again they were sitting in their canvas chairs watching the water. Both of them had books to read, but they liked just sitting next to each other and enjoying the day. And what a day it was. The sun was shining brilliantly and there was not a cloud in the sky. A flock of pelicans would cross their line of sight from time to time headed toward San Luis Pass. Every once in a while they would watch an individual pelican fly down to the surface of the water and catch a fish in its extended and world famous storage beak. The water would splash, and they could just barely see the fish disappear in the pelican's mouth. They had also seen some porpoises cresting the perpendicular waves as it appeared they were having a Gulf Coast run down to Corpus Christi or at least that's what Scott liked to think.

Scott said, "You know there are people who think the earth is flat."

"Well, yeah, we studied that in school and of course it was disproven by Columbus and several other explorers," Mary Jo replied.

"No, in the present tense. There is a large and growing group of people, fueled by access to the internet, who think the world is flat in defiance to all science."

"You've got to be kidding me."

"No, in fact I ran onto a guy in Lyric the other day who believes it. He's a Houston firefighter."

"Scott, you're smiling, and I think you're pulling my leg."

"No, I'm serious, even though I would like to pull your leg." He raised his eyebrow and looked at her.

She hit him on the arm and said, "Keep your mind on the subject."

"You can Google it and see. There is a Flat Earth Society. I think they even have a convention every year."

"How can they be that ignorant? Haven't they seen the pictures from outer space? How about the trips to the moon and the satellites that orbit? For God's sake, I've flown to China east from Houston and returned from the west. It's clearly obvious it's round."

"Their contention is that it is all fake. It was purposely done and perpetuated by higher powers than them who have some diabolical agenda."

"What is the diabolical agenda?"

"I don't know. I asked the firefighter the same thing and he didn't have any specifics, but it is a take-over-the-world scheme of some sort."

"Oh, kind of like in the James Bond or Austin Powers movies."

"I think Austin Powers is more like it."

Then Scott did his imitation of Dr. Evil and Mary Jo started laughing hard. He kept it up with Flat Earth philosophy until she could hardly catch her breath. He finally stopped and Mary Jo had tears running down her face.

He looked at her and said, "Thank you for coming with me."

She replied, "Oh, Scott, this is wonderful. It is one of the best days of my life."

"Let's go back to the hotel and get ready for dinner. Maybe, we'll have a little time to drive around the island and see the sights before we eat."

"Sounds like a plan."

Chapter 56

After they left the hotel, Scott asked Mary Jo if she had ever taken in the sights of downtown Galveston. She told him that she only had gone down Broadway to the beach and back home and once to the Strand to do some shopping with girlfriends. Scott told her she had missed the best part. As he drove along he talked about the 1900 hurricane and how it had changed the very nature of the island city. Galveston had been the economic center of Texas before the storm. Most of the structures in the town had been wiped out by it, and around six thousand people had been killed. Mary Jo had a vague memory of reading something about the storm and knew those facts, but she was content to let Scott tell the story because she saw his passion for the meaningfulness of what he was telling her.

"Very few buildings survived, but the ones that did, have become icons in the history of Galveston. The Grand, where we will see Willie tonight, is one of them, along with Ashton Villa, Bishop's Palace, and the Moody House. They were all part of Galveston's golden economic era," Scott stated in his Mayor's voice.

"Where are all of these buildings, specifically?" Mary Jo asked.

"Well, three of them are on Broadway. Every time in the past that you went down Broadway, you could see them from your car window."

"I've always noticed some very nice looking mansions, but I just thought they were the residences of wealthy people."

"They were built by wealthy people and were their residences in the late nineteenth century and early twentieth century, but now they are open to the public through some non-profit organizations and the Catholic Church."

"You mean we can go in and look at them?"

"Yes."

"I'd love to do that."

"Let's go to downtown and I'll show you around and then you can decide what you would like to see. We'll go tomorrow."

Mary Jo smiled, and her blue grey eyes were wide, "Oh, that would be fantastic. I love to look at older homes and know their history." She grabbed Scott's hand resting on the console and held it tight.

They toured downtown Galveston in Scott's pickup and then went back to the seawall with tour guide Scott explaining the engineering feat of building the famous engineering marvel. They went a little further past the seawall and pulled into Waterman's restaurant and walked inside. It was a first for Mary Jo to eat at Waterman's although she had heard about it. They sat at the window and could see the Galveston Bay. Scott looked at the coming sunset, but he couldn't help but also look at Mary Jo a lot. She knew it. She could feel it even when she looked at the Bay. She had never felt this good in her whole life. How could this man make her feel this way?

The meal was exquisite. The way the restaurant prepared the shrimp and the sides with the entrée was unique and delicious. The butterflied shrimp with its white meat turned golden brown was wrapped in bacon. Vegetables grilled in garlic oil rounded out the plate. The bread was something Mary Jo had never really experienced, and she had traveled a lot. It made her question why she had never made the effort to see what was right in front of her all the time.

Willie Nelson did not disappoint. Even at his age, he stood for an hour and half and sang hit song after hit song, "Whiskey River", "On the Road Again", "Blue Eyes Crying in the Rain", "Stardust". Then his son, Lukas Nelson, and his band, The Promise of Real, performed for thirty minutes with some very good music that neither Scott nor Mary Jo had ever heard. Willie came back for another hour and sang more of his hits but then he sang a song written by Kris Kristofferson called "Help Me Make It Through the Night". Mary Jo almost had to get up and leave during the song. She became overwhelmed emotionally and started twirling her hair. She wanted to grab Scott's hand and kiss him, especially when Willie sang it.

He ended the concert singing his own song, "Roll Me Up and Smoke Me When I Die". The crowd joined by clapping in time and Willie was laughing the entire time he was singing it.

They left the concert holding hands and Scott said, "Let's take a stroll on the beach before we go back to the hotel."

"This night" he continued as he pointed up at the full moon and all the stars over the ocean, "is just too beautiful to waste."

Scott parked the pickup at Stewart Beach. They walked to the water. Scott looked up and just could not believe the beauty he had all around him. The moon, the stars but especially this beautiful, strong woman beside him who had come into his life. It was a miracle and he was thanking God for it right now.

Mary Jo said, "You remember our second time around first date?

Scott laughed and she smiled, "Yes, very well."

"I will always remember you taking me to the patio windows and looking out into the sky like you had gone somewhere else and then you came back. You said to me, 'the most beautiful part, belongs to a mysterious and ultimately unexplainable God'. I'm beginning to understand more about what you mean by that statement. We are more than just ourselves. We are a part of a glorious creation that God has given us—ourselves and nature"

"And each of us has a different perspective on it. No one person owns the ultimate truth. God works in our individual lives so that we can live in freedom from evil that steals our joy. We can even do it when we are oppressed and struggling."

Mary Jo looked at him and he looked at her. He bent down and kissed her like he had never kissed her. It was long and passionate. She was taken to another place. A place of goodness she had never seen.

They strolled on the beach a while longer, got in the car and went back to the hotel. They kissed good night, somewhat awkwardly and then went to their individual rooms. Both of them kept thinking about the other person as they got ready for bed and then peered out the balcony window toward the ocean. Within thirty minutes they had gone to bed and turned out the lights.

After an hour of lying in bed, Scott turned on his bedside lamp and got his book to read. He couldn't get the day off his mind and the way it ended was not right. He started to read, put the book down, put on the hotel robe and opened the door. As he opened it, he saw Mary Jo outside her door. She looked at him and smiled. She had her hotel robe on, also.

"I'm glad you're up," Scott said, "I couldn't sleep, and I wanted to talk to you." He walked over to her and held her in his arms. She put her head on his shoulder and wrapped her arms around his neck.

"I know you said we should take it easy," she said as Scott felt a couple of her tears trickle down his neck, "but I can't get that song "Help Me Make It Through the Night" out of my head. I need you, Scott. I'm tired of being lonely, and I've been lonely a long time until you came into my life."

He pushed her back, looked down at her and lowered his face and said, "I was just about to say those very words to you." They kissed more passionately than they had at the beach. Then he led her to his bed.

Chapter 57

It was 5:30 a.m. on Sunday morning. Richard Breeden had just awakened. He was laying on his back in bed. He was in his apartment, his home after the prison stint. He was living in Ash, a town about seventy-five miles north of Lyric. He was thinking about all the things that had changed in life for him over the past several years. His anger would not abate. He had to do something to make things right so that he could keep his sanity. He had owned one of the largest logging companies in Texas and now he was driving a log truck for someone else. He didn't even have enough money to buy the log truck.

Mary Jo had taken him to the cleaners in the divorce. His conviction for timber theft had happened during the divorce trial. Mary Jo's lawyer had used that to convince the judge he was irresponsible, and she got more than she should have gotten, especially that beautiful piece of property and house. The company had gone bankrupt after he went to prison because neither Mary Jo nor any of the employees knew what they were doing. Of course, their excuse was he had taken all of the cash and they couldn't operate. Richard knew they could get a loan, but Mary Jo had tried to get a loan and the bank would not give it to her. Mary Jo was not speaking to him at the time but Eric, their son, had told Richard. After the company declared bankruptcy, the bankruptcy court settled all of the company debts, and there was extraordinarily little left for him or Mary Jo. She had her interior decorating business, but it was growing and she made more net income than his salary according to Eric. She got the house and property, since they had no debt on it, and he got some of the timberland. What he did get, he had to sell to pay his attorneys and to settle judgements against him for Buddy Parker's death. He was flat broke.

His mistress, Sonja Sabini, who lived in Atoy, had ditched him after he went to prison. He called her when he got out. The number had been disconnected and their mutual friends were not giving him any information about her. He was on his own. He had a few women since he came to Ash, but the one who had stayed around the most and was in bed with him now was Cassie Loren, a woman from Lyric. Cassie still lived in Lyric, but she would come to see him on the weekend from time to time. They would go to movies, eat at the local restaurants, and have sex most of the weekend and then she would go back to Lyric. Richard liked the sex and he liked Cassie keeping him abreast of the happenings and gossip in Lyric. Other than that, Cassie was beautiful but a little light on the intellect. Richard didn't think, at least on his part, that it would develop into a long term relationship.

Cassie had told him that Mary Jo and Scott Mitchum were an item now. That wasn't a complete surprise to him. They had dated in high school and had retained their friendship. He was somewhat jealous, but he didn't want Mary Jo back. She wasn't appealing to him anymore. However, the fact that the two people he had on his list for payback were together a lot had made his job a whole lot easier.

He and Skinny Merritt had been talking when they were in prison and since they had been out. Richard had bided his time with his revenge. He wanted to be cool and calculating. He didn't want to go back to the joint. On Day One out of prison, Skinny had been ready to exact retribution on Joe Bob Presswood, Scott Mitchum and Bucky Taylor.

Richard's hardest job was keeping Skinny from going off on a tangent. He knew that it would take about a year of planning before they could execute their plan. Skinny had been keeping tabs on all of his targets, their habits and what they were doing. Richard had been doing the thinking. The plan was coming together. There were a few more loose ends they needed to tie up, and they would be ready to act.

As Richard lay there and looked at Cassie's naked breasts, he thought about how none of this misery he had experienced was his fault. Mary Jo had not been supportive of him as her husband. She could have stepped up and helped him more with the business and showed she cared about him. He had to find his affection with Sonja. The kids had never been close to him. He supplied their every material need, and they didn't show any respect or gratitude for it. They were still distant. Eric had gotten a scholarship to Harvard to play football. When he graduated, he went to Harvard Law School and was now working for John Marsh in Washington D.C. Richard was proud of him, but Eric hardly called him and had seen him only a couple times since he went to prison. Amy had not talked to him since he left the house the day he told Mary Jo he wanted a divorce. She blamed him for her ordeal with Jack Rocker. She had to see a psychologist for her to deal with the trauma.

Mary Jo had talked to Richard a few times during the divorce and the bankruptcy but in the last several years, he had not heard from her. He was going to enjoy this payback. Out of all of them, his turncoat employees, his ungrateful kids, the ignorant people in Lyric, he wanted to hurt her most of all. She was just a woman who had used him and had it coming to her. And if he could get to Scott Mitchum in the bargain, that would make the revenge much sweeter.

Chapter 58

Bucky was reeling in a striper below the Lake Livingston dam as Tracey watched him from the other side of the boat. She asked, "Do you need some help?"

"Naw, I got him. He's pretty big but I'll take the net and put under him as soon as I get him to the surface," Bucky replied.

Tracey watched Bucky as he masterfully reeled in the fish. It broke the water several times on its journey to the boat. Bucky was smiling the entire time. She liked watching him fish. He seemed to have a deep sense of joy whenever he was near the water or on it. He especially liked fishing. She liked it, too. It was peaceful and rewarding. Not only was it nice to be a part of nature but the excitement of catching food was thrilling. Since they had been dating, it was the one thing they thoroughly enjoyed doing together. They had gone to some movies and found some of them to be worthwhile but others not so much. They mostly enjoyed just being companions and talking about things that mattered to them. The fishing, though, it was if it was a shared spiritual experience. Her kids loved to do it, also. The only reason they weren't here today is because Bucky had requested that just the two them spend some time together.

The relationship had grown. Tracey looked at the churning water coming out of the dam release gates and was awed, as she always was, by the power of the water coming through them. She had some understanding of that power being a teacher She had learned enough science to know that water was one of the most powerful natural forces on the planet. Water was the single most destructive part of hurricanes. Many people mistakenly thought that the wind was the most destructive but people who lived on the coast knew better. Storm surges wiped out complete communities. She had a lot of respect for water. She had learned to swim at an early age, and it had been helpful on more than one occasion . She had made sure her kids knew how to swim. Before they went on Bucky's boat, she asked Bucky if he knew how to swim. He told her he hadn't until about three years ago when he almost drowned fishing by himself in his boat. He had been on the Trinity River and his line got tangled on some tree limbs under the surface. His rod and reel had fallen overboard and also got tangled up. He was cautious and slipped over the side holding on to the boat. The current picked up and as he was reaching for the rod the boat slipped out from under his hand. The water was about ten foot deep and was taking him downstream. He fought to keep his head up and was going down the third time when a log hit him on the shoulder. He grabbed a limb on the log and then draped his arms over it, kicked his way to the shore and lay exhausted on the bank for about an hour. He got up and found his boat about a mile down river stopped by some brush on the same side of the bank. He was able to wade out to it and take it back upstream to the boat ramp. He loaded it up on his trailer and vowed he wouldn't get back in it until he learned to swim. He went to the YMCA the next day and signed up for swimming lessons. He got rather good at it and became a water safety instructor. He now taught water safety at the Lyric city pool for the local fishing club.

Bucky brought in the fish and he put it in the cooler with the other ten fish they had already caught. He looked at Tracey and said, "I think if we catch twenty, we should call it a day."

"Sounds good to me," she replied, smiling at him.

"Man, it's nice out here today," he exclaimed, "the sun, the wind, the water—it's all just beautiful."

Then he moved closer to where Tracey was standing, being careful not to tip the boat too much. He touched her shoulder, stroked her hair, and said, "But not as beautiful as you."

She turned and smiled at him, "Why, Bucky Taylor, you're simply providing a powerful distraction. I'm going to drop this rod if you don't stop."

Bucky laughed, "Then reel it in and come sit beside me, because I don't want to waste this fine day, just catching fish."

She reeled in the line and placed the rod in its holder. Bucky handed her a Diet Coke and he got one himself. They sat close together on the bench drinking their Cokes and watching the water. Tracey put down her Coke and Bucky put his arm around her, then pulled her to him and kissed her. At first it was just a light kiss, but she put her arms over his shoulders and pulled him to her. It became more passionate until they finally had to come up for air. She nuzzled her head under his chin.

"I am so happy being with you, today," Tracey said.

Bucky didn't know what to say. His love for her was so deep that he didn't know how to express it to her in words.

"What's on your mind, Bucky?" Tracey asked.

"You."

"What about me?"

"I—I—I don't know what to say, Tracey. I'm not good with talking. You know that, but the best thing I can do is explain it like I know fishing."

"Let me hear it."

"Well, I've spent so much time by myself that fishing is my way to be happy. I love to do it. And I used to do a lot more than I do now since we started dating."

She had picked up her head and was looking at him seriously.

Bucky met her eyes. "Now, I'd rather be with you than fish," he said sincerely.

She smiled at him and then kissed him. She pulled her mouth back and said, "Bucky that is the most wonderful thing any man has ever said to me."

"No, it's not because, Tracey, I know this much, and I don't mind saying it. I love you, and I will for the rest of my life."

She couldn't believe it. This handsome redneck boy had the courage to step up and not think about himself. He had taken the risk of telling her something she needed and had hoped for. She could tell he was deeply in love with her. It was something she had never experienced, and she was not going to let it go.

"Bucky, I love you, too, and I am grateful to God that He has brought us together."

Bucky smiled at her and said, "That's another thing I want to talk to you about."

"What?" she asked.

"God. Whether you know it or not, I've been listening to the lessons that I hear about Jesus and the Bible when I go with you to church. But mostly, I've been watching you and your church friends. Some of them are more sincere than others. However, I seen your actions and their actions, and those speak a lot louder to me than those Bible lessons. I know you struggle being a single mother and all, but you told me that you live out your faith. And what I'm seeing from you is that your life matches up with them Bible lessons. I know what you mean when you say you are living out your faith. I know another person who does the same thing."

Tracey had never heard such a deep and eloquent speech in her whole life, even though it was grammatically incorrect. Tears were welling up in her eyes. She said, "Who is this other person?"

"Scott Mitchum."

Tracey was bewildered. She didn't know Scott Mitchum. Sure, everybody in Lyric knew he was the Mayor and owned a business. She had never heard of him doing anything wrong. She knew some people disliked him, but she didn't listen to them because they had plenty of character flaws.

"I don't know him, but I'd like to meet him. I didn't know you had relationships with such important people."

"I'm not bragging, but I've known Scott all of my life. I'd trust him with my life, and he and you act out your faith. Both of you are the finest people I know, and you know something, I'd like to be like you and Scott. I want to learn how to act out my faith."

Tracey put her arms around him and kissed him. It was slow and passionate, and she hugged him like she would never see him again.

Chapter 59

Corncobs up their butts. Scott was thinking about Robert Ward. His simple yet vivid description of religionists and atheists. He was looking out his office window and admiring the beautiful day. Wayne Mahaffey had just left his office. He sang in the quartet with him at church and was its de facto leader. Wayne had organized the quartet, selected music for them to sing, found instrumentalists to accompany them, set the rehearsal times and coordinated the performance dates. They sang at Whispering Hope about once a month but would go to sing at other places in the region. They had a following even though they were all volunteers. Scott admired Wayne and his commitment to the group. He always enjoyed being with them and thought their music ministered to people.

Wayne had come to see him that morning. Scott knew he had something serious on his mind because this was his first time to come to the office and speak to Scott.. He was reluctant to begin the conversation. Scott helped him because he had a full day ahead of him and said, "What can I do for you, Wayne?"

"Well, Scott, I was talking to Bruce and he told me about your support for John Marsh," Wayne replied.

"Yeah, John, Bruce and I have been friends since we were kids."

"Well, I don't think John and Bruce are very friendly anymore," Wayne said with a firm tone in his voice.

"I understand they've had some disagreements but that doesn't negate friendship in my opinion."

"I'd have to disagree with you on that Scott. You see John believes in killing babies, and Bruce has every right to sever his friendship with a non-Christian."

Scott could see where this was going.

"Let's cut to the chase, Wayne. Are you here to tell me because I support John Marsh as a friend and a candidate for office that I'm not a Christian?" John said while boring his eyes into Wayne's flitting brown eyes. Wayne looked down.

"Well, something like that, Scott," Wayne replied.

"Well, come on Wayne, spit it out and be a man. Do you want to tell me to my face that I'm not a Christian?"

"Well, that's what our pastor is saying," Wayne said.

"Oh, he is. Well, maybe our pastor needs to read his Bible. He might find out that a person's relationship with God is determined by that person and God and not a Pharisaical pastor," Scott replied with his voice raised and his eyes still boring into Wayne.

Wayne's eyes went wide, and he was speechless. He had never seen Scott talk this way before. He could tell Scott was angry.

In a little louder voice with an accusing tone, Scott said, "And before you say it, I know you came here to request my resignation in the quartet. Let me make it easy on you, Wayne. I quit. Now, please leave my office."

Wayne's eyes were still wide. He got up slowly and turned and left. He didn't look back.

As Scott looked out the window trying to calm down from his encounter with Wayne, he got his journal out. He had written Robert's explanation of "corncobs up their butts' explanation. He thumbed through a few pages and found it:

> We are to bask in the Creator and his creation. There is no special instruction other than to bask in it. It's like dancing. Do it because you are living. Religionists and atheists are not fun people—they've got corncobs up their butts.

Allen Marshall, his Senior Engineer stuck his head in the door and said, "I need to talk to you a minute. Is now a good time?" Scott looked at Allen with his eyebrows up and knew that he must have heard some of the conversation with Wayne. Scott needed a diversion, and he motioned him to come into the office. Allen sat in the chair across the desk from Scott.

Scott responded, "What's up?"

"It's Eminence. They're doing a request for proposals for engineering services on this major wastewater treatment plant project and I'm concerned that we are not at the top of their list."

Eminence had been a long time client, and Scott had known they weren't happy with the way their last project had gone with Mitchum Engineering. Their recent City Manager, Jason Cannon, had not liked Scott from their first meeting. Scott didn't get it. However, he was uneasy with the guy. He had done some checking on him and found he had never been in one place for very long. There had also been some questionable associations with engineering firms not known for their ethical standards. Scott suspected that Jason Cannon knew he would not bend when it came to the law, engineering ethics and common courtesy. The last project had been a series of confrontations between Cannon, Scott, and Allen. They had told him several times that he was asking them to do things they would not do, and he got angry about it.

"What has the Mayor said about it," Scott replied.

"I've talked to him and he keeps referring me to Jason. Of course, Jason is giving me that song and dance about how it's something they need to do from time to time to get a fresh perspective on what engineering services are out there. I've asked him what else we could do for him, and he just smiles and tells me nothing. However, that's not what I'm hearing from Bobby Euless, the Public Works Director. Jason is telling him that he wants somebody besides Mitchum Engineering because we don't know what we are doing. Bobby disagrees, but he has to hold his fire, or he'll lose his job.

Scott thought to himself that this was developing into a real faith-testing day. He was glad he had thought about Robert this morning because sometimes he just needed to dance. He looked at Allen and said, "I'll call the Mayor and talk to him, but in the meantime, let's put together the best proposal we've ever done. They'll have to not give us this project based on their own prejudices and Jason's self-centered agenda. I'm going to trust the people of Eminence to give us a fair shake."

Allen looked at him and replied, "You know that Smith Engineering is going after it, don't you?"

"Why, of course, they'd love to have every one of our clients, but as long as I'm here it will be after the battle. Allen, let me tell you, we may lose this one, but we will find something else to do. It never fails. Don't beat yourself up over this client. They will be the one to lose if they don't choose us. We stay steady on our mission and our goals in this firm and that's what our real clients want us to be. We can't pursue the whims of some City Manager like Jason Cannon who is here today and gone tomorrow. Let's do this the Mitchum way."

Allen looked at him and smiled, "Scott, I wouldn't want to work anywhere else. This is the best job I've ever had and I'm not going to give up. Jason Cannon is going to have to live with the consequences if we're not around, and I'm like you, the people of Eminence will wake up to that someday."

Allen got out of his chair and looked at Scott. He said, "Looks like a bummer day for you."

"No, Allen, it's life and there's glory in it, even though it's difficult."

Allen smiled, turned, and left the office.

Chapter 60

Joe Bob was standing on the street looking at his lots. He had received the re-plat approval from the Council and had gone to work immediately. He knew the major hurdle was getting Ashley to agree to a design. He had learned enough in the home building business that women were the engine that designed homes. Men could draw them and had some practical ideas, but it was women who had the final say. It never failed. A man could talk all he wanted about where to put this room or how things such as appliances fit here and there. Women would listen and give the man a little consideration on such matters but in the end, it had to be the way the woman wanted it, or the builder was going to pay the price for it. He had changed too many things on too many houses after they were almost finished because the designer hadn't listened very well to the woman in the owner household.

Ashley was excited about the whole house venture and was excited about getting married. She had lost some weight and the same thing had happened to Joe Bob. She had started eating healthy and had encouraged him to do the same thing. They also did a lot of walking and talking with each other. Ashley told him that she had been pretty skinny in high school. She and Buddy Parker had just started going together when he got killed.

Her parents were also fighting a lot and ultimately got a divorce. Ashley got depressed and started eating to deal with her depression. She knew she was an emotional eater and had to be conscious of everything she put in her mouth. She taught Joe Bob some of those skills. Joe Bob never thought about being conscious with what he ate. He felt like he was a car engine, and he just filled up with fuel any time he was hungry. He definitely felt better, and he sure looked better than any time in his life. He loved Ashley. She was the best thing that ever happened to him.

With Ashley's blessing he had talked to Dan Robertson about building the house and Dan was about as excited as she was.

"Of course, Empire Homes wants to build your first house," Dan told him. "Let me tell you how I do this with all my employees. First of all, we'll do a free design at no cost to you. Then we'll give you an estimate and then discount it ten percent. You'll need to get the financing, and I'll even help you find some good lenders. Once you get approval for the financing, we can start to work."

"Thanks, Mr. Robertson. Do you know when me and my fiancé can meet with the designer? Joe Bob asked.

"How about tomorrow?" Dan replied.

"Wow, I didn't expect it to be that soon. Let me call Ashley and see if she can make it."

"You do that and let me know. Another thing, Joe Bob, I've been watching you and how you handle yourself and other people when you're working. I'm going to need another framing crew leader in the near future. How would you like to train on framing while working on your own house?"

Joe Bob was elated, "You mean after I get through with my house I would be a framing crew leader?"

"Well, yeah, if you show me you can do it."

"You won't be disappointed, Mr. Robertson. I've been hoping to get that kind of a break."

"First of all, start calling me Dan, and I'm glad to hear you say you're ready for some more responsibility. I don't hear that a lot these days from young people."

Joe Bob walked away from him feeling like he was going to burst. With Ashley's salary as a teacher and his job as a framing crew leader, they would have plenty of income to pay their house note and other bills and maybe even some left over to take a vacation from time to time.

Joe Bob was looking at the plans now as he stood in front of the lot. He could imagine the whole lot development in his mind. He had already flagged the trees he wanted to save. He knew exactly where the house was going to sit. He could see him and Ashley sitting on the front porch or the back patio where he would be grilling chicken. This was such a major moment in his life. The lot clearing was going to start in thirty days. Within a week, the slab would be poured. Thirty days later they would start framing and it could be, weather permitting that he could be sleeping on this lot in a beautiful new house within three months. It was unbelievable.

But first, he had to get married and that was something he knew nothing about. He was nervous. The only women he had known in his life were his mother and Ashley. He had dated some girls. He could count them on one hand, and it was only one date with each of them. He had been around some of Skinny's girlfriends, but he wanted nothing to do with that kind of woman. Ashley had been perfect. She was extremely nice to him, and she never seemed to be without some joy in her life. He had asked her about it.

"Well, Joe Bob, after Buddy died and I got depressed, deep down I knew I was going to have to get out of this funk or it would kill me. My parents couldn't help me. Buddy and I had gone to Whispering Hope church youth services on Wednesday night and Buddy got really deep into all of the stuff going on in the church. I was skeptical. I knew some of those church girls, and they seemed pretty superficial to me but there was one who was pretty and humble. Her name was Amy Breeden. She was also popular in school. She would talk to me and ask me how I was doing and would invite me to parties and get togethers at her house. I would go to some of them."

"Amy Breeden—wasn't she the one kidnapped by Jack Rocker?" asked Joe Bob.

"Yes. After Buddy got killed, she came to see me. She told me how brave Buddy had been and how he had only been involved because Jack had threatened him by telling him he would hurt his mother. Amy started sobbing and I did, too. It was such a waste having Buddy killed like that. She told me it had strengthened her faith, even though it was horrible. She said if it weren't for Buddy and Scott Mitchum, she probably wouldn't be alive. They both put themselves at great risk to save her and Bucky."

She continued. "I was still depressed but I began to see that this had not only affected me but Amy, too. It didn't matter who you were or what position you had in life; bad things can happen to you. I resolved then to find some joy in my life, every day. I went back to church about two months later. After a few years, I began to understand through the Bible and from the people in the church that you may not be happy all the time, but you can be joyful all the time in the faith you have in God who loves you as his creation."

As Joe Bob looked at the plans, he thought about how his life had changed from being a good-timin', good 'ol boy, drinking and cavorting with Skinny Merritt, to finding some meaning in this life he was living. It made him want to have kids so that he could show what he had learned to them. His loneliness had been cured by Ashley, but now she had showed him something more. He was important in a way that was just between him and God. Even if he lost Ashley, God forbid, he still had that confidence of worthiness.

He hadn't thought about Skinny in a long time and it was as if his thoughts were carried through some dimension to none other than the object of his thoughts because he looked north on the street where he was standing and saw Skinny's pickup coming toward him. He was alarmed but not afraid. He could handle Skinny, but he knew before the truck got to him that it was not going to be a congenial conversation.

Skinny pulled the truck up to the side of Joe Bob and lowered the passenger side window. Joe Bob had rolled up the plans and had them in his left hand. He turned and looked at Skinny.

Skinny said in a loud voice, "Hey Joe Bob. I guess you're finally glad to see your old buddy now that he's out of prison and all."

Joe Bob stared at Skinny and knew that if he didn't talk, it would rile Skinny more than if he did talk. He also knew that Skinny was up to something. He could smell it.

"When'd you get out Skinny?" Joe Bob asked.

"About a week ago. Been looking up old friends and trying to hustle some work. It ain't easy finding work being an ex-con and all. Got anything hanging where I can put a few bucks in my pocket?"

"No, I'm not metal scrapping anymore."

"Well, I can do lots of other kinds of work. I hear you working for Dan Robertson. Y'all fixing to build a house on that lot."

"Yeah."

"Are you going to need some extra help?

"Not right now, we've got a full crew for everything." Joe Bob knew Dan wouldn't hire Skinny and had even told Joe Bob that

Skinny wasn't welcome around Empire Homes. Evidently, they had a past of confrontations.

"Well, you really are a talkative one today."

"I've got lots of work to do, and I need to get to it."

"Yeah, I get you. Well you got a few dollars you can loan an old friend? They didn't give me much when I left prison."

Joe Bob was silent and then he said, "No, Skinny, I don't have any money to give you and quite frankly we didn't part on the best of terms when you went to jail." Then Joe Bob leaned into the truck window and held his gaze on Skinny's eyes. "And let me be clear, I don't want to be around you. You're trouble, and you always have been. This is the end of this conversation on my part."

"Well, Mr. High and Mighty, it may be the end of the conversation for you—you piece of shit--but I've got some big plans and you and some other people are going to wish you had been a tiny bit nicer to me." Skinny leered at Joe Bob and gave him that evil smile he had seen many times and then left rubber on the payment as he drove the pickup away.

"Good riddance," Joe Bob said.

Chapter 61

Richard Breeden smiled when he opened the cypress box. The money was all there. He wasn't a total fool. After he started having his affair with Sonja, he began to think what Mary Jo would do if she found out about it. She was an independent woman and wouldn't put up with his running around. She'd divorce him and get half of everything he owned. He had one of his loggers drop off a cypress log to a small hardwood sawmill in Pelican. He talked to the owner and told him he wanted some 1" X 8" X 12' lumber out of it. He picked up the lumber and took it to his barn at the ranch and took a small portion of it to a skilled cabinet maker. He asked him to make him a 2' X 2' X 2' box out of it with a lid. He wanted it done using center match connections and durable glue. When it was made, he brought it back to his barn and put several coats of outdoor urethane on it. He put a stainless steel hasp on it with a padlock. Then he hid the box in the barn in a corner under some hay. Every month, he would embezzle about 1,500 dollars from the company's huge checking account. He did it in such a way that no one would notice it. He basically called it miscellaneous expenses and reimbursed himself. Over three years, he had accumulated $54,000 and had put it all in the box. Fortunately, Mary Jo didn't find out about the affair until he was ready to divorce her. When he told her, he went straight to the barn, picked up the box and took it with him. The next day he had buried it on a tract of remote land he owned at the time next to a pine tree on a hill. The tree was distinctive because it was about ten feet from the southeast corner of the property and had a noticeable curve in the trunk caused by an ice storm when it was a young sapling. After he got out of prison, he had waited until now to come and get it because he didn't want anyone to be suspicious of unusual movements.

His current job paid his bills but now that Skinny was out of prison, he would need to finance his plan. This money would do the trick. He wouldn't use all of it because he was going to find a way to leave the country. His probation would be over in a week and then he and Skinny could go to work. That redneck was still on probation, but it didn't seem to matter to him. Richard had one use for Skinny and that was for Richard to exact revenge on three people. Then he was out of here. If Skinny got caught, that was his problem. He put the box in his pickup, a four year old Chevrolet Silverado. He had a portable safe in his apartment. He'd keep the money there until it was time to leave and then take it with him. The money was all in $100 bills. He took twenty and kept the rest in the box.

He stored the money at his apartment. He had told Skinny to meet him at a remote roadside park at 11:30 am and to bring some food. He stopped at Whataburger and got himself a hamburger and French fries with a Diet Coke. Making it look like they were eating lunch would be a good cover for planning their future crimes. Although Richard didn't consider it a crime. These people had done something to him, and they were going to pay for it.

Skinny was already there when he arrived and was sitting at a picnic table eating. Richard grabbed his food and sat down across from him. He hadn't seen him since prison. He had been in communication with him but for a variety of reasons he didn't want to be seen with him until he was ready to execute his plan. It had been about eighteen months and Skinny looked the same, except Richard thought he looked a little meaner.

Skinny looked up and said, "Hey, Richard." Richard thought it was a little odd he didn't call him Mr. Breeden but he was going to let it alone.

"Hey Skinny, how have you been?" Richard replied.

"Well, I might as well be back in prison. Can't find a job and no one will give me any money. My probation officer is a dick, and I've lost all of my friends mainly because they're a bunch of goody-two-shoes who never gave a rat's ass about me anyway. And on top of that I haven't been laid since before prison."

Richard was pleased. Skinny was angry and he needed him that way. If he could just keep him under control, he'd be perfect for this work.

Richard said, "I'm like you. I do have a job, but the rest of it sucks. I think it's time we got some revenge on the people who ruined our lives."

Skinny replied, "I'm ready but if I don't get some money, I'm going to have to leave this part of the country and find some work."

"How much do you need?"

"Well I need food and gas money, right now. Pretty soon I've got to pay the taxes on my acre and mobile home. I'd say $300 right now. That'll pay for food and gas for about a month. I'll need about $500 to pay my taxes in two weeks."

Richard reached for his wallet and took out $300 and gave it to Skinny. Skinny smiled and said, "Thanks, Richard. This'll do just fine."

"Okay, Skinny. Let's talk some business. I have three people I want to eliminate as we discussed in prison. I want you to help me with them."

"As long as one of them is still Scott Mitchum, I'll help you. I hate that sonofabitch."

"He is." Although Richard really could care less about Scott, he knew he could get Skinny to help him if he was included. Richard continued, "I want this to look like these people were in the woods, got bit by a venomous snake and then couldn't make it to the emergency room in time and died from the bite."

Skinny eyes lit up. "That's a great idea. Then it doesn't look like murder and it's hard to trace."

"Exactly. I figure that we can obtain two maybe three rattlesnakes, keep them like pets until the right time when we find these people alone in the woods. Then we'll forcibly make them put both of their legs into a bucket or some other container, which has the snakes in it. Let the snakes bite the person at least once each to ensure enough venom gets into the victim and then zip tie the person so that they can't get away. We'll keep them there until they die and then cut the zip ties. The zip ties will be covered with some pliable material so that they won't leave any marks."

"This'll work," Skinny said with his evil smile showing his pleasure at such brilliant meanness. "I met an 'ol boy in prison from Sweetwater . He hunts those bastards and sells them at the Rattlesnake Roundup every year. He got out before I did. I bet he would sell me three or four and teach me how to deal with them."

"Great!" exclaimed Richard. "Okay, that's our first move. Secondly, we need some guns. As convicted felons, we can't own guns but I'm sure we can get our hands on some. We'll need some pistols to carry out this plan. We'll also need a couple of stun guns."

"No problem there. This same 'ol boy lives out there in the boonies in north Texas. He used to buy and sell all kinds of guns. He can't own them either, but he told me he could get one if he needed one. Then he said winking at me that he'd need one once he got out of the joint."

"Even better," Richard said. "However, you will have to be very careful traveling with them in your truck. If you get stopped, you be immediately arrested."

"No problem, there. I'm being real careful—no alcohol, no weed, no driving fast, no criminal activity—while I'm in the truck. I also have a secret compartment under the passenger side near the tail gate where I hide things I don't want anybody to know about. Made it myself out of scrap metal." Skinny sat up straight and pushed his chest out on the last sentence.

Richard mused. This is working out better than he thought it would. He said to Skinny, "Are you ready to go to Sweetwater and get the rattlesnakes and the guns?"

"Yessir. I'm going to need some more money, though."

Richard said, "I figure about $1,000 for the two pistols and two stun guns, about $500 for the snakes and their food and containers and about $300 for your travel expenses. Altogether, about $1,800."

"That oughtta do it. One more thing, Richard. I want $15,000 to do this deed. I don't mind doing it, but I want to get paid for it."

Richard wasn't expecting him to ask for that much money. He thought $5,000 would satisfy the redneck and his simple lifestyle.

He responded, "That's a little high, Skinny. You can't drink that much beer in the next year. It'll kill you."

Skinny glared at him, "I'm not as stupid as you think I am, Richard. I know you've got the money. I don't want it now, but I want half of it when I get back from Sweetwater. Either agree to it now or find you somebody else."

Richard knew Skinny had him over a barrel and he said, "All right but let's get on with it. I'll meet you here tomorrow at 9:00 am with the $1,300."

They stood up, shook hands, and went to their respective pickup trucks. As they got in the truck, neither one of them noticed the car passing the roadside park.

Chapter 62

Mary Jo was wide awake at 3:00 am. She knew why she was awake. She was excited about the day before her. It was dark in the room because she liked it that way. However, she could see through the curtains that it was a full moon. She put on her robe and slippers and went to the back patio. She sat there watching the moon on this warm summer night. It reminded her of the night when Scott showed her the magnificence of and mysteriousness of the night sky. She could hear the concert of the frogs and crickets along with a barn owl chiming in with his African monkey hoot. She remembered the first time she had heard a barn owl as a little girl, and it sounded like the monkeys in the Tarzan movies she used to watch with her Dad. The sky was overpowering. Stars were everywhere. She tried to pick out some of the constellations and planets. They had become abundantly clearer to her when Scott had asked her to go with him to west Texas on a business trip. They had gone to McDonald Observatory on the top of one of the few mountains in Texas near Fort Davis. It had been a wonderful trip. On Tuesday night, there was a sky party and astronomers from the Observatory would take highly powered lights to outline the various astronomical features in the noticeably clear west Texas sky. She had been fascinated by it and continued to try and search for them on clear nights.

She sat down in the chair looking up at the sky and thought about what was about to happen in a few hours. Her children, Eric and Amy, and Scott's children, Matthew, and Elaine, would be here with her and Scott celebrating July 4th. She and Scott had privately and individually told their children about their relationship and that it was serious for both of them. They cautioned their children that they had not talked about marriage, but they would like for them to come to this party so all of them could get to know each other better. Matthew had agreed to do the grilling, and Amy told her mother she would be there the night before to help her set up for the gathering. Both Matthew and Amy were elated about their relationship. Matthew had seen her on several occasions since he lived in the community and was working as an EIT at his father's firm. Mary Jo thought the world of him and told him so. He had been immensely helpful to her after Hurricane Harvey, and they seemed to hit it off just like she and Scott. Amy adored Scott even though she lived in another community. After Scott had rescued her, Scott had made it a point to check on her often to see how she was doing. He also helped her during Richard and Mary Jo's divorce by just being an adult male figure she could talk to about life in general.

Eric and Elaine had taken the news soberly and didn't go as far as being skeptical, but Mary Jo knew that there would need to be some encouragement from both her and Scott with both children for them to come around about Scott and Mary Jo's need for each other. Mary Jo was not too concerned about Eric. He and Richard had never been really close, and she thought it was one reason that Eric had chosen not to come back to Texas after he started his career. Elaine, on the other hand, had been very close to her mother, and Mary Jo knew she must make the effort to understand her loss. She knew that it was something she had to do to establish a connection with Elaine, and she wasn't going to leave it entirely up to Scott. She looked up in the sky and then bowed her head and said, "Father, I know you hear my prayers. You have given me so much that I am overwhelmed by your blessings. I have this request. I ask you to open up this beautiful young woman's heart to me. Give me the right words to say to her and let her know that I love her father. Let her know that I will give my life to be his faithful companion." Mary Jo felt the peace and the contentment come over her when she knew she was in his presence. She looked up at the sky one more time and then looked at the clock in the living room. It was 5:30 am. She could see the pre-dawn light coming up in the east. No time to go back to bed. She would start getting ready for this glorious day.

Scott and Matthew arrived at 3:00 pm. Amy answered the door and smiled at Scott. She didn't say a word and stepped up and gave him a big hug.

"I am so glad to see you," she said into his shoulder. A couple of tears were coming down her cheeks. "I'm sorry. I'm just incredibly happy about you and Mom." She pulled away from him and wiped the tears from her face.

Matthew was grinning at her and she laughed. She stepped around Scott, gave Matthew a hug, and said, "Hey, Matthew."

"Hey, yourself and ditto about your Mom and my Dad. I just think it's cool as it can be. Your Mom and I have gotten to be pretty good friends."

Mary Jo was standing behind Amy, smiling, and said, "You can say that again. I don't think I would have ever gotten this place back together again, if not for him. Of course, he's a taskmaster. I've never been so sore in my life."

All of them laughed and Mary Jo led them into the living room. After some small talk and getting drinks, Matthew took charge and said, "I think

I remember the grill being on the south side of the patio. I've got all the steaks and potatoes in the truck. What time are we going to eat?"

Mary Jo said, "Well Eric is arriving about 4:00 pm. How about Elaine?" She looked at Scott.

"Same time," he replied.

"Okay, let's eat about 6:00 pm. That will give us time to eat and visit and then watch the community fireworks show at 9:00 pm from the patio," Mary Jo replied.

"All right, I'll get the food and bring it in, get the grill prepared and fired up," Matthew stated as he walked to the door.

Amy said, "I'll help you", as she followed him out the door."

"Well, that went well," Scott said.

"Yes. I wasn't concerned about them. I think it's the other two that are going to take some work," Mary Jo replied.

"Agreed. It'll happen—be hopeful." He bent down and kissed her.

They busied themselves with preparations while Amy and Matthew visited with each other. Scott could hear some of the conversation between the two of them and was intrigued by its content. Both seemed excited about seeing each other and had positive things to say about each other's parent. Later, he heard some skepticism about their siblings and then he detected a team sense between them about trying to convince Eric and Elaine of the positive outcome of Mary Jo and Scott's relationship. He smiled.

Eric arrived and not long after him, Elaine. After handshakes and hugs, Mary Jo and Scott told them that their siblings were on the patio. They both went outdoors and began visiting. Mary Jo was twirling her hair with her fingers and then she started wringing her hands. She looked at Scott and said, "Don't you think we should follow them and be sure everything goes okay?"

Scott smiled a crooked smile and replied, "Remember what I told you about faith. Some time you act and some time you just let things take their natural course. Our younger generation allies are making the case for us as we speak. It'll be much better coming from them than from us."

Mary Jo looked at him with an anxious face, "I hope you're right. Oh, I want this to go well."

"It will, Mary Jo, but it will also take some time beyond today. Let it be." And then he grabbed her and started dancing, singing into her ear the Paul McCartney song "Let It Be". Mary Jo started laughing and held him close. Then he pulled her around as he finished the song and dipped her. He looked up at the patio door and saw all four kids looking at them. They were all smiling and applauding. Mary Jo turned red but was still smiling.

Eric said, "Would you like for us to put on some oldies so that you can do an encore?"

"No." Mary Jo replied. "That is the only performance you will see from me."

Matthew said, "Well, I need a few things from the store. All of them wanted to go with me and cruise a little bit around Lyric since they hadn't been here in a while. We'll be back in about an hour. In the meantime, I got the potatoes baking. I'll grill the steaks when I get back."

"See you then," Scott replied.

Dinner was excellent. Everyone was in a good mood. Scott and Matthew regaled them with current stories about Lyric people and then everyone else joined in about past happenings that were humorous and unbelievable. It was the "truth is stranger than fiction" scenario as everyone chimed in with their favorite foible and funny story about the town of Lyric. Mary Jo thought as her stomach hurt from laughing so much that she had never had such a good time in her life. She was hoping the rest of the evening would go as well. They sat around the table until about 8:30 pm.

When the conversation lulled, Mary Jo said, "I have Blue Bell ice cream with brownies baked by Amy. Who wants some?" All hands were raised.

"Well, we'll eat out on the patio. The fireworks should start in about thirty minutes. Amy can you help me get it together?"

As soon as she said it, Elaine looked at her and said, "Can I help?"

Mary Jo looked at Elaine, smiled and said, "I'd love for you to help."

Elaine got up immediately and joined the other two women in the kitchen. Scott watched them as they walked away with Mary Jo complementing Elaine on her blouse and how it made her eyes stand out.

Eric looked at Scott with a serious look and said, "Mr. Mitchum, I wanted you to know that John Marsh always speaks highly of you, and I want you to know I appreciate you supporting his candidacy. He's taken a few blows this time around, but I've never seen him so determined about representing this district. He is pulling out all the stops."

"Well, John and I go back a long way and I like to be loyal. He's helped this town. I don't always agree with him but that's the beauty of good politics. We help each other by seeing the other side of the issue, right?"

"Exactly, we need a lot more of it."

Scott got up and said, "Let's move out to the patio. I think that ice cream is about to get there."

As they ate their ice cream, the fireworks show began. It was outstanding. The rockets would sail high in the air and burst into a kaleidoscope of lights, some multicolored and some brilliant white. They could even hear the patriotic music playing with the show. The evening was beginning to cool off. They could feel the East Texas breeze flowing over them. Having freedom always made Scott feel good. Fundamentally, he knew that's what they were celebrating. There were lots of things wrong in the USA, but there were more things right because of freedom.

After the fireworks, everyone pitched in and cleaned up and Matthew told Scott and Mary Jo they were all going to the July 4th dance at Bodittle's. He knew some of their Lyric friends would be there tonight. Scott told him and Elaine he would see them at home and excused himself to go to the bathroom. Elaine told Matthew to wait for her about five minutes and she would be at the car. As soon as they all left, she went to Mary Jo and said, "I want to tell you that I had a great time, tonight. I also want to thank you for how happy you have made my Dad. It's going to take some time for me, though. I still miss my mother a lot. No one can ever take her place, but you have made it a lot more bearable."

A tear rolled down her cheek and down Mary Jo's cheek. Mary Jo took in her arms and said, "Elaine, you'll never know how much that means for you to say that to me. Thank you."

Chapter 63

Megan McClelland sat on the outdoor platform as she watched her father speaking to the crowd of about five hundred. Her mind and soul were somewhere else as she also contemplated the beautiful blue sky and the fulfilling morning she had had with her two daughters and her husband. She was blessed. Although she had to endure some hardships in life, she had no complaints. She knew her life would change even more in a few minutes after she gave her speech. She was ready for it. The Creator, who had given her a beautiful family and this exquisite morning, was by her side now. She had a peaceful feeling. Her Dad was finishing his speech and she knew she was up next. She stood up as he started introducing her... "my daughter, an Army veteran of eight years awarded the Army Commendation Medal, Purple Heart and Bronze Star. She also is the mother of two beautiful little girls and the wife of another Army Veteran, Chris McClelland. Ladies and gentlemen, please welcome Megan McClelland." There was a round of heavy applause with some people standing out of respect for her service. Megan strode with purpose up to the stage and smiled at the audience.

"Thank you very much, Dad, and thank you." She pointed to the crowd. "It is good to be back home and seeing many of my Lyric friends and acquaintances. I leave politics mostly up to my father and generally stay out of the fray. However, this campaign has come to a point where it has invaded my personal life, and I'm here to tell you personally, face to face, my story so that you can get the facts from the source." Reporters started writing, TV cameras were zooming in on her and rapid fire digital cameras were doing their high pitched humming.

"When I was sixteen, I went on a date with a man who was eighteen years old, he raped me, and I became pregnant. The date was to a party where some teenage drinking was going on and he encouraged me to participate. I was reluctant because I had never drank alcohol, but I felt the pressure from this very handsome and charming college man who I wanted to impress. It was only my third date ever and I yielded to his pressure. I could tell after the second drink that I was not feeling right. After the party, he was taking me home. He stopped the car in a secluded place and being inebriated I wasn't paying much attention. He then got out of the car and opened my door. He wanted to take me for a moonlit walk and talk to me. It sounded romantic, and I went with him. We walked away and then he pulled me to him and started kissing me. He then pushed me down to the ground and even though I was drunk, I knew something was wrong. My mother taught me to always be a lady but to protect myself. I had been genuinely nice to this man, but I never gave him any indication I wanted to have sex with him. But that's what happened. I hit him, kicked him, and tried to get away from him, and it did no good. He was bigger, very strong, and knew exactly what he was doing. He raped me quickly and when he was through he pulled me up off the ground and pulled me back to the car. He put me in the seat. I couldn't stop crying. I didn't know what to do. He took me home. While I was still crying, he opened my door and pulled me out of the car. He brushed the dirt and leaves off my dress and left me in the driveway. He had not said a word to me since he raped me.

"I went in the house, still crying, not knowing what to do. I was ashamed, mostly. I thought I had done something wrong. I didn't want my parents to see me. I was glad they were already in bed. I went to my bathroom and looked in the mirror. I was a wreck and I hated myself. I tried to make myself look better but it didn't do any good. I went to my room, didn't change clothes, and got under the covers. When my mother later knocked on my door and peeked in, I pretended to be asleep.

"The next morning, I couldn't leave my room. I told my parents, who checked on me periodically, that I was feeling bad. After a while, added to my shame was a simmering anger that developed into depression. I perfunctorily went to school, but I was in a fog. I knew my mother thought something was wrong with me, but I didn't say anything to her until I was late with my menstrual period. After I told her, she brought my Dad in on the conversation. They were concerned about me and immediately took me to the doctor. That's when I found out I was pregnant. I just couldn't believe it. My future life had been determined for me by a man I hardly knew through his one selfish, violent act against me. I was consumed with anger. He had no concern for me whatsoever."

Megan looked down and was silent. After a few moments, she looked intently at her audience.

In an Army strong voice, she said, "My parents and I discussed the options. I knew they would love me and support me. I had never thought much about abortion, but I knew I could not live with bringing this child into this world after what this man had done to my life. Of course, I was having to make this decision as a sixteen year old girl and my parents, God bless them, continued to pour their love out for me.

"Afterwards, I channeled my anger into becoming a strong woman. I also wanted to be a lady, but I didn't want something like that to happen to me again. My parents and I did not press charges against him mainly because

I had virtually no evidence and the idea of a public trial with me on center stage was more than I could bear. I took martial arts classes and earned my black belt by the time I graduated from high school. I decided to join the Army when I graduated, which was a shock to my parents. I became a warrior. I also became strong because of my faith in God. That night after the rape, I asked God to help me. I have been in the hand of God since that night. My faith has sustained me during that time and to this day.

"I have only had sex with the man who raped me and my husband. You've been hearing a lot of rumors about me. Rest assured you are getting the facts today. The person who started those rumors is a man, and he will have to answer to God for that gossip, not me. Abortion is a very personal matter. None of us knows the individual lives of any woman who has had an abortion. I've never heard of or known a woman who gets pregnant so that she can have an abortion. We're just not wired that way. It is not for us as a community, as a minister, as a priest, as an attorney, as a judge or as a politician to decide how a woman wants to deal with her pregnancy. It is between her and God."

Megan paused. She had never heard a crowd be this quiet. She wasn't sure and she didn't care what kind of reaction she would get, but this was interesting. She concluded, "There are a lot of things I could be right now but bitter and depressed are not among them. I have personally experienced physical, mental, emotional, and spiritual turmoil. Life for me has been as the apostle Paul stated when he said, 'Now we see things imperfectly, like puzzling reflections in a mirror, but then we will see everything with perfect clarity. All that I know now is partial and incomplete, but then I will know everything completely, just as God now knows me completely'. I will continue to live my life to the fullest, to the best of my ability and through the grace of God. I hope you will be able to do the same thing."

Megan walked confidently back to her seat and sat down. She had not campaigned for her father. She had set the record straight. Scott Mitchum was with Mary Jo at the back of the crowd. He knew, politically, she had scored some big points for John. Most of all he was proud of her for being faithful, forthright, and strong.

Chapter 64

Jesse Henderson was researching prison records of felons convicted in State District Courts in the Lyric area. He was specifically zeroing in on Skinny Merritt and Richard Breeden. He was getting concerned about these two guys. Skinny had been back in town for a while. He didn't seem to be hanging around with his old buddies like Joe Bob Presswood and Bucky Taylor. He was either by himself or with some men who looked like they had spent time in prison. What was particularly concerning to him was that he had seen Skinny and Richard together in a remote roadside park near Ash, Texas. He was going fishing in a small lake near there with a friend of his from Pelican. They had been fishing in that lake for years and made a trip about twice a year. His buddy was taking a nap, and he was taking in the scenery when as plain as day he saw Richard and Skinny getting in their trucks to leave the roadside park.

He knew Richard was living outside of Lyric although he had seen him a couple of times in town with Cassie Loren. Since Richard was with Cassie, Jesse understood why he was here. If a man hadn't had a woman in a while, Cassie would be the right one to hook up with. However, he didn't get the connection with Skinny. Although their trials were in different District Courts, they could have spent time together in the same prison.

And there it was, both had been in the Beaumont unit and then the pre-release facility in Cleveland at about the same time. Jesse was wondering what that cracker Skinny wanted from Richard or was Richard wanting something from Skinny.

Jesse walked down to Harry Jenkins' office. Harry was sitting at his desk on the phone. Jesse walked in and sat down in the desk side chair. Harry got off the phone and Jesse with an eyebrow raised, said, "What's up, Harry?"

"Oh, I was checking up on some fingerprints we sent to the lab from the jewelry store burglary two days ago," Harry replied.

"Any leads?"

"Yeah, it's Charlie Stephens. Fingerprints just verified by the lab. There was also some hair at the scene. We'll pick him up for probable cause and get a DNA sample. He's at it again. He's already done time for burglary. The next time he's going to be three and gone." Harry was referring to a three time convicted felon getting twenty-five years or a life sentence on a third felony conviction. Jesse looked down and shook his head. He knew Charlie Stephens and liked him. He just couldn't keep his hands off that pretty jewelry. He had had one conviction overturned, but the last time they had plenty of evidence. There were two pawn shops and two jewelry stores in town. Now he had hit all of them except one.

He looked up at Harry and said, "I'm concerned about something that I can't get off my mind. Have you seen Skinny Merritt around town since he got out of prison?"

"I've seen him several times. His trailer is about a mile down the road from my house. But about a week ago I saw him leaving town and then he didn't come back until yesterday. I talked to Martin Dishongh down at Dairy Queen getting coffee one morning, and he told me that Skinny had gone out to Sweetwater. Skinny's not the same person he was before he went to prison. He always had a bit of a mean streak, but I think meanness is his total motivation now. The hair on the back of my neck starts standing up when I see him in his truck."

"What do you mean?"

"Well, Martin told me that Skinny had it out with Joe Bob Presswood the other day. I know they weren't on great terms before he went to prison. Evidently it's getting nastier. It was mostly a word fight, but Joe Bob told Martin that when Skinny drove off, he said something like he had big plans and Joe Bob was going to wish he had been nice to Skinny."

"That cracker is up to something and I think Richard Breeden is involved."

"Richard Breeden!" exclaimed Harry. "Oh, come on Jesse, what would Richard Breeden be doing with Skinny Merritt?"

"That's the same question I was asking myself when I saw the two of them together at a remote roadside park outside of Ash."

"Isn't that where Richard is living?"

"Precisely, and what is Skinny doing up there with just Richard? Having a picnic together? I don't think so."

Harry looked pensive, "Were they in prison together?"

"Uh-huh." Jesse looked directly into Harry's eyes.

"Uh-oh. Are we about to go through this again?" Harry replied.

"I don't know, but I'm going to alert our patrol officers to keep an eye on Skinny and his movements. I want them reporting to me if he does anything unusual. I also want you to do a little digging to see if Richard has any designs on getting back into a life of crime. I know he's been sleeping with Cassie Loren. Maybe she might be a source of information."

Harry looked down and said. "You'd think these guys like Charlie, Skinny and especially Richard would learn."

"Some of them do and some of them don't," Jesse replied as he got up out of the chair. "Our job is to protect the people of this town from them when they decide that crime does pay. How they think it pays is beyond my comprehension."

Chapter 65

"Now, that's yer tong and it's the most important part of keeping a rattlesnake under control when you pick it up. Don't be a stupid ass and try to pick these thangs up like you see in the movies. You'll get yourself bit, and you'll be in a world of hurt," explained Johnny Cook as he was showing Skinny how to handle rattlesnakes.

"Now, you grab him about eighteen inches away from his head with these tongs." Johnny carefully grabbed the snake out of the five gallon bucket and let it go on the ground. He then grabbed it again from behind at the same spot and put it in its hard plastic and plexiglass carrier. He locked the door.

"Your turn, Skinny," Johnny said mirthlessly.

Skinny was fascinated and wasn't afraid. These snakes were powerful and beautiful. He had never seen one like it. He had once happened on a timber rattler when he was logging. It had moved away from him quickly. He didn't get a good look at it. This was his first time to look at a rattlesnake up close and personal, and he liked it.

He practiced with Johnny for about an hour and got the handling and transporting part of it down quickly. Johnny told him to make sure they had food. Skinny asked him if they needed water. Johnny told him that they drink their body weight in water in a year. For the trip to Lyric, they wouldn't need any water. He did tell Skinny to build a habitat for them where they had access to water. He gave Skinny some written instructions on snake handling and building a habitat for them.

"Okay, you're all set. That'll be $1,500 for the pistols, stun guns, snakes, and snake transportation," Johnny said as he handed Skinny the box of guns. Skinny was proud of himself. He spent $300 less for the guns and snakes than Richard had given him. He was going to keep it and enjoy himself on the way back from Sweetwater. He handed Johnny the cash money. They then put the snakes in a secure tied-down wooden box in the bed of his truck. The snakes were each in their own transport container inside the wooden box. Then Skinny placed the guns in his secret compartment on the truck.

The next day as he was driving back to Lyric, he thought about what a smart guy he had been, getting guns and ammo, three nasty looking rattlesnakes and saving $300. He had put some of that money to good use last night at a bar in Fort Worth. They had a great local country band playing and there were several fine cowgirls looking for love. He was able to hook up with one of them and she had spent the night with him in his hotel room. And what a night!! That woman knew every sex trick in the book. He was worn out. She told him she needed some spending money when she left this morning because she needed a cab to get back home. He gave her a $100 and she smiled really big at him and gave him her phone number. Told him to call her next time he was in Fort Worth.

He met Richard Breeden in Ash and showed him all his contraband and the snakes. Richard appeared to be happy. He told Skinny their first target was Don Miller, his former contract forester who had blown the whistle on him about stealing timber, which had led to the discovery of other improprieties and had put him in prison. Richard had been following Miller and knew he was working by himself on a big timber tract. They could catch him, get two snakes to bite him and leave him out in the middle of the woods. By the time someone found him, it would be too late to save him. The authorities would just think he had been bitten by a snake and couldn't get back to his truck to go to the hospital or call for help. Richard told Skinny they could do it tomorrow or the next day. He would call Skinny tomorrow and set it up. Skinny drove back to Lyric. When he got home, he immediately started building a home for his snakes. He hadn't been this excited about doing something since he had learned about Santa Anna's gold from Bucky Taylor.

Two days later, as Don Miller lay dying on the forest floor, Richard and Skinny were walking away to Skinny's truck on the main road. Skinny said, "Man, that was easy. They'll never figure out we had anything to do with it."

Richard smiled and said, "Yeah, 'ol Don just never figured I'd pay him back. But I did and now we go after the best targets."

"Yeah Scott Mitchum and who is the other one?" Skinny replied.

"My ex-wife, Mary Jo,"

Skinny's eyes went wide. Probably the most beautiful, smart woman in Lyric and he was going to be a part of ending her life. He looked seriously at Richard.

"Are you sure about that?" Skinny said.

Richard stopped and looked at him with a cloud of anger that Skinny had never seen. It was pure evil. Not just bad human behavior. This was unworldly, psychotic, and downright pure wrath.

"I'm so goddamn sure about it that I'll kill you if you try to stop me."

"Hey, calm down," Skinny said backing up with his arms out in front of him and feeling scared, "I was just asking a question."

"Well, quit asking 'em and let's get out of here"

They rode in silence all the way back to Ash. Skinny took Richard back to his house. When the truck stopped, Skinny said, "I want half my money now."

Richard narrowed his eyes and looked at him. Skinny didn't flinch as he looked right back at him.

"All right," Richard replied. "Wait here and I'll bring it to you."

Skinny took the Glock out of the secret compartment and put it in the back of his waistband under his t shirt. He didn't trust Richard. For that matter, he didn't know any ex-cons who trusted one another.

Richard came out with a brown paper bag, looked at Skinny and said, "Count it."

Skinny counted $7,500.

Richard said, "I want you to follow Scott and Mary Jo. We'll need to get them together in a secluded place like we did Don. Scott owns several timber tracts and he's bound to take her with him some time to look at them. Just keep your eyes and ears open for an opportunity. Call me when you find one. We have time. Don't rush it."

Skinny nodded, got back in the truck and drove toward Lyric. He stopped at the secluded roadside park and put the pistol back in the secret compartment.

Chapter 66

The thunder clouds began forming north of Lyric around 3:30 pm. It had been hot all day, and nature was going to cool down. The wind had shifted from the southeast to northwest. It was a bluish black along the north horizon, full of rain. The wind was refreshing after the hot day and residents of Lyric knew what was coming. In south Louisiana, it was called a garden shower, which meant a lot of rain for a short period of time. It was always welcomed by construction workers and other people who worked outside, except farmers cutting hay. In that case, if hay were on the ground, farmers put every piece of equipment they could on the field to try and bale it before it got wet. The construction workers usually got the rest of the day off and in summertime, it was a nice break from the 60 hour work week.

The rain began about 5:00 pm. It continued until 7:00 pm. The thunder and lightning put on a spectacular show. John Marsh was watching it out his office window. Long streaks of lightning in the north accompanied by a delayed sonic boom caused by the thunder. John was impressed by the power and magnificence of a summer thunderstorm. It was a nice respite from campaigning and thinking about the upcoming appointment with Bruce Jones. John didn't know what Bruce wanted, and he was expecting the worst, based on their relationship in recent years. He was getting weary of politics and even though he was in this race until the end, he might not run again regardless if he won or lost.

Bruce came through the front door of the office and tentatively looked in John's office to see if was at his desk. He noticed he was standing looking out the window at the thunderstorm. It was an image he would remember for a long time. Bruce said, "I think that was more than a garden shower."

John, without turning around, said, "I agree. It was a true Texas thunderstorm. Quite a show."

John slowly turned around and looked at Bruce, "What can I do for you, Bruce?"

Bruce said, "Do you mind if we sit? This may take a few minutes."

"Sure," John motioned to the side chair in front of his desk and then took a seat in his desk chair.

Bruce looked at John and could feel the emotion of sadness coming up in him. His years of ministry had trained him to control his emotions, but it was hard for him not to cry in front of his old friend.

"First of all, I want to thank you for agreeing to meet with me. I know I have been oppressive and acerbic with you over the last several years, and I want to apologize. After Megan told her story in public, I have had to do some very deep introspection. I know you had confided in me as a counselor and friend. I did tell someone else that she had an abortion, but I never called her a-a-a……..slut." Tears started coming out of his eyes. He was silent for a few minutes. "I held her when she was a baby. I have always admired her as she grew up and still admire her. I began to……" He couldn't control it any longer and in deep heaving sobs he bowed his head and cried his heart out.

John watched and felt for his old friend. He didn't console him, and he didn't say any vacuous words. He knew this was a time of repentance.

He stayed in his chair, not gloating but understanding. Bruce needed to get this off his chest. Bruce somewhat composed himself and wiped his face with his handkerchief.

He continued with a low voice, head bowed, "I began to get intoxicated with the power of politics. I couldn't see anything except what it was going to do for me." He looked up at John and said, "Ideas I had once believed in and people who were close to me were discarded to reach this goal of being recognized for being on top. And now I know how much that has cost me. Thank God, it happened to me now and I can repent before I go any further. I'm truly sorry, John. I not only wanted to tell you this in person, but I really need to tell it to Megan, Chris, Paula and Rachel."

John said, "I can arrange that meeting."

"Thank you. I still have strong views on abortion, but Megan's speech not only made me contrite, it made me think. I need to re-examine this "pro-life" position. God revealed to me that if I want to take that position, then I need to not be entirely focused on birth but life after birth. Specifically, the untenable situations like poverty and domestic abuse, mass shootings and their causes, food and medical assistance for pregnant mothers, immigrants seeking political asylum and capital punishment." He hesitated and looked away. Then he looked at John again. "I really think what got me off track to start with is the bitterness Peggy and I felt because we couldn't have children. I was angry and didn't know it. I was angry at God and jealous of other people my age who had that joy in their life and that included you and Scott. I am also going to visit Scott."

"I also want to tell you; I've resigned my position as Pastor at Whispering Hope. I'll be there another two months so that the church can find an interim pastor. Over the years, I've had offers to teach at several seminaries, and I think I'll do it. Right now, I'm going to take a sabbatical and reinvigorate my first love with Jesus."

He paused and looked at John, "I know how this works, John, and you and your family have every right to expose this wrong I have done to you. I'm asking you for some mercy. I would like to spend the remainder of my life making this right for Megan but also for myself in my actions and not my words. Anyhow, thank you for listening to me. I would like to shake your hand as we leave each other, but I'll understand if you don't want to do it."

John got out his chair and went around his desk. Bruce extended his hand. John ignored it, walked up to him, and hugged him. Bruce put his arms around John, and they both wept.

Chapter 67

Bucky Taylor and Joe Bob Presswood watched the kids playing in the backyard pool of Don and Sherry McAdams as they sat in lounge chairs in their swim trunks sipping Dr. Pepper. It was hot and being able to take a dip in the pool occasionally to cool off was nice. The umbrella over the table was a respite from the heat. They were attending a church party. All the people here were in a group at church led by Don and Sherry. Most of them were close to the same age as Bucky and Joe Bob. They studied the Bible together on Wednesday nights and usually had some get together once a month. All of it, including the Bible study, was very informal and had a come and go atmosphere. Bucky and Joe Bob didn't attend everything but their girlfriends, Tracey and Ashley, had asked them to come to this group function. Both of them wouldn't openly admit it, but they had enjoyed the social interaction and the acceptance they got from everyone, even though both of them had dubious reputations.

Bucky was watching Tracey and Ashley. It looked like they were in a serious discussion. Both of them were sitting on the side of the pool in their bathing suits watching Tracey's kids in the pool. He also noticed how Ashley had turned into a particularly good looking woman. He remembered her as being skinny when she was younger and then putting on quite a bit of weight. She had changed and that went the same for Joe Bob. He had lost some weight, put some definition in those abs and really broadened his shoulders. In fact, he wanted to talk seriously to Joe Bob about something and now was as good a time as any. He opened the conversation with a compliment.

"Hey, man. It looks like you've shed a few pounds. You're looking really jacked, dude."

Joe Bob turned and looked at him and smiled, "Thanks, Bucky. Looks like you've been listening to all that teaching from Don and Sherry about being positive."

They both laughed. They knew that the opposite had been true a few years ago when everything was a put-down between them and their friends.

Bucky replied, "Yeah, well I'd rather be that way than what I used to be. It just took too much out of me. Being defensive all the time, trying to one up each other, looking over your shoulder and sometimes just being downright mean. It was exhausting."

"Tell me about it," said Joe Bob.

"Hey, man I wanted to ask you something. I know you and Ashley are getting married. Well, I-I-I" He paused. "I never've been real good talking and everything and can you tell me how you asked her?"

Joe Bob got this sly look on his face, "Yeah, not much to it. I just said, 'Will you marry me'?"

"Okay, smart guy." Bucky knew Joe Bob was giving him the business. "You know what I mean. When, where and how did you ask that question. There's more to it than just the question. She's a woman, and you know she's got to have some atmosphere with it."

"First of all, I guess you're going to ask Tracey, right?"

"Yeah, but don't you tell Ashley. I want it to be a surprise."

"Okay, this is what I did. You know that pretty spot down by Lucy's Bayou that has all those cypress trees where we used to go fishing and swimming as kids?"

"Of, course."

"I always liked that spot. Ashley had been wanting to go on a picnic for a while and one day when it was real pretty I took her out there. After we ate, I asked her hand in marriage and gave her an engagement ring."

"Simple as that?"

"Well, it took a lot of thought, courage and prayer on my part before I could do it. I mean this was a big step for me."

"How'd she like it?"

"Oh, man. She can't stop talking about it. She said it was so sweet and beautiful and perfect. She tells all her girlfriends. You're right. You can't just ask the question."

Bucky looked pensive. A plan was beginning to form in his mind. He had a good idea about how he could ask Tracey to marry him and it would mean a lot to both of them.

Joe Bob said, "You okay, man?"

"Yeah, just thinking. Thanks Joe Bob. I've got an idea about what to do."

They sat there a little longer without saying anything. Joe Bob watched Ashley and Tracey and thought about how much difference the two women had made in his and Bucky's lives. He was grateful. He had been through some rough patches and had a lot of people to thank for helping him to get out of them. He was taking to heart some of the things he had learned at church, especially about helping other people. He got a lot of satisfaction out of it. Some were grateful and some were not, but he knew what he had done for them and that in itself was reward enough. He thought about Scott Mitchum and his unselfish attitude about everything and then he compared it to Skinny Merritt—man what a difference. Thinking of Skinny reminded him of something he wanted to discuss with Bucky.

"Hey, Buck, have you seen Skinny?" Joe Bob asked.

"Yeah, I saw him at Bodittle's one night about a week ago. I was with Tracey, and I just said-"Hi"- to him as I walked by his table. He barely acknowledged me. He was with Joanne Roberts. I never thought I would see that. Of course, Joanne has been married four times—hard for her to hold onto a man—but it may be because of her expensive tastes. I know because I had a date with her once and that was enough. I could tell Skinny was shelling out a lot of money for the meal and drinks—probably about a $100. Where'd he get that kind of money?"

That news percolated something in Joe Bob's mind. "I don't know but I have a bad feeling about it. I wouldn't put it past him to be doing something illegal. You know he and I had a word fight and when he left me, he issued a warning and a veiled threat that went 'you and some other people are going to wish they had been nicer to me'. I've been keeping my eye out for him ever since."

"Well, I wouldn't trust him with nothin'. I'm trying to stop cussing because Tracey doesn't like it, but that guy has turned into a no good sonofabitch."

"I'm concerned that he might try something to hurt some people who he thinks have wronged him. I know how to look out for him, but I think he might try to do something to Scott. I know how Skinny thinks. He's so self-centered that I'm ninety-nine percent sure he thinks Scott put him in prison. I wonder if Scott needs to be warned."

"I actually know something better we can do and that's to tell Jesse Henderson our concerns. At least tell him what he said to you and what I've heard and seen. He does not like Skinny. I'll call Jesse and tell him we want to talk to him about Skinny. I'll let you know when we need to go see him."

"Good idea." Joe Bob and Bucky continued to watch the pool as Ashley and Tracey came toward them smiling.

Chapter 68

Scott and Mary Jo were eating lunch at the Hwy 116 Diner. They had a history here. The diner had been in Lyric since they were kids and whether it was after a football game or just hanging out, it had been a part of their lives. It was still in good shape due to renovations over the years, but the atmosphere was the same—inexpensive meals with good service. There was always a crowd. In the bank of booths along the front picture windows facing State Highway 116, they were sitting in one nearest the door. It had been the only vacant one when they entered the local icon of comfort food.

As they were eating, Scott was contemplating sharing something with Mary Jo and as a testament to the growing love they had for each other, she responded verbally.

"What's on your mind?" Mary Jo said in a casual way.

Scott was still amazed at how women could read other people. He was trying to be nonchalant, but she knew.

"Well, as well as you read my mind, I figured you already knew what was going on," Scott said with a sly grin on his face and twinkling eyes.

"Scott Mitchum, don't you try to be presumptuous about me. It's my prerogative as a woman to be empathetic."

"I'm teasing. I was just thinking I would like to show you my timber tracts. It's dry enough and although it's hot there is some nice shade. I especially wanted to show you one near the Tanner Woods. It has a nice creek and lake on it with some beautiful cypress trees. We could have a picnic."

She stopped eating, smiled at him, and said. "I'd love to do it. When?"

"How about day after tomorrow, Thursday, at noon? I need to go a little early and you could meet me out there. There's a road to it, but it's not traveled much. I'll have to give you directions."

"Sounds good. I'm glad you convinced me to buy that four wheel drive truck when I needed to get a new vehicle. Now I won't have to be concerned as much when I go places like that."

"Yeah, if you had only listened to me about buying a Ford instead of a Dodge," he responded with an eyebrow raised.

"You boys and your competition with your toy brands."

Scott laughed. He was beginning to like the idea of spending a lot of time with Mary Jo. They finished their meal, paid the cashier and were in the parking lot when Scott paused. He looked at Mary Jo and said, "Did you see Skinny Merritt in the diner?"

"No," she replied.

"Well, that's his truck over there, but I didn't see him either. I try to watch out for him. I don't want to get punched again."

They both looked around. Scott shrugged his shoulders and told Mary Jo he would see her on Thursday. He would call her tonight with the directions to the timber tract.

Richard Breeden was sitting in his living room watching an old rerun of Mannix on television when his phone rang. It was Skinny Merritt.

"Okay, it's set up," Skinny said immediately without any small talk.

"What's set up?" Richard replied thinking that this redneck was a tad low on the IQ and communication skills scale.

"The hit on Scott Mitchum and your ex-wife."

Richard sat up in his easy chair. "Do you mean we can make this happen soon?"

"Day after tomorrow on one of Mitchum's tracts out by the Tanner Woods. They set it up themselves. They're going on a picnic. Now ain't that quick work on my part and romantic on their part," Skinny was proud of his clever description of the situation.

"Is it remote?"

"Damn straight. I helped him clear out that little picnic area and put a table on it. There's just a pig trail going to it, although you can get there in a four wheel drive. They're going to be there at noon. He's going early."

"All right, I'll meet you at your place tomorrow at 6:00 pm, and we'll work on the details of our plan to take care of them."

"See ya then."

Harry Jenkins was standing in Jesse Henderson's door waiting for him to get off the phone. He was concerned about something. He wanted to talk to Jesse about it. They had a good working relationship because Jesse had been on the street a lot more than Harry. He personally knew criminals and had an uncanny insight about how their mind worked. He saw things about a crime that put motive and opportunity together. He had a high percentage when it came to solving crime and had been recognized for it several times. Jesse got off the phone and motioned for Harry to come in and sit down.

"I wanted to show you something," Harry said as he sat down. "It's about Don Miller."

"Yeah, snakebite, right?" Jesse replied.

"Yeah, well the family is suspicious as most families are when someone dies in an isolated place. And you know that nine times out of ten, it's obvious the person made a mistake and it cost him his life. They are convinced that there was some foul play. Don, they said, was always incredibly careful in the woods. He was bitten by a copperhead when he was a kid and almost died. Well, he would wear good boots and heavy denim, watch where he was walking and had a good understanding of snakes in their habitat. The fact that he was bit twice is what triggered their suspicions. I agree that it is very unusual for a person to get bit twice by one snake and or even once by two snakes for that matter. Well, the family wanted an autopsy, and I agreed to it just to be sure. The coroner said the venom did kill him, but he also found this right under his arm." Harry showed Jesse a picture of two small dots that looked like a burn.

"That looks like it's from a taser." Jesse observed.

"My feelings exactly," Harry replied.

Jesse looked up in the air, thinking. "Where have I heard the name Don Miller prior to his dying?"

"He was the forester who turned state's evidence on Richard Breeden for stealing timber." Harry looked intently at Jesse.

"Ohhhhh, shit," Jesse exclaimed. "Did we treat that as a crime scene?"

"Well, yes and no. When the officers were called out there by the owner of the property and saw him lying on the ground with no obvious signs of violence, they thought he might have had a heart attack. They examined him and felt the swelling on his legs and puffiness all over his body. They looked at his legs and determined it was a snake bite and called EMS. Of course, he was already dead, but they wanted to make sure it was a snake bite."

"So, we didn't examine tire tracks, look for evidence, etc. to see if there was foul play."

"They treated the body that way but not anything else."

"And it has rained since then, right?"

"Yes."

"Okay, ask the coroner about the red dots and get back out there to see if you can find anything. I told you Richard Breeden and Skinny Merritt are probably up to something, but I need something to arrest them. I'm afraid they may not be finished."

Jesse was moving from low gear to high gear. It was Wednesday afternoon, hump day, but the adrenaline was kicking in after the telephone call he had just received and his meeting with Harry. He needed to take a ride to calm down before his next appointment in twenty minutes with Bucky Taylor and Joe Bob Presswood. Bucky had called him about Skinny Merritt and wanted to tell him a few things. He got in his car and went to Sonic to get a diet cherry limeade. There were few things in this world that could calm him down better on a hot day than a Sonic cherry limeade. He pulled into their drive through and noticed Skinny Merritt's truck parked in an ordering space. He kept his eyes on the truck and noticed a couple of box-like items in the back. He could just barely see them. He got his order and then made a pass by Skinny's truck and saw that the box-like items had a Plexiglas front. He wondered what in the world was Skinny doing with something like those things. However, he had his suspicions after hearing about Don Miller.

When he got back to the PD, Bucky and Joe Bob were in his office. They exchanged pleasantries and then Jesse said, "You guys given up on finding Santa Anna's gold?"

Bucky and Joe Bob looked at each other and laughed. Bucky said, "Yeah, I think we've been too busy working and getting married to do anything else."

"Getting married! Now don't you lie to me, Bucky Taylor." Jesse exclaimed.

"Yep, it's true Jesse. We're both getting hitched. My fiancé is Tracey King and Joe Bob's is Ashley Wilson."

"Now I know you're lying to me. There's no way you two ugly mugs could find beautiful women like that to marry you."

Bucky laughed and Joe Bob was silent. Bucky prodded Joe Bob with his elbow. "He's just kidding Joe Bob. Jesse only does that to people he likes and if he doesn't do it, he probably doesn't like you."

"You got that right, brother. Speaking of someone I wouldn't kid is Skinny Merritt. Now what do you want to tell me about him."

Bucky said, "Well, I'll let Joe Bob go first."

"Well, it's like this, Chief Henderson, Skinny found me after he got out of prison and I basically didn't want to have anything to do with him. I told him that and he made this statement to me like 'I've got some big plans and you and some other people are going to wish you had been a tiny bit nicer to me.' I just passed it off with him being Skinny, but Bucky thought we should tell you."

Bucky said, "Yeah, Jesse, I saw him with Joanne Roberts at Bodittle's one night, and he must've had a $100 worth of food and alcohol on the table. As far as I know, he's not working. I don't know how he can afford a meal like that or Joanne Roberts for that matter."

Jesse looked up, thinking. Some things were coming together now, and Jesse was beginning to see connections. He looked at both of them, "Do you boys know if Skinny has ever had a fascination with snakes or handled them?"

"I've seen him pick up grass snakes or garter snakes when we are kids and try to pop their heads off," Joe Bob responded.

"How about poisonous snakes?" Jesse queried.

"I know they don't scare him. I've seen him get real close to them and kill them. He almost got to the point of picking one up one time, and it jumped toward him. He killed it after that," Joe Bob said.

"I can't tell you why I want to know that information, but I appreciate both of you coming in today to tell me about Skinny. I want you to do something for me. Since both of you know him pretty well, if you see him around town and it looks like he's doing something suspicious, please call me on my phone, not the PD number. I want to know immediately what he's doing."

"Just one more thing before we go, Chief," Joe Bob added, "Skinny hates Scott Mitchum and I think if anybody should look out for him, it should be Scott." Bucky nodded his head in agreement.

They exchanged phone numbers, then Jesse stood up and shook their hands and walked them to the door of his office. He watched them walk down the hall and mused about how some things do change for the better.

Chapter 69

Skinny slowed the truck down as they got into the Tanner Woods. He was on a county road that had extraordinarily little traffic ever. He looked at Richard in the passenger seat and said, "I'm going to park the truck in that temporary logging road right before you get to Mitchum's place. We can park it off the road so's nobody will notice it. Then we can walk up through the woods to his little picnic spot. I know a trail to it, and he'll never know we are coming."

"You better be right because I don't want to fuck this up. Mitchum is sharp and we better be on our p's and q's," Richard answered.

"What the hell does p's and q's mean, anyway? Skinny queried.

Richard looked at Skinny with exasperation and said in a loud voice, "I don't know, Daniel Webster, but goddammit you know what I'm talking about."

"Okay, okay. You don't have to get your panties in a wad."

"I don't wear panties you stupid motherfucker," Richard fumed.

"I know, just an expression, kinda like p's and q's."

Richard thought to himself that he may just have to pull his gun and shoot Skinny when they parked the truck. If he had to listen to any more of his bullshit, he was going to go insane.

They rode silently and then Skinny parked right off the road in the temporary logging road. Neither one of them checked to see if the truck could be seen from the county road. They grabbed the snakes and started hiking up the trail to the picnic area. As they approached, they could hear Scott singing Blessed Assurance. They both looked at each other and smiled, both thinking he's never going to believe what's about to happen to him.

Scott was sitting on the bench of the picnic table looking up through the luscious green canopy of oak and pine trees. The sky was a brilliant blue with a few puffy clouds. Richard stepped out and trained the Glock on Scott. Scott didn't notice him until he was about twenty feet away. He looked at Richard curiously and didn't seem startled. Richard calmly walked up to him and said, "Hello, Scott."

"Hello, Richard," Scott said calmly. "What's with the gun?"

"Well, you see Scott, Skinny Merritt and I want to visit with you for a while and we need your cooperation. However, I doubt that you're going to want to cooperate."

Scott looked around and saw Skinny behind him.

"Now, real easy, Scott, take off your shirt."

Scott remained calm and knew he was in an untenable situation and needed to look for opportunity.

"Okay, what are you guys planning to do?" He asked.

"We'll explain it as we go and you ain't going to be so calm when it's over," advised Skinny.

Scott slowly took off his shirt. Skinny stepped up, grabbed his right arm, and hit him with the stun gun right under his arm. Scott started spasming and fell on the ground. Skinny went and got the snakes he had previously put in five gallon plastic buckets. He took the lids off them and then pulled up Scott's pants on both legs above his knees. As he continued to be immobile, he and Richard stood him up and put his right leg in one of the buckets. The rattlesnake immediately struck him, and Scott flinched and cried out with an inner muffled pain. Then the put his left leg in the other bucket and the rattler struck. Scott flinched again and emitted the same cry. Skinny and Richard laid him on the ground face down and then zip tied his hands behind him and then zip tied his feet.

Mary Jo was running a little early for the picnic with Scott. She was looking forward to it on such a beautiful day. She never tired of being with him and was excited to share the day with him in nature and on his property. He was always a breath of fresh air. She was getting close to the turnoff for his property and turned into the temporary logging road which didn't seem like the one Scott had described. As she drove up the road, she noticed a truck parked on it. It wasn't Scott's. Then she decided this was the wrong road, stopped and started to back out to the county road. She paused and looked at the truck in front of her again.

It was Skinny Merritt's truck. Her heart started beating fast. What was Skinny doing here, she thought?

Fear crept into her. She then knew intuitively that something was wrong. She tried to remember what Scott had told her about faith and fear. He had said that we are destined to have trouble in our life, but our faith will always, always help us to overcome that trouble. She took deep breaths and calmed herself. She reached into the console and took out the Smith and Wesson MP Shield. She placed it on top of the console.

She backed the truck out and got back on the county road again, heading north. She found the entrance described by Scott seed drove the truck at a steady pace up the road. She didn't know what awaited her, but she was not going to back away from it. She had weathered a lot of things in the last several years. She was going to help Scott if he was in trouble.

She thought about calling the police, but she didn't think she had enough information to make that call. She got to the clearing, parked the truck, and saw the picnic table to her right about a hundred feet away. It looked like Scott was sitting on the bench facing out with his hands behind his back. Although it didn't look right, she got out of the truck and went around the front to head toward the picnic bench.

"Hello, Mary Jo," said Richard off to her left.

She was startled. Richard was standing about twenty feet away pointing a gun at her. She didn't say anything.

"Well, aren't you going to come give your former lover a big hug? Richard laughed.

She looked at him with disdain and then observed Skinny coming out of the woods near the picnic table.

"Richard, what's going on?" Mary Jo gave him a loathing glare.

"Well, I'm glad you asked. It's payback time darling. Skinny over there is paying back Scott, and I'm going to payback you. Both of you are responsible for sending us to prison, and you know in prison you learn a lot about paybacks."

"Richard, you'll never get away with this."

"Yeah, that's what Don Miller said."

Her heart started beating rapidly again. She had gone to Don's funeral. He had died of a snakebite. She looked over at Scott again, and he almost looked catatonic. Then she saw the five-gallon buckets. She knew what they had done. She focused on her faith and a solution.

Richard was smiling, "Mary Jo you sure are looking good today and you know it would be nice if we could have a little fun for old times' sake."

Mary Jo knew what he had in mind, and it was something to do with sex. She had lived with him long enough. She remained silent.

"Why don't you take off your shirt," he said.

"In your dreams, Richard."

"Skinny, give Mary Jo's boyfriend a little stimulus so that she'll get aroused enough to take off her clothes."

Skinny reached under Scott's shirt and hit him with the stun gun under his left arm. Scott started convulsing and slid off the bench.

Mary Jo was aghast but kept her face composed. She had found her opportunity and her solution. She had used sex in the past to manipulate Richard, mostly in the later years when the love between them had gone. She was going to use it now to help Scott and herself out of this predicament.

"Okay, Richard," she said as she started unbuttoning her shirt.

She got the shirt off and was standing there in her Victoria Secret's finest. Skinny was moving away from Scott so that he could get a good look. Richard came a little closer and waved the gun, "Off with that fine looking bra," he said.

She gradually took off the bra. She wanted this to get their full attention. She could tell that both men were getting erections. Skinny's mouth was hanging open.

"Okay, slip off the shoes and the jeans."

Mary Jo took her time and watched as both gave her their eyes full. She knew where this was going. Richard always wanted a blowjob before he engaged in vaginal intercourse. She was thinking ahead and considering her options. She acted somewhat disgusted but not enough for them to avert their attention.

She took off her shoes and jeans and stood there in her very skimpy panties. She had their full attention. Their erections were very noticeable.

"The final piece of this wonderful puzzle—the panties—which I must say do not cover much, but let's see you without them."

She took them off and Skinny Merritt could not believe his eyes. The most beautiful woman in Lyric was standing in front of him naked. It couldn't get any better, except for her to have sex with him, but he didn't think Richard would let that happen.

Richard started to unbuckle his belt. Mary Jo saw him.

"Stop right there, Richard. I know what you want to do, but I don't want Skinny to see it. I'll do it, but over here on the driver's side of the truck so that I can have a little privacy." Mary Jo knew Skinny would see it. This was just a distraction.

Richard moved to the driver's side of the truck unbuckled his pants and pulled out his erect penis. Mary Jo told him to come over in front of her where she was on her knees. Richard had not noticed the dead two foot piece of pine limb about an inch in diameter between his legs.

Mary Jo took his penis in her left hand and began to slide it up and down his erect cock. She then took her right hand and wrapped it around the pine limb. Richard had his eyes halfway closed. The gun was still in his hand, but he was mesmerized. She also noticed Skinny in the background moving around the front of the truck, watching. He was holding the stun gun in his right hand, and it was perilously close to his crotch. Mary Jo put the head of Richard's cock in her mouth and watched as he closed his eyes. She then took the pine limb and rammed into his balls with all the force she could manage. He screamed, fell back, and she dove under the truck and crawled to the other side, opened the passenger door, and took out the Smith and Wesson. She looked over at Skinny. He was convulsing on the ground. She surmised he must have shot himself in the crotch with the stun gun.

"You bitch," Richard screamed, "I'm going to enjoy killing you."

He hobbled around the front of the truck and saw her standing in a firing stance.

"Richard, put the gun down. I don't want to shoot you, and we both don't want that for our kids."

He hesitated and brought the gun up. She shot him in the arm above the gun hand. He screamed again and looked at her in amazement. "You shot me."

"Yes, you bastard," she shouted. "You should never have insisted I take that concealed carry class. I like to shoot guns, now. You're the only person I've ever shot, and I'll shoot you again if you don't lay down on the ground."

He got on his knees and laid face down on the ground. She stood with her right foot on his back and told him to bring his hands together in the back while she pointed the gun at him. She stood on his right arm where she shot him and got a zip tie out of his back pocket. She put the gun on the ground and brought over his left hand and tied them together, picked up the gun and then tied his feet. She did the same thing with Skinny who was immobile. She immediately went to Scott. He was on the ground. She checked his pulse, and he was still alive. She saw his legs were swollen from the snake bites She ran back to get her phone out of her jeans when Jesse Henderson and Harry Jenkins pulled up in his police cruiser.

"Oh God, Jesse," she exclaimed, "Scott's been bitten by two rattlesnakes. They used a stun gun on him. He needs to get to the hospital as soon as possible."

Jesse and Harry went into action. They picked up Scott and got him in the cruiser. Harry took off and Mary Jo went back to where her clothes were on the ground. She put them on as Jesse dealt with Skinny and Richard. He told both they were under arrest for the murder of Don Miller and the attempted murder of Scott Mitchum. He read them their Miranda rights. As he finished, he said to both of them, "..and if I can find anything else to hang on you, I will, including the sexual assault of Mary Jo Breeden. If Scott Mitchum dies, I'll make it my mission to see that you get the most punishment the State of Texas will allow."

He handcuffed both of them, took them to the picnic table and put zip ties on their feet. He put compression on Richard's arm and bandaged it. He leaned on the side of Mary Jo's truck as he called the PD for a cruiser to come pick up Richard, Skinny and him. Mary Jo came around the front of the truck and hugged him.

"Thank you, Jesse. Maybe they can get the anti-venom to Scott soon enough and he'll be all right." Then she started sobbing. He patted her on the back and said, "You did good, Mary Jo. You did good."

Chapter 70

"Yeah, your boys, Bucky and Joe Bob, are looking out for you, Scott," Jesse Henderson said as he sat next to Scott's hospital bed. "After they came into the office and warned me about Skinny being up to something, they called me and told me they had seen Skinny's truck going to the Tanner Woods. They observed that there was another man in the truck with him. Harry and I had been suspicious of Skinny for awhile but when we began to doubt Don Miller's death being just an accidental snakebite, we thought they may be together again to do a number on somebody else. I knew you had that timber tract near the Tanner Woods. Harry and I got in the car to cruise out there to see if they were engaged in some criminal activity and bingo!" Jesse looked over at Mary Jo sitting on the other side of the bed.

"Now as for your real rescuer, I can truthfully say I have never seen anything like it," Jesse continued his gaze on Mary Jo and turned to Scott when her face turned red. "That is one tough woman and neither me nor you need to ever get on the wrong side of her."

Scott gave him a weak smile and Mary Jo looked at him with concern. Jesse could tell it was time for him to go. He got up and said, "Get well, Scott. This community needs you. There are a lot of people praying for you because I hear it every day. They may not be overt about it, but they sincerely care for you. I'll see both of you soon." He immediately turned and went out the door.

Mary Jo walked over to him and put her hand on his head. "How are you doing?"

"I'm still pretty tired and right now I'm hungry. Maybe I should eat some lunch and take a nap," Scott replied.

"I'll go check on your lunch. Be right back."

Scott reflected on the last several days after Mary Jo left. It had been rough. He almost didn't get the anti-venom in time and the doctors were worried he might have a stroke. They had kept him in the hospital for three days now, observing him. He felt better now. He was grateful for all of the attention he was getting, and the sincere sympathy people had for him. He was worn out, though, from the snakebites, from all the publicity and from trying to understand why Skinny and Richard had gone to such elaborate lengths for revenge. It puzzled him that he was the object of their hate. In his mind he had done nothing to deserve this action on their part. Then he thought neither had Don Miller. Scott had only casually known Don but liked him. Don had a wife and two young children. Scott quit moping and smiled at Mary Jo when she came in the room.

"Now, you look better. Lunch is on the way," Mary Jo said as she closed the door.

"I was just feeling sorry for myself, and I shouldn't have been doing it," Scott replied as he reached for her hand.

"Why are you feeling sorry for yourself?"

"It's not the injury, I just don't seem to understand why I have this problem with people like Skinny and Richard wanting to hurt me."

Mary Jo was silent for a few minutes. She put her other hand on top of the hand she was holding. "Yes, you do, Scott. You've taught me about it. It's jealousy, it's anger, it's self-centeredness. Both Skinny and Richard just couldn't stand you because you loved the life you were living even after overcoming problems. They want to be like you, but they live in their own small world so much that they can't see the beauty of introspection and engaging the world through self-honest eyes. They want to blame all their problems on other people, the rich people, the black people, the government, the immigrants and take no responsibility for anything they do that wrongs someone else or infringes on their rights. They want what you have, but don't know how to get it."

"You're right. I just need somebody to remind me, especially someone as smart and beautiful as you." He pulled her to him and kissed her. It was a nice long deep kiss. They needed to kiss and touch. Scott needed it to heal, and Mary Jo needed it to stay sane.

There was a knock on the door. Mary Jo slowly let go of Scott's embrace and went to the door. She opened it, and the aide brought in Scott's lunch—roast beef and gravy with rice, carrots and onions. Scott looked at Mary Jo and said, "This is remarkable. My second favorite meal."

"Yeah." She replied with a glint in her eye.

He whispered a "thank you" as the aide got it ready for him to eat in bed. Scott devoured it. Mary Jo watched him and read her book as she waited for him to finish. He laid his head back after he ate. She watched him as he immediately fell asleep. He didn't wake up for two hours. Mary Jo went to the cafeteria to get herself some food and came right back. She didn't want to be away from him. Since he had been in the hospital, she had only gone home to bathe and change clothes. She had asked Matthew and Elaine if they were okay with her staying in his room at night. They were thankful that she wanted to do it.

He had been awake for about fifteen minutes when there was another knock on the door. Mary Jo got up and answered it. It was Bruce Jones.

"Oh, I didn't know you were here, Mary Jo. I'll come back another time."

"No, it's all right, Bruce. Come in," she replied.

Bruce walked in and hugged her, saw Scott, and nodded his head. Scott was expressionless. It was a bit awkward and Bruce sensed it. He looked at Mary Jo to try and relieve the tension, "How are you doing? I understand this has been quite an ordeal for you."

"I'm doing fine, physically. It's going to take a little time for me to understand what happened and cope with it. I've talked with the kids. They are incredibly supportive, but it's a stain on our family."

Bruce nodded and was pensive for a moment as if he were trying to find the right words to say. "I've been praying for both of you and your families. After what you went through several years ago and now these circumstances, humanly speaking I cannot imagine your turmoil."

"Thank you," Mary Jo said. Scott remained silent as he looked at Bruce.

Bruce looked at Scott, and they held each other's gaze. Mary Jo watched them and said, "I need to call Amy and Eric. You two visit and I'll be back in a little while."

She left the room and Bruce took a seat. He sat with his head down for some time and then he lifted it and tears were rolling down his cheeks.

"Scott, first I want to apologize to you for being arrogant and mean to you and John over the last several years. It was sinful. It was not only a grievance against God but against two long-time good friends. I've already apologized to John, Paula, Megan, Chris and Rachel. What I did to them was inexcusable. You didn't have to be included, but I stepped over the line. I wanted the power of the temporary life of this world, I was seduced by its strong pull, and it became an addiction. I came here today to tell you. I wanted to tell you before this egregious thing happened to you, but I just came to this realization of my sin a few days ago. I didn't want to upset you as you were recovering, and that's the second reason I'm here. I want to ask your forgiveness and minister to you if you will allow me. But I will leave if it will upset you."

Scott remained silent. Bruce got up and walked to the door.

"Wait, Bruce," Scott said quietly.

Bruce turned to him by the bed and Scott sat up in the bed, "You know what Jesus said to Peter about the number of times we should forgive people?"

"Yes, seventy times seven."

"Okay, that's already been done with me to you, and you have four hundred and eighty-eight left," he advised with a playful tone in his voice.

Bruce grabbed Scott's right hand with a firm grip and placed his left hand on his shoulder as if he wanted to pull him out of the bed. Bruce closed his eyes and whispered, "Thank you." Tears came streaming down his face for a couple of minutes, as they both uttered no sound. He composed himself and let go of Scott's shoulder, wiped the tears from his cheeks and then looked at Scott.

"Four hundred and eighty-eight left?" queried Bruce.

"Yeah, I've already had to forgive you once for stealing my girlfriend in the seventh grade."

They both laughed for a long time.

Chapter 71

Mary Jo was going to pick up Scott and bring him home from the hospital. She had been at her house to bathe and change clothes. She was excited but also anxious. She, Matthew, and Elaine had wanted to have a homecoming party for him at his house, and it had soon turned into a community party. The only thing she could remember taking this much effort in planning was her wedding. Bodittle wanted to cater the food at no cost. Two florists in town had wanted to decorate at no cost. A local band, which played a variety of rock, country, blues and gospel music, and Scott dearly liked, wanted to provide some entertainment at no cost. She had left most of the details up to Matthew and Elaine, but advised them on some of the invitees, managing parking and how long to have the event since their Dad was going to need to rest for a while. Scott's house was not built for entertainment like hers, but she had done enough of similar smaller events that she was confident they could pull it off. It was amazing how the people of Lyric loved this man. She just wanted it to be good for him.

The doctor had told Scott to take it easy for two weeks, no driving, walking after one week, no City business and no work. She'd believe that when she saw it. Although he did look at Mary Jo and told her to stay with him, keep an eye on his health and report any abnormalities to her. He also told her privately that she should probably stay with him twenty-four hours, since she had worked as an EMT in college, and help him if he did have a medical emergency. She had talked to Matthew and Elaine about that arrangement, and they were happy for her to be in the house with him and them. It was all set up.

As Mary Jo walked to Scott's room, she felt complete. She had never loved a man this much. He had consumed her thoughts and her daily activities. She had to stop occasionally and think about herself and her needs. Although Scott had never said he loved her, she knew it. She knew he had to deal with the past and coming to that point was difficult for him. Mary Jo was patient. She had learned in her spiritual growth; it was a fruit of the Holy Spirit. That was the other part of him that she loved. He never was preachy or demanding about spiritual matters. He lived it.

She walked into his room where he was dressed and sitting in the chair, "Are you ready?", she asked.

"Yes. I'm ready to go home. I've had enough of hospitals for a lifetime," he said circumspectly.

"We took your truck home. We'll go in mine."

"The one with the gun in it?", he smiled and raised his eyebrows.

"Yes." She looked questioningly at him.

"Good, I need an armed escort. I don't want to come back here."

They smiled at each other and then walked out of the hospital. Scott was using a cane. His muscles were still sore from the bites, and he had to get used to walking again. They drove in silence with just the songs on her Ipod playing. It was a nice fall day. The sun was mixing with the multicolored leaves and shadows to effectively present the coolness of autumn atmosphere. Scott was immersed in observing the trees and the sky and began singing "Amazing Grace" with Judy Collins as the song begin filling the cab of the truck. The song ended right before the turnoff to his house and he said to Mary Jo, "Go to the cemetery. I want to visit Robert and Fran's graves before I go home."

Mary Jo complied and pulled into Berry cemetery about a half mile beyond the turnoff. They both got out of the truck. Scott grabbed Mary Jo's hand, and they slowly walked to the graves. He took in the names on headstones, many he had known while they were here on this earth. He stood with Mary Jo in front of Robert's grave for a while. He turned and walked two rows to his family's area of the cemetery and stopped for a moment at his mother's and father's graves and then stepped over to Fran's. He was still holding Mary Jo's hand. He pulled her close to him and looked into her eyes.

"I want to thank you for saving my life, in more ways than one."

She put her head on his chest, and he held her close.

"I'm the one who should be thanking you. I have never known such completeness with a person. God has given you to me and I'm not going to let anyone interfere with it." She paused and said, "How do you do it, Scott?"

"What?" he asked.

"How do you come back from such hateful, spiteful assaults on your life and your character? I don't know what possessed me to marry Richard, but he was different then. He changed, and I didn't see until it was too late. I hate him now, and I hate Skinny Merritt. I can tell you don't hate them, and I don't understand why."

Scott continued to hold her.

"I can't let my life be burdened with hate. It takes too much energy. That's why I pray for Richard, and I pray for Skinny."

She grabbed him above his hips, held herself back from him and looked intently in his eyes and exclaimed sharply, "Pray for them! After what they did to you? How can you do it? I'd just as soon see them suffer and be put to death."

Scott put his fingers on her lips and pulled her closer. "I pray for them because it's what Jesus did and would do if he were in my shoes. But here is something I want you to know. Praying for your enemies rids you of energy-sucking hate, and God either changes you or them so that you can continue to live out your faith instead of being involved with destructive thoughts and activities that lead to poor mental and emotional health. Try it."

She put her head back on his chest. They were silent and still for a long time. Then Scott gently pushed her away and told her to look at the sunset. It was definitely God's artwork this evening. The shades of red, orange, yellow and blue were mixed in a kaleidoscope of color that was fascinating and calming. It was a celebration of mystery. Scott put his arm around Mary Jo as they looked to the west together.

"I love you, Mary Jo," he said continuing to look at the sunset.

"I know, and you know I love you," she replied looking in the same direction.

"We still have a lot of good years left on this journey. I want to spend them with you. Will you marry me?"

"Yes."

The wind picked up and brushed past their cheeks moving their hair all over their heads. It was constant and dependable. It was there to remind them of something permanent.